BLACK FLAMES

Ember 1

MADILYNN DALE

COPYRIGHT

This book is a work of fiction. Names, characters, businesses, organizations, places, events, and incidents are either an idea from the author's personal creativity or used fictitiously. Any resemblance to actual places, persons, events, or locales is completely coincidental.

Trigger warnings: sex, violence, kidnapping, blood, alcohol, vulgar language, some nudity, toxic relationship, death, violence

DEDICATION

This book is dedicated to Dwayne, Lainie and Traz. Thank you all for the inspiration.

CHAPTER ONE

My breath huffs out as I push myself to keep up with the lean male ahead of me. My legs burn with fatigue, and my body begs for me to stop. Sweat drips down my back in what feels like waves as I continue ahead, one foot in front of the other. Running is torture.

"Come on, keep it up, Ember. You can't slack off. You have to be strong. We need to see if we can't force the change."

I huff, giving his back the stink eye. "Give me a break, Corey. I think I'm doing alright keeping up with a male shifter who's already had his first transition into a wolf."

"You know that isn't good enough. The Alpha's already putting pressure on your family because you're still unchanged. The next Luna needs to be prepared for anything. Your betrothed is concerned."

"My betrothed can kiss my ass. He knows I don't want to be with him. We just don't want to disappoint our parents. Hell, I'm nineteen. I can choose who I want to be with." I stop, doubling over, attempting to catch my breath. My stomach burns, and my mouth is dry. Why didn't I bring a bottle of water with me? "I have to stop."

I hear Corey stop, and the dirt shifts as he whips around. I take in deep breaths, doing my best to fight the cramps in my sides. "You can't stop, Ember. We're almost finished. Just another mile or two."

I stand as straight as possible and place my hands on my hips. I glare menacingly at him. "No, I need a break. You can't push me like this. It's not fair. None of this is fair. I didn't choose this. Adam can find someone else. We don't even know if we're meant to be mates."

He walks to me and puts his hand on my shoulder. "I know it's not fair, and I hate to push you. Hell, I'm the one keeping secrets from him about you, but you have to try. You don't have a way out of this, even if he isn't your mate. Unless he chooses to break the contract your parents made with the Alpha at your birth, you're stuck. You know the rules. We can't go against the Alpha."

I frown and reach up, placing my hand on his cheek. "But where does that leave us? What if you're my mate? The attraction and the sex are there. That's all we need to seal the deal, right?"

"No, even if you're my mate, you know I can't claim you. That's not how this pack works. As the next Beta to the future Alpha, I have to do what I'm ordered. Those orders will include not touching the Luna once it's official."

"That's stupid. I know he's been sleeping with Lacy. What if she's his mate?"

"I think he'd know if she was. There isn't a bond between them like that, from what he's said."

"Fine, but until we find a way to get me out of this shit, I'm still going to enjoy who I want and whatever I want. That includes you." I step into him and place my lips against his. What better way to distract him from our training than to put his mind elsewhere?

After a minute, he pulls away. "I know what you're trying to do. Come on, let's keep moving. They did put me in charge of your training for a reason, you know. I can't fail this task."

I roll my eyes. "Fine."

I push off at a slow pace as Corey sprints ahead of me. I let my gaze drop to his ass as he moves. The way those sweatpants hang, showing off the muscles of his core, makes my mouth water. We have known each other since we were kids. He was my best friend for a long time until I took a chance to kiss him. Things quickly escalated from there, but we've had to keep our relationship a secret, especially since he and Adam are close. Well, somewhat tight.

Adam is a prick and my pack's next Alpha. Our parents agreed we should lead the pack one day together and decided to sign a contract stating it. They even had it approved by the council of elders residing over all the paranormal communities —vampires, witches, shifters, and the like. They have done a decent job of keeping our world hidden, but will there ever be a time where we don't have to hide who we truly are?

I grumble loudly as I continue following Corey. No matter how much training we've done, it's yet to encourage my wolf to surface. She's in there. I've felt her presence a few times, but she refuses to appear. I've no idea why. My mother says I'm just a late bloomer, but I haven't been that in any other areas in life. Why can't I make the shift happen so she can do all this running?

My legs continue to burn as we make it another mile, and the gentle breeze pushes the smell of smoke in our direction. It has another faint scent that I can't place, but my steps falter as Corey suddenly stops ahead of me, cursing.

"What's wrong?" I reorient myself and slow my pace to a walk, stopping at his side.

"You don't recognize the smell?" He turns to me with a concerned expression. It sends flutters of trepidation through my belly.

"Smoke? Yeah, why?"

"It's not just smoke. The smell of death is in it. I need to check it out, then alert the pack. Stay close." He motions for me to follow behind him, and I roll my eyes. There is no way someone died. Nothing exciting ever happens in this pack, other than an occasional squabble.

"It's probably just a typical house fire. Supernatural beings aren't the only ones that live around here, after all. It's probably just an old man that fell asleep and left the stove on." I shrug as Corey shakes his head.

"I wouldn't put hope into that idea."

We walk a few minutes in silence after that, and I cherish the time to catch my breath. The street around us seems fine with tall trees and evenly spaced plots with houses on them. It's unusually quiet, though, and unease makes its presence known as we continue to follow the trail of smoke.

"See that ahead?" Corey's voice startles me, and I follow his line of sight to the house half a block away, covered in flames.

"Oh shit! That's Amber's house!" I take off at a sprint toward my childhood friend's home. Fear screams in the back of my mind, and all reason leaves me as I move with unnatural speed. She has to be okay. Maybe they're all standing in the backyard or calling the fire department from another house.

I reach the house as flames crackle, and something to my right crashes. I run toward the noise and see Mrs. Bane, Amber's mother, attempting to crawl out from beneath a board. The board is covered in flames, but they're different. These flames are black.

I move toward her and grasp the board, ignoring the fire, and lift it off of her as she collapses to the ground. She looks up at me from her position and then at my arm as I hold the board. I follow her gaze and gasp as the black flames lick up my arm and disappear. I shriek a second later and fling the board away from me.

4

A howl fills the air, and I turn my gaze back to Mrs. Bane, whose eyes have turned a creepy black. Her body begins to change and elongate, but it's different from her usual shift from human to wolf. Slime leaks from her eyes and coats her entire body as talons bust from her hands.

She lunges for me, only to be stopped by a large body barreling into her. Her body flies back into the burning house, and I stare in shock as the house collapses on top of her.

I turn, glaring at the dark red and brown wolf whose fur is bristled. He growls toward the house as if Mrs. Bane is going to come back.

"What the hell, Corey! She needs our help!"

He turns and glares over his shoulder at me. Shrieking noises come from the pile of fiery rubble, pulling his attention back. I follow him and stare at what I thought was Mrs. Bane rising on wings with four talons beneath her. She flies toward us, and I scream as I'm yanked back. Wind surrounds me as arms encircle my waist in a familiar hold.

"Calm down. It's me. I'm getting you out of here. I beat the rest of the wolves here. You're one lucky lady," a voice drawls out in my ear.

"Zeke! Oh my God! We can't leave Corey! We have to go back!" I start hitting his back with my fists. He just chuckles and repositions me.

A sharp squeal follows us from the burning fire, and I hear growling from multiple wolves. Hopefully they got there before that thing destroys Corey.

"He's going to be okay, Ember. He's the next Beta for a reason. He's strong. You'll see." He begins to slow down, and I take in our surroundings. We traveled miles in what seems like only a few seconds. I guess that's one thing vampires have over us wolves is their intense speed. We may be fast, but they're always faster.

"What was that thing? Did you see it?" I feel the adrenaline moving through my body, and something in me stirs.

"That was an Imp, a creature from hell. They aren't the friendliest creatures. They normally don't reveal themselves. Did it hurt you or anything?" He stops suddenly, jolting me, and sets me on my feet. He looks me over and lifts my arms, then puts them down. "Do you need healing? Do you need some of my blood?"

I slap his shoulder. "No, I don't need any blood. I'm fine. She didn't touch me."

He looks me dead in the eye, as if trying to discern if I'm genuinely hurt or not. "Did anything else happen?"

I go to speak when I hear a door open from somewhere close. I turn and realize we're standing in the front yard of my parents' house. It's not too far from the pack house where the Alpha and his family reside, as well as several enforcers and the Beta's family.

"Oh, honey, are you okay? Your father just told me what happened through our bond. Are you hurt? Zeke, did you look her over?"

"She's perfectly fine, Kyra. Not a single hair was touched," Zeke says, resting a hand on my shoulder.

"Thank the goddess. Come inside. We can have some coffee. Your father will be around after a while," Mom says and turns, ushering us to follow her.

"Did he mention if Corey was alright?" I ask, and I notice my mother's shoulders stiffen. She's always been concerned about how close I am to him, but we've never let on that we're together. Even Zeke has kept it quiet.

"He didn't say, but he did mention that the pack uncovered the bodies of the entire Bane family. I'm sorry, honey, I know you and Amber were once close." Her voice seems to move through a fog as memories of playing Barbies with Amber in the backyard surface from the recesses of my brain.

Her long blond curls would bounce around her when we laughed as kids. She had an early transition and began training to be a Sentinel on the pack borders shortly after. It made finding time to hang out difficult.

I feel a gentle nudge as Zeke's hand pushes me forward. He then proceeds to pull me into his side. I look over at him and offer him a small smile of thanks, and we follow my mom the rest of the way into the house.

Zeke has been around since I turned fourteen. He and my mother met back when she was young, and he deemed himself a guardian for the family at that time. I'm not sure why and none of the specifics have ever been shared, but he went away for a time to do who knows what. Mom claimed he was like a different man when he returned.

Zeke's always seems to appear when I need him the most or right when I am about to do something stupid that I probably would regret later on. Like the time I got dared to jump off the roof of another family's home into their pool in the dead of night, and he stopped me from completing it.

I knew it wasn't a good idea, but I had to show that stupid Lacy up. I know I don't want to be with Adam, but it pisses me off that she gloats about it in front of other shifters that she and he are an item. It doesn't look good for me when she does it. If Zeke hadn't stopped me, I probably would have broken something, and considering I haven't fully transitioned into my wolf yet, my healing is barely above that of a human. It would have taken me weeks, or possibly months, to recover from that.

He also kissed me that night and told me that he would always be here waiting, no matter how things end up. I wasn't sure how to take that at the time, but things haven't been awkward, and he hasn't kissed me since. I don't know if he still feels that way or what, but it doesn't matter because I'm with Corey and tied to Adam.

I'm brought out of my thoughts when I feel something cold

hit the back of my legs. I blink and look down to find the couch behind me and plop down on it. I look up and see Zeke's concerned expression, but he remains silent as my mom busies herself in the kitchen. I watch his eyes, which are the most gorgeous brown I have ever seen. They are like molten chocolate in one of those chocolate desserts that ooze chocolate out when you cut into it with a fork. His curly black hair hangs loosely around his face, and his dark skin seems to glisten with power. Wait, when have I ever been able to see his power?

My eyes widen, and I look him up and down as if taking him in for the first time. There is definitely a sheen of magic that seems to hover over his skin, and a colorful aura surrounds him. It varies in colors, and his brows droop low as he frowns.

"What?" His voice seems to calm me, and I meet his gaze. My cheeks heat, and I know I'm blushing. His brows shoot up. "What in the world? Why are you blushing?"

"I can see your magic. I've never been able to see it before. Why can I now? Are you doing something to make it visible?" My breath rushes out with my words as I word vomit. What is going on with me?

"Are you sure nothing else happened back there at the fire? I'm not doing anything different from what I usually do around you," he quietly whispers and glances in the direction of the kitchen.

My mom is still shuffling around in there. I thought she was just getting coffee, but now it sounds like she's making food. I don't feel like eating, so maybe that means we have company coming. Great.

"Well, yeah, something weird happened. Mrs. Bane, I mean the Imp thing, was under a board that was lit up with black flames and regular flames. I picked it up to let her out, and the flames ran up my arm and disappeared. I didn't have any burns or anything, but I threw it away from me. The thing's eyes changed from those of Mrs. Bane to black, and then Corey appeared. It all happened so fast."

"Wait, did you absorb the flames?" Zeke's expression is serious, which causes me to squirm.

I look down at my right arm and stare at it as if the answer would appear on it. Nothing happens, of course, so I meet Zeke's gaze again as I say, "I guess I did."

He stands quickly as he curses and begins pacing the room. My mother, I guess, having heard his cussing fit, comes running and stares at us both for a second.

"Did something happen?" she asks, looking between Zeke and me.

"She touched hellfire, Kyra. She absorbed it," Zeke says, coming to a stop and staring at my mother, whose face has paled.

"What is hellfire? Is it bad?" I ask in confusion, staring at the two of them.

"You want to tell her what hellfire is, Kyra? Why the hell did you never tell me what she was? I knew there was a reason I was drawn to her." Zeke's voice grows, and I sit shocked at the edge of the sofa, having never heard him raise his voice at me or Mom.

"I couldn't tell you, Zeke! Her father knows, but no one else," my mother retorts and runs a hand through her hair. It's her usual sign of stress.

"What's going on? Is there something you're keeping from me?" I ask my mom, who stares at me for a whole two seconds before she begins to pace.

A bell chimes from the kitchen, and the scent of coffee and cookies fills the air.

"Is the Alpha coming back with Dad?" I ask, praying she says no.

"Yes, your father, the Alpha, and Adam will be here soon.

MADILYNN DALE

After they leave, we will continue this discussion. Not until then. Zeke, you can go." My mother attempts to dismiss him.

"Like hell, I will! You might as well consider me a permanent fixture at this point. I'm not leaving her side." He moves away from my mother and returns to the couch next to me.

"Fine, but not a word of anything until after the Alpha leaves. Not a word." My mother storms out of the kitchen, and I watch her retreating figure until it disappears through another door.

"What just happened?" I ask, turning and pinning Zeke with a glare.

"You, my darling, are so much more than just a wolf. You will know soon enough. I hear that awful betrothed of yours approaching with his father. We'll continue this conversation later," Zeke says, patting my shoulder before pulling me into him. He places a gentle kiss on my head as he whispers, "I'll keep you safe. Remember that, always."

I roll my eyes at his overdramatic words and rest my head on his shoulder. A knock on the front door startles me before I hear my father push it open. His footsteps seem to echo, but as he enters the room, I notice that he moves as he always has.

"It'll all be fine," Zeke whispers for only my ears to hear as I watch the Alpha and Adam file in behind my dad.

CHAPTER TWO

I stare at Adam as he moves gracefully, striding into the room behind his father, Alpha Gale. Adam smiles at me, and he's the spitting image of his father before him. His silver eyes seem to glow as his silver-blond hair falls to his shoulders. It gives him a rugged look with the five o'clock shadow he's got going on.

The Alpha, on the other hand, is clean-shaven with a short cut of hair that is gray. He, too, has silver eyes that glow and, for being in his mid-fifties, still maintains a youthful appearance thanks to his shifter genes. He doesn't look a day over thirty, and his muscles are strong and lean.

My father looks small standing next to them, when really there are only a few inches of difference between all of their six-foot-something frames. My dad, with his red hair, stands out like a sore thumb next to them. I never understood how my hair could be so dark if he was a redhead, but biology has never been my strongest area. He is bulkier than the Alphas with him and works as a Sentinel on the edge of our neighborhood, remaining close to the pack house where the Alpha's family resides.

"Hello, everyone. I wanted to pop in to check on my soon-to-be daughter-in-law. It appeared that Corey did an excellent job in protecting you until Zeke here could get you away. Thank you for that, Zeke." The Alpha nods at Zeke.

"Anytime," Zeke responds with a graceful nod.

"It appears we've had an increase in demon attacks as of late. I hate that you got mixed into one. It concerns me that it was so close to home, though." The Alpha moves to sit on another sofa in the sitting room as he appears lost in thought. Adam follows, remaining silent and watchful as he does. He stands next to the sofa his father claimed.

I guess Adam has taken it upon himself to be a guard or something. I watch him with a curious expression, and the Alpha remains quiet, as if contemplating. My father mumbles and steps out of the room for a few minutes before returning with my mother, who has a plate of cookies and a tray of coffee for everyone. She smiles as she sets it down on the table before us and the two of them squeeze onto the couch next to Zeke and me. It makes me wonder where my twin sisters are. Shouldn't they be home? Are they still at Mona's house across the street?

The Alpha clears his throat, pulling our attention back to him.

"With the demon attack on the rise, I fear that we may need to act soon to stop them from gaining further ground. They've always plagued some of the other packs but never ours." He frowns, and I feel my mother stiffen beside me.

I glance out of the corner of my eye and notice a grimace on her face. What's that about?

"I'm going to begin a new training regimen for all of the younger pack members. Your twins will need to attend as well. Any child ten and up will begin to train. They may not necessarily be fighting any time soon, but we need to be prepared for the worst-case scenarios." Alpha Gale shifts his weight on the couch and looks at Adam to suggest he sit.

Adam sits, and I stare at him. I didn't realize how much taller he was than his father or how much broader his shoulders are. Seated together, the two Alpha males dwarf the couch and make it appear like one of those toddler couches you see kids with.

"Adam and Ember, you will be training with an advanced group of Betas who typically only handle covert missions. As the next in line to lead, I need you two to prepare for anything and work together in sync. It should help your wolf surface, my dear, and strengthen your bond." Alpha Gale smiles at me, expecting me to be pleased with this plan, but I fight the growl threatening to rip from my throat.

What the hell is this? I want to find a way out of this shit with him, not willingly move to lead the pack. I need to figure this out.

"May I join in on this training, sir? I think I could provide more insight when it comes to facing other creatures. I've been around for a long time. Would that be acceptable?" Zeke's southern accent breaks me from the glare I didn't realize I was giving Adam, who I notice smirking in response. I know he doesn't want this, so why doesn't he stop it?

"That's an excellent idea, Zeke. Would you be opposed to working with all of them?" Alpha Gale shifts his attention to Zeke and my parents to my left. I take a brief moment to offer a vulgar gesture to Adam, who only smiles bigger in response. Asshole.

Zeke pinches me, making me focus. I plaster a fake smile on my face and listen in as my parents talk with the Alpha about the training my sisters will be doing. They'll mostly be doing basic self-defense maneuvers and simple attack combos. They're fifteen, so they should be fine.

After my parents talk with the Alpha about my sisters for a

solid thirty minutes while I pretend to be excited about all the new plans, the Alpha returns his focus to me.

"Ember, you'll meet with the group in front of the pack house tomorrow morning at seven to begin your new training. I may have you continue to work with Corey some outside of it, but he'll also begin training. I need him to be able to follow both you and Adam wherever you go in the future. I'm looking to recruit another Beta to create a team for you, but I've yet to find someone to fill that role. I want to be able to trust them completely, and I'll find them in time. Until then, you'll focus on that training," he says with an authoritative voice that sends chills down my spine.

"What about my college classes?" I ask, hoping I can continue with them when they start up in a few weeks.

Alpha Gale frowns and looks down at me over his nose. "You'll need to change them to an online schedule. I don't want you far from the pack lands while the demons remain active. It could be dangerous for you to attend."

"Even if I take someone to protect me?" I ask, hoping he'll let me have this little freedom.

"Yes, even if you have someone with you, the risk is too high. So, you will remain here," he says with finality.

Anger surges through me at the freedom he just took away from me. The Rose Moon pack used to be different at one time, but Alpha Gale has slowly been making it a living hell since Adam's mother died. I get why he wants me safe, but I don't want the role of Luna. I've no interest in his son, and I don't think he's my mate. I don't want to be forced into an arranged marriage or mating. I know there's someone out there for me, maybe even another life outside this pack.

Despite my anger, I keep my mouth shut and nod in response to the Alpha's decision. I don't want to cause trouble for my family, who are happy with the way their life is. Also, my sisters are attending the pack school as I did before them.

They get along well with all the other pack members at the school, and I know if I cause trouble, it could cause problems for them.

"Now, the day is getting late. Adam and I have to make several stops in preparation before tomorrow. Thank you, Mrs. Benedict, for the coffee and cookies. They were delicious, as always. We'll talk again soon." We all stand as the Alpha stands, and my dad offers to walk him out.

"May I have a word, sweetheart?" Adam's voice is cool as he requests my attention.

Zeke reaches with a hand and squeezes my shoulder for encouragement. I smile back at Adam. "Yes, shall I walk you out then?"

He smirks. "Please."

I walk toward him, and he grabs my hand, putting on a show for my parents and his father. My dad smiles, and he and the Alpha remain where they are to give us a few minutes of privacy.

Adam squeezes my hand, and we step through the front door into the late afternoon sunlight. He turns to face me and drops my hand. "We need to get our shit together if we're going to make this work. Neither one of us needs to be screwing around anymore." His voice grates on my nerves.

"Neither one of us wants this, Adam. There has to be a way to break that stupid contract our families created," I grumble.

He runs a hand through his hair. "You think that if there were a way, I wouldn't have already done it? We're stuck in this, Ember. It's time we face the facts. There's no way out. We need to start acting like the betrothed couple we are."

I grimace. "What if you find your true mate?"

"What if you are my true mate? We won't know anything until after your wolf surfaces. Has there been any changes?"

I pause, thinking through today's events. Should I tell him yes that there are some new advancements? What if they aren't related to my wolf at all but are a delayed reaction to all the adrenaline from my near-death experience with a demon?

"Not yet, but hopefully soon. Maybe the new training will coax her out."

He frowns. "I hope so. I'll see you in the morning." He leans in and kisses me softly, and I let him. His lips are gentle as he kisses me, and I know I can count on one hand the number of times we've kissed. So, if he's willing to try to make this work, maybe I should as well.

As we pull away from each other, Alpha Gale opens the door and breaks into a radiant smile. "Ah, young love. How precious. We'll see you bright and early, dear Ember." He gently pushes Adam forward and away from me. I nod in response and return to the house.

As I enter the living room, I find my parents have dispersed, and Zeke lounges on the couch. I rejoin him, feeling moody, and sit at his side before I pick up a cookie from the coffee table before us.

As I toss it into my mouth and begin to chew, he says, "Your mom is calling the Carolines to see if the twins can spend the night tonight. She's using your event from earlier as an excuse. Apparently, the talk we're going to have in the next few minutes may get tense."

I shrug and finish chewing my cookie. Zeke watches me, assessing my movements.

"Are you okay?"

I swallow and cross my arms across my chest. "No. I'm pissed because things are moving faster than I want toward tying me to Adam for the rest of eternity."

"Oh," is all he says before my parents return to the room with grim faces.

I quirk my brow and tilt my head as they sit across the room from us on the sofa the Alphas had claimed while they were here. If they're sitting that far away from us, whatever they're about to tell me must be bad.

"Okay, darling, there are some secrets we've kept that I need you to understand were for your safety." My mother places her hands in her lap. I watch as she tries not to pick at the cuticle on her thumb. It's been her nervous tick for all my life. She looks over at my father, finally, with a sad smile.

He meets her gaze and nods before turning to focus on me. Then, with a sigh, he says, "I'm not your real father."

I gape at him, confused, and look over at my mother, who is staring at her lap. I silently will her to look up at me and deny what he claimed, but she doesn't. I turn my gaze back to my father—who is not my father—as he continues.

"When your mother and I found each other, she was already pregnant with you. We didn't find out until after we had been dating for a few weeks. We knew we were mates right off the bat, but wanted to learn more about each other before taking the next step to complete the mating. Your mother came to me with tears in her eyes when she found out. She had hoped it wouldn't happen." He reaches over and grabs my mother's hand, squeezing it.

"Your real father was someone I met at a party. He was sweet and every girl's dream. I will never know why he took an interest in me, but he picked me that night, and we slept together. I was about your age at the time. I didn't find out who he was until the next morning." She glances at Zeke.

I feel Zeke tense around me, and he tightens his hold on me.

My mother continues, "I had hoped to try and turn that one night into more when I woke the following day, but your real father revealed to me who he was. He told me he only ventures out from his realm on occasion to attempt to procreate. He has never had a true mate and will most likely never have one. He also told me that there was a chance I could become pregnant after our night together despite contraceptives and that if I find myself pregnant, to call for him, and he would come to take the child. He said the babe would be the next heir to the throne of Hell."

Zeke's grip on me becomes uncomfortable, so I elbow him to ease up as I continue to stare at my mother. "What are you trying to say?"

She lets go of my father's hand and begins to shake them as if shaking water. Her eyes dart to my father, who is frowning, before coming back to mine. "Your father is Lucifer, the leader of Hell."

"This has to be a joke," I state, trying to push up from the sofa, only to be held back by Zeke.

"This isn't a joke, Ember. I never called out to him because I didn't want him to take you away from me. Will agreed to claim you as his own, and no one ever knew that you were conceived before we found each other. They just assumed we got overly excited to have found our mate, and you were conceived from our first time. With the attacks that have been happening, though, I can't help but worry that he's looking for you." I watch as my mother stares down at her lap in defeat. My father begins rubbing circles on her back.

"How could you keep a secret like this from me my entire life? I've lived a lie! Am I even a shifter? Do I even have a wolf inside of me?" My voice rises to a scream, and I begin fighting against Zeke's grip. "Let me up!" My body heats, and I feel something stir inside of me.

"Honey, calm down. Yes, there has to be a wolf in you. You have not lived a lie. You're still the sweet little girl who entered this world. You're my little girl even though you're not truly of my blood." My father's words move across my raging fire within and settle me. Tears spring to my eyes, and I quit fighting Zeke.

"What am I? If you knew this, why did you tie me to Adam?" I ask, my voice softer this time.

"Your father and I made that contract with the Alpha in

hopes of keeping you here if the day were ever to arise when Lucifer discovered your existence. We could sense great power in you early on. It's just taking its sweet time to surface," my mother states.

"Does Alpha Gale know that she's not fully a wolf shifter?" Zeke asks quietly.

"No, we never told him. We have been the only ones to know. Not even your grandparents know." My mother offers me a slight smile, but I drop my gaze and stare at my hands that rest in my lap.

What am I? Who am I? I look up, feeling Zeke move and meet his gaze.

"It's going to be okay, Ember," he says, sensing my turbulent emotions.

I push my thoughts of what I could be to the back of my mind and refocus on my parents. "Is there anything else you've kept from me that I need to know?" I stare both my parents down, feeling the anger that was calm only a second ago, stirring to life again.

"No, you're our daughter, and eventually, your wolf will surface. Lucifer won't take you from us." My mother's words are strong and seem to bring an end to the conversation as she pushes to stand. "Now, I'm going to clean up. Zeke, you can stay, but Ember, you'll need your rest for what is to come. I know Alpha Gale has a lot of plans for your training tomorrow."

"Fine, I'm going to my room then," I say. I feel Zeke's gaze burning holes into the back of my head as I move away from everyone and down the hall.

"I'm going to do a sweep to make sure there are no lingering demons that the wolves missed. Just expect me to hang out here rather than at my own home, Kyra." Zeke's words follow me down the hall and irritate me. I don't understand why he is suddenly so protective and needs to be at my side or near me twenty-four seven. The encounter with the demon was a fluke, and I highly doubt anyone is looking for me. Lucifer doesn't even know I exist.

I hear my mother's soft words but can't distinguish them as I enter my room and close the door behind me. I move to the bed and flop down on top of my comforter. I stare at the ceiling fan as it rotates above me and mull over the information my parents shared with me.

Why would Lucifer be looking for me now, after all these years? It doesn't make sense. There has to be something else going on.

I roll to my stomach and stare out my window across the room from me. The evening light of the sun causes shadows to dance on my light gray walls. Pictures of my family and me hang in small clusters next to the window while my dresser dominates the wall to the right of me. I close my eyes as the last of the sun's rays fill the room, and something seems to come alive inside of me. An urge to run hits me like no other, and I know I can't stay in this room. I need out.

Opening my eyes, I push from the bed and move toward the window. The sun sinks even lower, casting everything into dark shadows as night begins to take over for the day. I rest my head against the glass as my skin heats, and I know I need to get outside. Something is happening, but I'm not sure what.

I quietly lift the window and slip into the bed of flowers resting below it. My mother will be upset that I have trampled a few, but I'll deal with that later. As the evening air hits me, I sigh, and my blood seems to cool.

I take in the trees around me and mentally create the shortest route from here to Corey's house. I might as well run and check on him. I know he got banged up today, and that shifter healing should have kicked in to help him heal, but I have to see for myself.

I take off at a sprint and feel my body moving faster than usual. The new sensation causes me to stumble, but I quickly regain my footing and continue. The wind whipping past me feels exhilarating, and I feel a heat bubble up inside of me. It moves up and seems to dance around me as I speed between trees. Cutting through the forest is the quickest route to where I want to go.

I giggle to myself as I move lightly on my feet, but the sound of a branch cracking as if someone has stepped on it catches my attention. I slow my pace to a walk before finally stopping and remain still. I listen and pick up on sounds I've never been able to hear before. Then, fighting the urge to take it all in, I focus like they teach young shifters to do and pick out the faintest footsteps.

It sounds like someone is approaching me from behind, and heat swirls around me as I whip around to face my supposed attacker. As I stand, preparing to attack, Zeke walks from between the trees with a smirk.

"I knew you wouldn't stay in your room, but this isn't what I expected, Ember," he says, approaching even closer and stopping an arm's width away.

I place my hands on my hips. "What do you mean? I just wanted to run."

He laughs and reaches to pluck something from my hair. I gape as he holds a small black flame. "This, my dear, means you are not just out for a run. Your beast is surfacing. It makes sense after what your mother revealed. I knew there was something about you that pulled me to you, and this is it. We are similar, both you and I, but not."

"What do you mean?" I drop my hands and move closer to his hand that holds the flame. I poke at it with a finger, and it jumps to me and dances up my arm. It doesn't burn, but it dissolves into my skin a second later.

"You and I are both creatures from hell. Vampires were created in hell, and we broke free to roam the human world, leading to different vampires being made. Vampire hunters were also created in hell to help control our numbers because we got out of hand. With your heritage, though, Ember, I can't help but be curious about your beast. What will it be? Will it be a wolf or something else?"

"I would like to know that as well. Why are you so cryptic? Do you not know what I am if you're from hell?" I can't help but glare at Zeke, as I fight the urge to run some more.

He shrugs and ignores the question. "Were you headed to Corey's place? You know you need to end things with him. Not only because of the thing with the Alpha but because it would be good for him to move on."

I drop my gaze to the ground, feeling defeated. I knew that eventually, Corey and I would have to call it quits, but I don't want to. I love him, but I also don't want to hurt him. Hell, I don't want to hurt. "I know, but it's not that simple."

Zeke lifts my chin and meets my gaze. "I know it's not, but maybe you just need the right distraction." He leans in and presses his lips to mine.

My eyes widen in shock momentarily as a strong pulse rushes through my body, almost like when I grabbed the electric fence as a kid. I feel lightning in my toes, and it dances up my spine. I close my eyes and lean into Zeke's kiss as more electricity explodes around us. He pulls me closer, wrapping his arms around me, and I feel him move us. In seconds, my back is pressed against a tree, and I wrap my legs around him.

We deepen the kiss, and the scent of burning wood surrounds us. I pull back for air and blink as tendrils of black smoke flow around us. Perplexed, I look over my shoulder to see black flames burning the tree Zeke has me pressed against.

"Well, that was unexpected. Maybe we should revisit this when you have more control of your powers," Zeke says, lowering me to the ground. I stare up at him.

"How did I do that? All you did was push me against it. Wait, we kissed! Oh shit, Zeke, we fucked up! What is this going to do to our friendship? What if this doesn't work out? Shit!" I push away from him and begin to pace.

He chuckles and grabs me, pulling me close to him. "It'll be fine, Ember. Just wait and see. You aren't a normal supernatural being, love. Our friendship will be fine. Let's get you back home before your parents realize you're gone. You can end things with Corey in the morning."

I frown up at him but don't say anything. My mind is too cluttered right now to address the Corey thing. I'm utterly confused. I just kissed my lifelong best friend. What the hell? I'm super fucked.

We walk in silence at a slow pace back to my home. Zeke holds my hand the entire time, rubbing calming circles on it with his thumb. He lets me sit in my thoughts as I process what the hell we just did and how the hell I managed to get myself tangled up with three men. One I want nothing to do with, one I'm in love with, and the other is my best friend. What should I do?

We stop after a time, and I realize we're standing outside my window. I look down at the flowers I trampled on my way out and see they have burned to ash. Well, hell, what am I going to do about this new flame thing I have going on?

"Go in and get some rest. I'll come up with some ideas on how to work with your powers. I think we need to keep this between us right now," Zeke says, lifting my hand to his lips and placing a kiss on it.

"The powers thing or the kissing thing?" I ask snarkily.

"Both." He smirks. "I'll be in the living room on the couch if you need me. Don't try to sneak out again."

I smile, and mock salute him. "Yes, sir!"

He rolls his eyes. "Goodnight, Ember. I'll see you at dawn."

"Goodnight," I respond with a soft smile, letting all my sass go. I feel drained. This day has wreaked havoc on my emotions and my mind.

Zeke nods, and I take that as my cue to climb back through the window. I check my palms before pushing up and through it to make sure I'm not going to leave scorch marks and promptly land on the floor in a crouch. I sigh with relief and surprise as I notice how quiet I landed. I listen for my parents for a few seconds. I can faintly hear their breaths down the hall as they sleep and wonder if normal shifter hearing is that good.

I then register light steps as Zeke moves away from the window and moments later hear the front door open and close. He's in the house. I push from the floor and walk toward my dresser. I rest my hands on its surface and stare into the mirror before me. I don't see any differences, but I feel them. It's an odd sensation, and a sad feeling of loss weighs heavy on me. There is no turning back from what I learned today, and I know I can only move forward.

I shake my head and reach into the dresser to pull out a tank top and shorts for bed. I quickly change and move over to the bed. It's late, and tomorrow is going to be a long day. Who knows how it will go.

CHAPTER THREE

The next morning arrives quickly, and Zeke and I walk down the road to the pack house. He seems all bright-eyed and bushy-tailed this morning while nerves fill my stomach with butterflies once again.

When Zeke and I first met when I was younger, I was amazed that he could move around in daylight. I thought all vampires would burn in the sunlight, but it turns out that was only a myth. He once told me that it's not comfortable walking in the daylight but manageable. It makes it easier on vamps if they wear long-sleeved clothing and cover all their skin. Non-supernaturals tend to throw him weird looks when they see him dressed like he is today in the summer heat. It's a good thing we aren't going to be around many of them for a while.

After several minutes of walking in silence, Zeke forces me to stop. He rests his hand on my shoulder. "I'm not sure how today is going to go, but I need you to make sure to keep any hint of that fire you displayed last night under control. I don't think we need the Alpha picking up on the deception your parents have created."

"Isn't it going to come out eventually that I'm more than

what they expect? I know I have increased abilities since touching that flame and that I can't hide, but what if I'm not a wolf at all? We won't be able to hide whatever beast I am in time," I say, bristling. I don't see a way to keep my secret safe for long, especially from my lover and future spouse.

"We'll figure it out. In the meantime, focus on the training, and don't forget to have that talk with Corey." Zeke drops his hand and begins to turn.

"I'm not sure I want to drop what I have with him, Zeke. It's not that easy." I frown and look down at my hands. The idea of ending things makes my heart ache even though it seems to be the most logical thing to do.

"Life isn't easy, Ember. Do it before he's ordered to end it. It'll hurt less," he says as he continues to walk forward.

I grit my teeth and hold my tongue. There's no arguing that, so I just follow quietly and remain silent as we walk the remainder of the trek to the pack house.

As we near, I take in the beautiful exterior of the plantation-style home. Its white paint and trim look new, and the flower beds are filled to the brim with flowers. It reminds me of something you would find in *HGTV* magazines.

Everything looks perfect except the large group of burly men standing before it. The sight causes me to pause. It throws everything off, but I know that's the group we're meeting. There are maybe fifteen males gathered around, chatting. I recognize a few of them from some pack meetings, but none of them pay Zeke and me any attention as we approach.

We stop near the group's back, and I look around, trying to find Corey or even Adam. I feel awkward, nervous, and out of place. The butterflies flitting in my stomach turn to something else, and it feels like my power is trying to rise to the surface like it did last night. As if sensing a change, Zeke whips around to face me.

"Breath and calm yourself, love. We don't need any of that

power coming out. It's already starting to cloud your scent. Mine should be able to mask it for a time in this group but get it together," he whispers, for only my ears to hear.

I nod and close my eyes, taking deep breaths. It calms my heart rate, and I feel the power recede and settle. It's almost like it closed its eyes and went to sleep. I open my eyes and meet Zeke's gaze. He offers me a kind smile, and we turn as the door to the pack house creaks open.

I can't fight the smile that breaks out on my face as Corey walks out, followed by Adam. As if sensing me, Corey seeks me out, and my smile widens as our eyes meet. Relief fills him, and he looks to his right as Adam places a hand on his shoulder. Corey frowns at him as they speak, but I can't hear what's said. A moment later, a burly black-haired male exits the pack house.

He stares at our group, and the men around me get quiet. He must be our trainer.

"Good morning, everyone. For those of you who don't know who I am, my name is Seth. I'll be training you from here on out. We have several newbies today, but we will not be taking it easy. We will begin this morning by working with our resident vamp and focusing on hand-to-hand combat. Now, everyone will head to the training area behind the house. Let's get to work." He claps, and everyone begins to move.

I glance at Corey and Adam on the porch and try to make my way to them, but a hand on my shoulder stops me.

"No, let's go," Zeke urges and turns me toward the direction the crowd is moving.

"But I need to talk to them. Why not?"

"You need to focus. Save it for later," he growls.

I roll my eyes. "Fine."

I trudge along behind Zeke, fighting the urge to stomp my feet like a child. We move from the grassy lawn to a brick walk that leads us to the back of the pack house. The area for training has raised platforms for sparring and other necessary equipment. There is a rack with imitation weapons as well as one for weights.

The group makes its way to a raised platform in the center of the training area. We watch as one while Seth climbs the steps and stands before everyone. I hear Adam and Corey speaking in hushed tones and turn to watch as they move in place behind me. They stop their chatter, and both offer me a smile. It seems suspicious, but with those two, one can never know.

I turn my focus back to Seth as he motions to Zeke. Zeke moves with his vampire speed and stops at Seth's side. We remain standing as a group as Zeke launches into a quick lesson on vampires and other creatures that we may encounter from Hell. He shares some information about the Imp from the attack yesterday, and I'm surprised with how much he knows. Then again, as he said last night, he is a creature of Hell. It may be a requirement for his people to have this type of knowledge before roaming the human world.

At the end of the speech, Seth returns and pairs us off into groups. I'm excited that he pairs me off with Corey, but I don't miss the warning look from Zeke. Instead, I offer him a mischievous smile as I follow Corey toward another raised platform to begin practicing.

As Corey and I climb the steps of our platform, he says softly over his shoulder, "I'm glad you're okay after last night, Ember. I was worried about you."

"Thanks, I was worried about you too. The Alpha visited with Adam last night to check on me. I tried to sneak out to check on you last night but got caught by Zeke."

Corey reaches the center of the platform and turns to me. "Yeah, they came by my place after they left there. Adam said they're going to push the arrangement between you both to strengthen his place in the pack."

I grimace and move into a fighting stance to begin practicing. Corey has been teaching me some moves for years now, but it's nothing compared to what the Betas around me know. We'll need to up our game to take on demons. "I'm not excited about that. You know how I feel about it."

"I do, and that's why we need to talk." His face drops into a frown, and I know what's going to follow.

"Don't say it. I get it. It sucks." I move forward to attack, and he parries.

"You know what we need to do then," he says, blocking my attack.

"Yes. I don't want to, though." I make a move toward his left side.

He blocks me. "We have to call it quits."

Anger surges through me, and I move to hit him in the stomach. I nail my target, and surprise fills me as Corey flies back a few feet.

"That's new," he states as he regains his footing. "Did the anger bring that out?"

"I don't know," I respond and move to attack again.

"Ember, say something about this. Are you okay with being friends? Unfortunately, we don't have much of a choice." He blocks, and I try to increase my speed.

"I'm not okay with this, no. Does it need to be done? Yeah. It doesn't mean I have to like it." We move in circles, and Corey steps forward, taking more of an offensive position. I try my best to recall the bit he's taught me over the years and block.

"So, we're good?" he asks, a little breathless.

I smile broadly as excitement courses through me at how breathless he is. But, of course, I've always been the one breathless when we practice. It's a nice change not to be winded for once.

"I guess." I get another hit in, but it's off a little and lands on his shoulder.

"Why are your punches so much stronger today? Did something happen after the attack?" We've picked up speed, and I faintly notice that people are starting to stare.

"I guess we're finally getting what we've been pushing for. I don't know. I don't feel any different," I respond, dodging a punch.

"Hmph," is all he gets out as we continue to spar. We block, punch, kick, and parry like this for a good hour.

Sweat drips off of me in rivulets when Seth's words pierce the air. "All right, you two. Everyone else has been done for at least ten minutes. Take a break."

Corey and I both stop, panting, and look around. Adam stands next to Zeke with an impressed smile on his face while the other males around us gawk with their mouths open. They act as if they've never seen a woman fight before. It's not my fault that the Beta females train separately, but then again, the Alpha handpicked this group.

"I think we can keep going if that's okay, Seth," I say boldly and turn back to face Corey. I still have some frustration to take out on him. I'm not ready to end this.

He looks surprised but resets in preparation to spar.

"How about I step in and give you a break, Corey?" Zeke asks and then clears his throat as I whip around and glare at him. "It would be good for her to practice with another opponent with a different set of skills. She has been working with you and knows how you fight. It gives her an advantage."

I turn back to look at Corey, who shrugs. "That's true. Okay, let's see how you guys do."

I glare at Corey as he walks off and turn my focus on Zeke. "Really?" I ask him as he moves into the place where Corey stood.

"Really. Now let's see you face off against me. Don't hold back but control your emotions." He winks and shifts into a fighting position.

I roll my eyes and mirror him, but in the blink of an eye, he moves and has me pinned to the ground. "What the?"

"I told you to be ready. Come on now, love." He helps me back to my feet, and I growl.

I take a deep breath and let myself focus. I let the anger toward Corey and the fact that he ended things before I had a chance to talk it out with him go. My bruised feelings will heal. Facing Zeke now will help me later, especially if we run into other beings from Hell.

Feeling settled, I focus on Zeke and let my power roll through me but not to the point where flames come to life. Instead, I feel it sink into my bones like a soft blanket wrapping around me. It warms me from the inside, and I smile as Zeke makes his move.

This time I stop him, and I push myself, managing to meet each blow and block it. I let my confidence boost me and attempt to move from the defensive, but he is quicker at blocking me than I am him, and I take a step back.

We circle and punch, parry and jump, round and round. I faintly hear hoots and yells from others around me, but the noise barely registers as I focus on Zeke. It's almost like a string keeps me tied to him, and we move almost in sync.

I go to punch Zeke on his right side when an odd emotion fills me. It's almost as if I grabbed an electric fence. Sparks shoot through my body, and I stumble, which gives Zeke an advantage. In seconds, he has me pinned to the ground, knees straddling me, with his fist at my chin.

He pants, trying to catch his breath. "Got you."

I stare up at him, stunned at what just happened and also confused. Where did those emotions come from? Was that my mate? What the hell?

Clapping pulls me from my thoughts, and Zeke slides off me. He offers me a hand to help me up, and once I stand, I look around at the group of guys around us.

Corey and Adam are beaming as they take me in, and I can't help but wonder if maybe I let too much power out. I do an internal check and feel it still resting in my bones. I try to push it back, but it doesn't budge. I sniff the air, trying to pick up if my scent has changed, but with all the sweaty males around, all I get is salt and wet dog.

I look over at Zeke, who frowns and shakes his head. "You're fine. I have you covered," he says softly for only me to hear.

"Well, that was a magnificent display of power, my dear," a voice drawls, and I turn to find Alpha Gale behind me, standing next to Seth. "I guess she's finally surfacing?"

I bow my head. "Yes, I think so."

"Good. You all take a break. I need to speak with Seth. We have a mission for you that you'll be briefed on this afternoon. Grab lunch and meet with us in the conference room at two p.m. Don't be late," Alpha says, and we all bow our heads in acknowledgment.

We keep our heads bowed as he turns with Seth, and they head back toward the rear of the pack house. I let out a sigh of relief but tense up when Adam's hand lands on my shoulder.

"It's about time, Ember. I knew you would push after that talk last night. Corey told me you two were good and that we're clear to move forward," Adam says, smiling at me.

I turn and glare at Corey for a second before refocusing on Adam. "I guess so. Things seem to be moving in the right direction." I feel Zeke come up behind me, and I fight the urge to look at him.

A few of the other males smile at me and wave to the guys as they pass us. None of them get too close, though, knowing I'm supposed to be with Adam and that males can be territorial.

"I know this isn't exactly what you want, Ember, but please try and make the best of it, for both of us. I think we could grow to care for each other like a truly mated pair if we aren't," Adam says quietly for only our small group to hear.

I feel Zeke place a hand on the small of my back, and a jolt shoots through me, similar to what I felt earlier. *What the hell?* Instead of turning to look at him, though, I hang my head and say, "I'll try."

"Good. We need to have a united front, like I said last night. I'll see you after lunch," Adam says and starts walking toward the house.

Corey pauses as if to add something but shakes his head instead. He has reminded me repeatedly that if it came to it, he would have to follow orders. Seeing it hurts worse than him telling me that things are over.

I fight the tears that threaten to flow as my heart breaks and turn to Zeke. "Let's get out of here." I grab his hand, and instead of pulling him in the direction that will take us back to my house, he swings me up into his arms and sprints us there.

"Thanks," I say as he sets me down on the step. "I needed that."

"Anytime, love. Now let's get some refreshments. We have a busy afternoon ahead." He smiles and pushes the front door open for me.

"Do you know anything about the mission Alpha mentioned?" I ask curiously, trying to distract myself from my aching heart.

"I don't, but I'm sure it isn't anything serious. He wouldn't send us out if it were. I'm sure he has another team already trained for this." He shrugs, and we make our way into the kitchen.

I walk to the fridge and grab sandwich stuff and a bag of blood for him. I toss it to him, and he catches it and quickly rips the corner of the bag. I plop my sandwich stuff down and throw my sandwich together.

Zeke's blood-drinking habit quit bothering me years ago. "I hope you're right. Did I do okay today?" I glance up at him as he pauses his drinking.

"You did amazing. Now eat."

I roll my eyes as he goes back to drinking. "Fine, but I have questions for later."

Zeke nods and takes his bag to the other room.

I take my sandwich and follow.

CHAPTER FOUR

That afternoon rain moves in, and my mood sours. Zeke has been avoiding me since lunch, and I don't understand why. I want to ask him about the strange sensation that occurred during our fight.

I make my way back to the pack house with him at my side, but we remain silent. It's not an uncomfortable silence, but something's different. I can't put my finger on it. Rain drips down our hoods, but we remain predominantly dry.

We leave our jackets hanging on hooks to the left of the front door and head to the main conference room once we reach the house. The air is humid and smells of lemon. Nevertheless, it's pleasant and seems to lighten my mood.

Zeke and I pick seats at the back of the room in an attempt to remain low-key. A couple of the males glance at me curiously, but they don't try to start a conversation. Corey and Adam take the two open seats next to me moments later, and Seth quiets us all to get our attention.

"Reports have come in that something has been lurking in the woods on the north side of town. The Sentinels found a scent similar to putrid fish lingering near a bush where something had discarded part of a rabbit carcass. We are assuming it's a creature similar to what we saw at yesterday's attack. This assignment, yet simple, will be your first task, trainees. You'll go in groups to seek out and take down whatever it is. Per the Alpha's orders, Adam, Corey, and Ember will be together while I will divide the rest of you. Zeke, you will not be part of this attack. We want to see how the groups do."

Seth looks over us all as we nod, and I can't fight the frown that comes to my face. "You'll go from here to begin tracking the beast or beasts. Work as a pack and if you find nothing by midnight tonight, call it a night, and return to the task in the morning."

We all nod again, and Seth continues to give us instructions. We are to pick up weapons from the weapons room and head out.

As he dismisses us, I turn to Zeke. "Will you be close?"

"I'll do what I can. Stay focused and work as a pack." He nods and slips out before I can ask anything else.

I stand from my chair, as do Corey and Adam beside me.

"Are you worried, Ember?" Adam asks curiously.

"You should be fine after how you trained today," Corey says with a frown and perplexed expression.

"I'm nervous, that's all. But I can do this." I square my shoulders and smile, feigning confidence.

"Great. We'll do well as a team. That's what my father wants us to work as in the future, anyway. It's about time we start doing this, am I right?" Adam looks to me and then Corey.

Corey nods. "Yes, we'll be strong together. Let's head to where the fight was yesterday and start from there."

"Great idea. Ember, we'll follow you in our wolf forms while we hunt for the beasts. We won't be far from you. If you see something before us, though, don't engage, we'll take it down." Adam grabs my hand and squeezes it.

"Okay," I respond, pulling my hand from his.

We walk from the conference room and down the hall to the weapons room. I grab a couple of items before we head back to the front of the pack house, pausing on the front porch as the rain falls. Its light tempo makes me feel at peace, but I don't miss the noises of the guys transitioning into their wolves.

Now more than ever, I can hear their bones crack and pop as they change forms. But, thanks to some shifter magic, they can maintain their clothes following a shift. The process is strange to me since I haven't experienced it myself, but the pain from the first shift is excruciating from the stories I have heard from others. It's supposed to be better with each change after, but I think each person finally adapts to the pain or maybe even compartmentalizes it.

I shake my head, clearing my thoughts as two wolves stare at me from the rain at the bottom of the porch. They are larger than a typical wolf, but thanks to our pack, and many others like us, people believe the red wolves are making a comeback in their former historic home in the US. It's allowed our pack to grow and live safely here in eastern Oklahoma. The difference between the two is that Adam has streaks of silver in his hair while Corey has some darker, almost black fur added to his. Both have hints of the red coloring, typical to the old red wolf.

"I'm coming," I mutter, and they huff at me, then take off at a trot. I roll my eyes and jog to keep up with them, thankful my new strength has also led to more stamina.

I follow the two wolves as we make our way into the woods. A path leads to the northern part of our territory that keeps us away from prying human eyes. We move along quickly and arrive at the burned remains of Amber's family home. The sight of it breaks open the wound I have been trying to ignore since yesterday, and a lump forms in my throat.

As I fight from letting the tears roll down my cheeks, Corey's voice floats into my mind, *It's okay to be sad, Ember. You can cry around Adam and me.* Somehow, all our minds are linked when we are accepted into the pack, and they teach us at an early age how to block to keep from sharing with everyone all the time.

I'll be fine. Do either of you smell anything? I ask and look at the two wolves who are watching me closely. They huff and begin sniffing the ground.

I have a faint trace of something, but it's not anything like what Seth described. It smells more of burned hair. It leads off into the woods there, Adam says through my mind and points with his nose.

Let's follow it and see where it leads us, Corey suggests, and I nod.

We move forward into the trees with Corey in front, nose to the ground, and Adam trailing behind me. I feel protected between them, but I can't fight the unease that creeps in. Something tells me we are walking into a trap, but I don't have anything to prove it.

We step into a clearing, and the smell of burned hair and spoiled milk hit me in the face. I fight the urge to gag as I hear Adam wretch behind me.

Shit, the smell is horrible, he says, and a loud crack fills the air.

A yelp draws my attention, and I watch as Corey is yanked into the air by a rope. It's a snare that he walked right into. I pull out one of the hunting knives I grabbed earlier and begin to walk toward him to cut him down when a shriek fills the air.

Three black beasts with webbed wings similar to bats wings fly down from the tops of the trees. Their maws are opened wide and filled with razor-like teeth as they scream. I instinctively throw my knife at one, but it misses and embeds itself in the trunk of a tree behind it.

I duck and feel a slight breeze move over me and glance up to find Adam meeting them head-on. He grabs one with his jaws and brings it to the ground, causing the other two to scatter.

Get Corey down and hide. His voice is loud as it bangs around in my head, but I react and follow his orders.

I pull another knife out and run to Corey. I begin sawing at the rope as another of the beings flies toward me. I saw faster, my heart racing, and my newfound power responds. Without control, black flame lashes out at the rope, and Corey drops to the ground. He is on the beast within seconds, and I push back into the trunk of the tree where the trap originated.

I watch, utterly terrified, as Corey faces it head-on. I glance over at Adam and see he is faring pretty well, at least until I see the third creature above him with a giant branch.

"Adam! Look out!" I scream, but it's too late. As he rips the throat out of the beast before him on the ground, the one above him swings the branch hard, knocking him in the head. Adam flies sideways and lands in a heap against a tree, and the beast turns its attention on me.

"What is that I smell mixed with fear? Could that be what I think it is? Who are you, little girl?" the beast coos, sending chills down my spine.

He flies toward me, and I push away from the tree, prepared to do what I can. I glance over at Corey, who has his hands tied with his beast and take a deep breath. My power pulses in my hands, and I spread my feet.

"I'm just a latent wolf, ugly creature," I say, pulling a dagger from my side and attack.

The beast and I clash, and it drags its claws down my arm, trying to get me to release my weapon. I cry out but turn into it, hitting it with my opposite arm. The force causes it to stagger back, and it takes a minute to right itself.

As its wings speed up in an attempt to steady it, I launch myself at him with my arm extended. My new strength propels me forward at a speed I wasn't prepared for, and my guard drops, causing black flames to erupt down my arm and across the blade.

The beast screams in pain as my dagger slices through its torso, followed by my flaming arm. It creates a hole the size of a softball, and I land on the ground atop the beast as it takes its final breath. I pull my arm back and stare, bewildered at what just happened. I sit back on my heels and startle as a hand lands on my shoulder.

I turn and stare up into Corey's eyes, now in his human form, as he asks, "What the hell was that, Ember?"

I continue to look at him and turn back to the beast lying on the ground. "What do you mean?"

"You just burned a hole through that thing."

"I guess I did." I keep my gaze down, refusing to look at him. "We need to check on Adam."

"I already did. Now, care to tell me what the hell just happened? Seriously, did this come as a result of yesterday? You have strength, speed, and powers that were not there twenty-four hours ago. I should know. So look me in the eye and tell me," Corey demands.

I turn to face him and push myself up from the ground. "You don't have the right to demand things from me. We ended things this morning, remember? I'll tell you when I'm ready. Now, alert the others, and let's finish this."

"Fine, but we will talk about this. You're not getting out of it that easily."

"Fine," I say, crossing my arms and watching him shift back into his wolf. I can almost feel his anger toward me, but I ignore it. Now's not the time to deal with this.

Corey's howl echoes around me, and I hear Adam grunt as he comes to in his wolf form. I turn and meet his concerned gaze as he moves toward me. I rest a hand on his head. *I'm fine. Are you okay?*

My head hurts, but I'll get over it. Why is Corey pissed? he asks, and I turn to look at Corey as he watches us. I shrug and remain silent.

Minutes later, more wolves appear around us, with Seth and Alpha Gale behind them. I remain quiet as Corey relays what happened telepathically.

No one questions Corey when he covers for me, saying that my dagger burst into flames when it met the demon's flesh. I don't offer anything to say otherwise and make a mental note of what he did. I need to talk to Zeke about this before I share anything with Corey.

After another two hours, trucks are brought in, and we load the demon carcasses up to take back with us. Alpha Gale wants to look them over and run tests to see if someone can create a weapon to take them out. The thought of such tests creeps me out, and I walk back to the pack house with Corey and Adam in silence.

We're dismissed and told to be ready for training at the same time again tomorrow, and I head home. I don't say anything to my family as I walk in the front door and find them all gathered on the couch watching television. Instead, I offer them a smile and murmur something about needing to shower.

I head up the stairs and quickly peel my soaked and bloody clothes off of me. I smell something awful after fighting those things, and I crank my shower on. I give it a moment to heat up before stepping in. As the spray lands on me, my muscles relax, and I let my tears fall. The shock of everything that happened both yesterday and today washes through me.

As I let it all out, I force myself to grab the bar of soap and start scrubbing the blood off my arms. I take extra care around the gashes that are beginning to heal. My tears finally stop as the last bit of blood washes down the drain.

I step out to grab a towel and stumble as I spy Zeke sitting cross-legged on the counter by the sink.

"What in the hell are you doing in here? You couldn't have waited until I was out?" I ask, but not loud enough where my parents can pick it up with their heightened hearing.

"I was worried about you. Corey hunted me down and asked about your black-flaming hand trick, so I sought you out. What happened?"

"My control slipped in the fight. I didn't have any other choice but to let it happen. This new magic saved my life," I seethe and pull my hands through my hair.

He grabs my hands and pulls me into his chest. I put my forehead against him, and he wraps me in his arms, sending tiny tingles down my spine.

"It's okay. We'll work on it. This is new territory for everyone. We'll figure it out together."

"Thanks, Zeke. Now, can I ask you something?" I pull back and look up at him.

"You just did, didn't you?" he says with a smirk, lightening the mood.

"Yes, but something else. What are these electrical tingles I feel when I touch you now and what was that during our sparring today?" My words rush out, and I wrap my arms around him and hold tight. I need to know what this means.

He looks at me, and I hold my breath. "I think it's because we have similarities. I'm not sure, but that would make sense, especially now that your powers are surfacing."

"Oh. Okay," I say, feeling somewhat defeated.

"Did you think it was something else?" he asks, lifting one of his brows.

"I was just curious. We need to get some rest. Are you going to train with us again in the morning?" I drop my arms from around him and move to grab my clothes. I feel sad, not getting the answer I was seeking.

He slides off the counter and grabs my hand. "Yes, I'll be there for the morning session, and then I have to go meet with some acquaintances. Your Alpha has asked me to call in some friends to help prepare your group for stronger opponents. I'll be gone for a few days, but then I shouldn't have to leave for a while."

"Great. Then I'll see you in the morning." I squeeze his hand, and he lets go of mine. Before I can turn away, though, he grabs me and pulls me into a kiss. The kiss is eager but soft, and I melt in his arms. I shouldn't be this way after the breakup with Corey this morning, but something in me calls to him.

The kiss ends before I'm ready, and I hold on to Zeke.

He looks down at me with longing in his eyes, but I know now is not the time for what his eyes ask.

"Goodnight, Zeke," I say and grab my clothes from where I dropped them on the floor.

"Goodnight, Ember."

I turn my back to him as I drop my towel and begin to dress. A light breeze and the faint click of the door alert me to his departure. I smile as I quickly finish my nighttime routine and fall into bed with ease. Thoughts of Zeke's kiss keep the events of the day at bay, and I fall into slumber easily.

CHAPTER FIVE

The following day I roll out of bed, feeling like I've been hit by a Mack truck. I hurt all over and even feel feverish. I've never been sick before, so I write it off to exhaustion from the new magic I used yesterday and the fight between the demons. But I can't help but wonder if this thing with the demons will be my new normal. Am I going to be seeing them regularly?

After pushing myself through my morning routine, I grab a protein bar and some coffee from the kitchen. I take it with me as I begin the trek to the pack house for today's training. My feet feel heavy, and my heart sinks when I arrive at the pack house, only to find Corey waiting for me.

"Morning, sunshine, care if we talk a minute?" he asks, grabbing my arm and pulling me off into the trees on the right side of the house.

I frown as he pulls me to a stop a minute later. "I guess I don't have much of an option. What's this about?"

"I think you know what this is about. What happened yesterday, and don't lie to me? I can tell when you lie." He crosses his arms and glares at me.

I cross my arms, mimicking his posture. "Why should I tell you? I told you I'd fill you in when I was ready."

"I find that hard to believe. You're pissed at me. I know how you get."

"Hell yes, I'm pissed at you, Corey! You think I want any of what's going on? I feel like I don't have control of anything anymore. My life is a lie," I all but yell at him.

"Jeez, calm down. Is there more going on? Despite things that have happened, you know I'm always here, but I can't defy orders, Em." He reaches out and pulls me into a hug.

I soften at the use of my nickname and let him hold me for a second.

"Everything okay here?" Zeke's voice startles me, and I force myself to step back away from Corey.

"Yeah, just talking," I say and offer him a sheepish smile.

"Is that why you were yelling a second ago?" He's leaning against one of the trees, casually looking both Corey and me over.

"Well, no." I stop and look at Corey.

"I was asking her about the attack yesterday. She skewered one of those demons with a black-flaming dagger. Do you know what's going on, Zeke?" Corey turns his focus on Zeke, crossing his arms again.

Zeke lifts his brow and looks at me, gauging me for my reaction. I shrug in response.

"Well, it's not my place to share things like that. If you're ready to tell him, Ember, it's your call," Zeke says, pushing away from the tree and moving closer to me. He reaches up and tucks a loose strand of hair behind my ear as he stops in front of me.

"I don't know if we should," I mumble, and Zeke tilts my chin up, bringing my focus to him.

"If you trust him and you think he can keep the secret, tell him. We don't have much of a choice on keeping it under wraps if you let it loose yesterday," he says quietly.

"Hello, still here. Why are you two being weird? Wait, are you with him now?" Corey interrupts, and I roll my eyes.

"If I tell you, Corey, you have to promise not to share this. You could die if this secret gets out." I turn and stare Corey down, willing him to understand how serious this is.

"If it's that big, then I'll guard it with my life unless the secret puts Adam or you in harm's way. Then I can't guarantee it."

I sigh and stare up at the sky for a second as I gather my wits. Then, I meet his gaze once again. "Apparently, I'm Lucifer's daughter and may be a creature from Hell."

He blinks, letting the words sink in for a second before bursting into laughter. I stare at him, and Zeke remains beside me, quiet and assuasive.

"That's hilarious. Now seriously, what is it?" Corey asks after several minutes.

"Seriously, I'm Lucifer's daughter. So that's where this," I pause and lift my hand, bringing a black flame to life, "comes from. At least, I assume so."

"It is. Lucifer has a power something similar to that," Zeke says, reinforcing my words, and I snap my attention to him.

"Wait, you've met him?" I stare dumbfounded and drop my arm.

He shrugs. "Eh, yes and no. It's not like I know him, know him. I've just seen him use his magic."

"Holy shit, you're not kidding. So, what are you then?" Corey draws my attention from Zeke.

I shrug. "I hope to find that out, but I think we need to get to the practice area. We're going to be late."

"Fine, but I need to know more," Corey says, and we move back toward the house to walk around to the practice area in the back.

"I don't know much, honestly. Zeke's going to train me," I state, keeping my gaze forward.

"Is he, now? I guess I may need to get in on that training, too, then. But wait, aren't you leaving today, Zeke?" Corey asks quietly to keep our discussion from prying ears.

"Yes, and now that you know our secret, you can help work with her until I get back. Just keep it G-rated. No more of what you've been doing," Zeke says quietly, but I sense a bit of possessiveness in his voice.

Corey doesn't say a word, and I look over my shoulder to see him with his brow lifted but nodding. *Did I miss something?* I turn my focus back to what's in front of me, and we enter the training area.

Groups of men are already warming up, and I get the sense that we're late. I look over and spy Adam talking with Seth, who has a grim expression on his face. The two of them see us and wave us over.

I tense as we approach, preparing to be scolded for yesterday's attack.

"Good morning, guys. Zeke, I'm going to have you do a few demonstrations, but first, I need to talk with these three. The Alpha wants to send them on a special training assignment in Alaska," Seth says.

"Alaska? What could he possibly have for us up there?" I ask without thinking, and Adam frowns at me.

Seth doesn't let it faze him. "He wants you three to train against a special supernatural being that is causing a friend of his some trouble. They are called Kushtaka. They are a type of Skinwalker that takes on the form of an otter."

"How can an otter be dangerous? They're so cute," I say, confused.

"These are not cute. The Kushtaka have been luring citizens to their death for centuries. A contract was struck between the Alpha of the pack there and the Kushtaka's leader at one of the elder council meetings, but that leader has been missing. The rest of the Kushtaka have started breaking the rules, so Alpha Gale wants you three to go in and take out the rebel leader.

You'll leave next week," Seth says, and I feel Zeke tense beside me.

"That's too soon. I'm not sure they're ready for that." Zeke places his hand on my back. It's comforting, but his concern causes worry to flutter inside me.

"We should be fine. It can't be that hard if we're to go. My father wouldn't put us in harm's way. I'm sure a few others will be accompanying us on the trip. You can join as soon as you're free, Zeke," Adam adds with a smirk.

"We'll be fine, Zeke. We won't let anything happen to Ember, I promise," Corey adds, and I turn to look at his face. His expression is determined, and I know he'll fight tooth and nail to keep me safe. He still cares despite his orders. I hate the position we're in. Life really is unfair sometimes.

"The Alpha is sending a handful of the other warriors with them. They'll be fine. I'll be joining the small team as well. It'll be an easy training experience. The rest will remain here to keep the demons off our land. If we continue to be successful with this small group, we'll branch out to teach the other packs in the future. That's why it's also important to contact your friends to see if they'll help us out," Seth declares with a light shrug. "Now, you all need to warm up before we work with Zeke. You have several days of intense training to complete before you go. You need to be in top form."

"Right," I say sarcastically and turn away from them, shrugging out of Zeke's touch as well. I glance over my shoulder as I walk away and see he has begun to argue with Seth. I leave him to it and begin to do laps around the practice area to warm up.

After a single lap, Corey falls into place beside me. "Zeke's pissed about this mission. I get it, though. Yesterday was intense, but I think we can handle it."

We keep pace with each other as we continue to run. "I hope you're right. I've got a bad feeling about this."

"We will. After we're done today, I hope you can meet me in

the woods behind your house. Zeke is right that you need to get your magic under control."

"Do you have a method in mind of how to train with it? I don't recall anyone ever having powers around here like this before."

"I have some ideas, but it stems from books, mostly. The fantasy books I've read over the years have characters with powers, so maybe we could try some of what they did."

I stop and drop to the ground to begin stretching as I eye him. "I guess that could work. We have to start somewhere. Okay, it's a date."

"You mean it's a plan. We can't do that anymore, Em. Adam ordered me to back off, despite him saying that he was okay with it. You aren't the only one hurt by the Alpha's decisions."

I close my eyes and remain quiet for a moment as I hold my stretch, letting his words sink in. I thought this would be easier than it was when we began messing around years ago. Now it sucks.

I open my eyes and meet his gaze. "A plan, we have a plan."

The rest of the morning goes smoothly, and Corey and I stay paired up. Zeke throws glances my way frequently with a concerned look in his eye, but he doesn't interfere. I don't know if he doesn't trust Corey with our secret or what, but I know he'll keep it.

Zeke walks with me back to my house at lunch, and the silence around us is heavy. Then, as my house comes into sight, he grabs my hand and pulls me into the trees.

"I don't like that the Alpha is sending you to Alaska. I don't feel comfortable with it, but Seth assures me that it's just a simple training exercise and nothing more. As soon as I get done speaking with my associates, I'll join you there, I promise." He leans down and kisses my forehead.

"Zeke, we'll be fine. Have faith in me. Maybe it'll bring my wolf out, or what I hope is my wolf," I say with a smile and an uncertain shrug.

He stares me in the eye as he says, "There is a wolf in you, but it's different. She's close to the surface. I can almost feel her, but it's not time yet." He closes his eyes and inhales deeply. When he opens them again, they faintly glow with a red hue. "Yes, she's close."

He drops his gaze to my lips, and I watch him curiously. In the second it takes for me to blink, his lips are on mine. I open to him and eagerly accept his kiss. I can sense his need and desire in that kiss, and heat swirls around us.

I wrap my arms around his neck, and he lifts me and moves us against a tree. Instinctively, I wrap my legs around his waist, and he drops his hands to my ass.

"Promise me you will not let Corey touch you like this while I'm gone. You are mine now, Ember. Mine." He returns to kissing me deeply, and I moan against his lips. He pulls back, and I look at him, confused. "Promise me."

I blink and tilt my head to the side as I take him in. "What about Adam? The contract?"

"I'll figure something out." He leans in and kisses me again, biting my lip softly.

I pull back as another question surfaces in my mind. "Are we mates?"

He moves to kiss the side of my neck, and I arch to let him have better access. "I'm not sure. Creatures of Hell take mates differently. It's not the same as what the wolf world is used to. We might be, but we'll have to wait and see." The sound of his words rumbles on my skin, and he bites into my shoulder.

I feel his teeth pierce my skin, and instead of pain, there's pleasure. Heat pools in my lower abdomen, and I feel him harden against me. I tilt my hips forward in encouragement as my mind spirals into a place of need.

"Are you okay with this?" he asks as he licks across the spot where he bit me, and I moan as my core tightens.

"I need this, Zeke. I don't know why we've never tried this." I lean in and bite his ear, and he moans.

"You were always distracted with Corey. I didn't want to interfere, but I can't help myself now. Everything about you calls to me, and I don't want to fight it anymore. I don't want to take you against this tree, though. I think we need to move it elsewhere."

"My room is free. There shouldn't be anyone home, I hope, anyway." I wiggle my hips, causing friction between us, and he groans again. He presses one more kiss into the side of my neck, and then we're moving.

Faster than I have ever felt him move me before, we breeze through the front door, down the hall, and stop in my room with my back resting on my bed.

"Holy hell, that was fast," I breathe out breathless, and Zeke leans back away from me.

"I'm a vampire, love, and you're about to find out what it's like to have sex with one." He leans in and pulls my top off, trailing kisses along my skin as he does.

I let my mind focus on the moment and feel a warm breeze around us with the scent of a small fire. My body feels alive, just with Zeke's touch, in a way it's never felt before.

He continues to trail kisses down my body as he removes my clothes. Once he has everything removed, he sits back on his heels and looks me over. "Stunning. Every inch of you is gorgeous and perfect."

I blush at his words, and all train of thought leaves my mind as he begins to pull his clothes off. His dark, ebony skin glows as I take him in, and his lean, chiseled body is ripped in a way I never realized it was. As I let my eyes drift lower, the size of his member makes me pause. *Holy hell!*

My gaze snaps back up to his as he says, "Eyes up here." He

pulls me down the bed toward him. Before I can process what he's doing, his mouth is on my sex. Pleasure seizes me, and I lose myself to it.

He sucks my clit in and slides a finger into me as he begins to work me toward my first climax. In no time, I shatter and scream out his name. Instead of switching positions to finish himself, he holds me steady and begins building me back up again. Climax after climax bursts through me until I see stars, and only then does he pull away.

He proceeds to slide back up my sweaty body, kissing and licking as he does. I whimper as he trails his tongue across my nipples, and then he bites his way back up to the spot on my shoulder. He slides his fingers back into my fold, teasing me again before he bites down on my shoulder again. His bite is a little harder this time, and I feel him lap at the blood pooling from the punctures. My core tightens around his fingers as he plunges them in and out as he continues to lap at my blood, bringing me to another climax.

He moves his mouth away from my shoulder and pulls me into a passionate kiss. I can taste myself on his lips, both the blood and juices of my sex. It's sweet, and the blood doesn't taste like I thought it would.

He slides his knee between my legs as he takes a breath, and I gasp as he enters me. He edges his member in slowly until he fills me and then pushes a little further.

"Oh gods, you feel wonderful," he says breathlessly as he begins to pump in and out.

I wrap my legs around his torso and moan his name. He begins to move harder and faster as I encourage him. I scream his name and bite into his shoulder, tasting blood. I lap it up with my tongue, noticing the sweet flavor, and my body tenses around him. The amount of pleasure is almost unbearable, and Zeke pumps even faster.

The friction sends me over the edge, and I once again bite

into his shoulder as I mumble out his name. Seconds later, he joins me over the edge, crying out my name. Still connected, we collapse in a heap of sweat on my bed, breathing heavily.

I stare at the ceiling, trying to regulate my breathing as I say, "That was..." I pause, trying to come up with the proper word. "I have no words. Holy hell, Zeke."

"Agreed. Gods, I don't want to go on this trip now."

"Can't you just stay and go another day?" I ask, rolling to my side. I wrap my arms around him.

He smiles at me and kisses my forehead. "No, unfortunately, I can't. I am going to make it as fast as possible, though. I don't want to be away from you for too long."

"Ugh," I say and roll onto to my back.

"You need to eat, Ember, before this afternoon's work. I know Seth doesn't have formal practice, but you need to work on your magic."

"Oh shit. I need to shower. Your scent is all over me now." I roll to stand and pause as Zeke laughs.

He has me in his arms again seconds later. "I know my scent is all over you. No one will touch you now. You're mine."

I slap him playfully. "Territorial bastard. What do you plan to do about Adam? Do you have a way to break that contract?"

"I'll find a way. Now get cleaned up before I take you again. You're a temptress, Ember."

I give him a vulgar gesture, causing him to laugh again, and dart into the bathroom. I take a quick shower and step out to find him once again in my bathroom.

"I need to go, but I want to tell you goodbye first. We'll talk soon. Keep your phone on you while I'm away." He drops my cell on the counter. It's been resting on my charger for the last few days.

"Okay. I'll see you soon." I lean in and kiss him.

He pulls me into a hug regardless that I'm dripping wet and in my towel. I feel his hand twitch on my side, and I know he's resisting the urge to remove it. "Work hard. I'll find you as soon as I'm done."

"I know," I say, and then he zips out of the bathroom.

I sigh and look at myself in the mirror. I smile at myself and ignore the nagging thoughts of the disaster this could cause. I have to find a way to get out of that contract.

CHAPTER SIX

An hour later, I'm cleaned and dressed with an extra layer of perfume on. I can only hope that it'll mess with Corey's senses enough that he won't pick up on the subtle scent of sex and Zeke on my skin.

I took extra time after my shower to toss my bedding in the laundry as well. I don't want to face that conversation with my parents yet. They know I'm sexually active and have been for years but revealing that I'm now with Zeke will put them on edge, especially with everything they announced. I don't need that right now.

As I walk into the clearing not far from my house, my stomach drops as Corey scrunches up his nose. "What's with all the perfume?"

"I wanted to smell nice, why? You don't like it?" I wink, and he smirks.

"It's pleasant, but why? You're going to sweat."

I shrug and continue walking toward him. He scans me up and down and pauses at my neck. He blinks, and seconds later, he has me against a tree. I'm starting to think I should have bark put on me permanently at this rate.

"You slept with him? Are you crazy? Ember, what the hell?" he snarls into my face, and I wince.

"Who I sleep with is none of your business, Corey. You're following orders and leaving me alone, remember?" I say, letting sarcasm coat my words like a second skin.

He growls, and instead of pushing away from me, he kisses me. My shocked brain blanks, and my sex does a happy dance. I don't fight him as he pushes his hands up my shirt, sliding my bra up.

I wrap my legs around him in response and deepen the kiss. Zeke's words float away from me, and I let my pleasure brain take over once again as Corey tweaks my now hard nipples.

I stare at him breathlessly and whimper as he pulls back. "You can't go around smelling like him. The perfume won't work. I'm going to fix that. You were mine first." He growls again and then removes my shorts.

I fight to get his down his legs, and he steps out of them, pushing me back into the tree. Sex with Corey has always been a heated, passionate mess. It's nothing like what I did with Zeke, but Corey is large and pushes into me deep, causing me to moan.

He holds nothing back as he pumps into me. Bark scrapes against the exposed portion of my back where my bra and shirt remain pushed up, allowing him ample access to my breasts. I grind into him, increasing the friction between us, and reach my climax.

He slides a hand down between us as I begin to spiral down from my high and uses his hand to stimulate me. I begin to build once again as he groans out, "I'm marking you, Em, as mine. You may not remain mine, but I will fight like hell to keep the Alphas from harming you for going against their plans." He bites into my other shoulder, and I feel his canines lengthen to that of his wolf.

He howls in pleasure after releasing me from his teeth, and I tighten around him. Magic swirls around us, and I open my eyes to see black flames dancing around us. Corey eyes them but doesn't halt. He is close. I can tell by the fierce look in his eye.

He leans in again and clamps down on my shoulder, and I close my eyes, feeling the pressure build between us. Seconds later, we climax, and he slides us to the ground. I roll off of him, panting, and stare at the sky.

"Fuck, you men are going to be the death of me. Death by sex. Is that a thing?" I ask aloud, and Corey chuckles beside me.

"At least you'll die happy. Now you have mine and Zeke's scent all over you. Hopefully, Adam and any of the other wolves won't pick up on anything."

"Oh gods, Zeke is going to be pissed."

"I'll handle him. Now let's get dressed and do what we are actually supposed to be doing. You need to get a handle on things. Don't think I didn't see the flame show in the middle of that. Do you plan on telling Adam anytime soon?" Corey pushes off the ground and grabs his clothes.

I stand and grab mine as I say, "I don't know. My parents don't think it would be a good idea."

"Yeah, I don't know if we should take your parents' advice. How long did they keep all this information about Lucifer from you?"

"You do have a point." I sigh as I fix my top. "I'll tell Adam only if I need to or when I get my magic under control. I haven't given up hope of getting out of that contract."

Corey stares at me for a moment. "I'll do what I can to find a way. If they know about your power, though, I highly doubt they will let you out of it. You'll become the most coveted Luna to exist. There has never been a Luna with anything like what you have."

"How would you know if there was?" I ask, eyeing him curiously.

"Adam and I were required to sit in on a pack history class

for two summers. They never told us why you weren't taking it with us, but I assumed it was a male thing." He shrugs.

"Oh, well, then, I guess we better find something." I roll my shoulders back. "So where do we start, boss man?"

He rolls his eyes at the nickname. "Try to conjure a flame to one hand and then throw it at a target. Here, I'm going to draw an X in the dirt. Try to toss your flame at the X."

"So, balls of flame? I think I can do that." I smile and square up with the X. I think of it as if I were going to throw a baseball.

"Okay, go," Corey says encouragingly, and I lift my hand, expecting flames to dance in my hand, but nothing happens.

I stare at my hand and snap my fingers but still nothing. I lift my other hand and do the same thing.

"What are you doing?"

"Trying to sprout wings, what do you think I'm doing?" I ask with a hinge of frustration in my voice. I grit my teeth and toss my hand as if I were throwing a ball but still nothing.

"Are you visualizing your flame? Do you feel anything inside?"

"No, I didn't know I needed to visualize. Will it work?"

"I don't know. I've never done this before. Maybe calm your mind and then try it? Take some deep breaths," Corey says soothingly, and I close my eyes.

Thoughts of sex with him and Zeke float in the forefront of my mind, and I push those to the side. I breathe in and out, trying to settle my heart rate, and as it calms, my magic stirs. I open my eyes, feeling more focused and imagine a black flame dancing in my hand.

A warm tingle spreads up my arm, and a small flame bursts to life. I smile, feeling confident, and toss my gaze to the X several feet away. Focusing again, I visualize the ball of fire landing on it before trying to throw it. The flame miraculously lifts from my hand and lands close to the target with a sizzle.

"Great! Now do that again until you hit the X, and then do it ten more times without missing," he says, and I whip around to stare at him.

"What? Why so many times?" I gape.

"In my stories, they always had to master control. You, Em, do not have control of it. This is a start. We'll build on it." He shrugs, and I roll my eyes in response.

I turn my gaze back to the X. "Fine. I'll get the hang of this. You'll see."

We spend the rest of the afternoon and late into the evening working on tossing a ball of fire at the X. Corey watches from the side, occasionally offering tips while he works on conditioning. Sweat coats my body, and my head hurts from the amount of effort controlling my flame requires.

As dusk rolls in, I finally land my tenth ball on the X in a row, and I let myself plop on the ground. I lay back in the dirt and stare at the darkening sky. "I did it."

Corey lies down next to me and grabs my hand. "Yes, you did. Now we'll do this every day until we leave for Alaska. Once we get there, we'll figure out a new schedule, but you'll need to keep working. You're going to get this, Em."

I squeeze his hand. "Thanks. I love you, Corey."

"I love you too, Em. Now let's call it a night. We still have to train in the morning with everyone else."

I groan and push up. "Don't remind me. I'll see you in the morning."

He stands and pulls me into him, planting a kiss on my lips. "Goodnight."

He turns away, and I touch my lips, feeling the heat of the kiss lingering. I turn and begin to walk back toward my house as thoughts of the colossal mess of hotness I am now sitting in dance around. I don't even know what's going on with me anymore. I have Corey, Zeke, and Adam all hanging on to me. What the hell am I going to do?

CHAPTER SEVEN

I drag myself to training the next morning, feeling exhausted. I tossed and turned all night, feeling like I was on fire. Thoughts of Zeke and Corey bombarded me as I tried to rest, and confusion weighed heavily on me. I'm not sure how to feel for either of them.

I have loved Corey for years, but something is pulling me to Zeke that is like a live wire. It wasn't there until after my magic woke up, and it's got my head a mess, my heart even more so.

I drag my feet along the path leading around the pack house to the training area. Several of the males are already sparring, and I look for Corey. He's sparring with another male, and I frown. I glance around again, and Adam catches my eye. He waves me over, and I oblige.

"Good morning, gorgeous," he says cheerily.

"Good morning. Why are you so upbeat? I didn't think you were a morning person," I remark as I take a big sip of coffee from the thermos I have with me.

"You're right. I'm usually not a morning person, but this morning we get to practice together. I also needed to chat with you about this weekend. We have tomorrow off from training, and my father needs us to attend an event with him. He wants to present us to the rest of the shifter leaders as a couple and future leaders."

"Oh, so soon?" I try not to cringe.

He lifts a brow curiously. "Yes. I thought you understood that we needed to get with it on this, Ember. There's no breaking the contract. We need to embrace it."

"I do. I didn't know we would be doing things like this. What about the trip to Alaska? That's coming up soon."

"Yes, it is, and that's fine. He was the one that set it up, but he has things planned for us that we'll need to do beforehand. The life of a leader and his mate is never idle. I thought you knew that." Adam scowls at me.

"I do, but that doesn't mean I have to like it." I frown.

"It'll be fine. I'll keep you entertained. It's not like we have to do too much. Anyway, I have to ask, did you get a new perfume? Your scent is different today." He moves in closer to me and sniffs the air.

"No, maybe it's my wolf surfacing. I have newfound strength and stamina, so, yeah." I smile, hoping he doesn't question it further. I guess the events of yesterday muddled my scent as Corey hoped.

"Hm, well, I like it. Hopefully, soon, you'll let mine mingle with it. We need to discuss that as well." He drops his voice as if talking about sex is taboo.

I fight the urge to growl. "Let's talk about it later and start training. I want to be on top of my game when we go to Alaska."

"Why? It's supposed to be a walk in the park. Nothing like what we faced with the demons. You shouldn't have to worry about it. Corey and I both will be there to protect you."

"I don't want you two to always have to protect me. I need to be able to protect myself. Your father once told me how important it is. If this is a test of my skills, then I want to pass with flying colors, and if it brings my wolf forward, even better." I place my hands on my hips, and he lifts his brows in surprise.

"Okay, I get it. I want you to be strong too, but I also want you to know that I would die before I let anything ever happen to you. We may not have love yet, Ember, but I do care for you." He steps closer and pulls me to him. I look up into his eyes, knowing what will come next. "You are to be my mate, and even if you aren't my true mate, you're still mine." He leans in and kisses me.

I break the kiss and step back. "We need to get to work, Adam. Thank you for understanding."

He frowns. "Okay, I get it. You're not in the mood. Fine. Let's practice this morning with you facing my wolf form."

"That sounds like an excellent challenge," I say and stride toward a vacant training mat. I place my thermos on the ground and turn as Adam finishes his shift.

He moves to the other end of the mat and takes up a defensive stance. I move to my place and take my stance. I then take several deep breaths to focus my mind and check to make sure my magic is under control. I don't need to let any of it show this morning.

Opening my eyes, I'm forced to step to the side as Adam surprises me by attacking first. I stumble but quickly regain my footing and turn as he comes back at me. He jumps to tackle me, and I catch him with my hand and push him away from me.

He sails through the air to my left and lands on his feet with a grunt. I smirk as he begins to pace, looking for an opening.

Your skills are getting better, his voice sounds in my head, and I get the feeling he's keeping his voice from being picked up by the others.

Thanks. I've been practicing. I smile proudly.

Good. I thought you and Corey were done? he asks, and I try not to freeze. He launches himself at me, and I punch him in the side.

We are, I say as he regains his footing and attacks again. This time, he nips me on the ass and darts away.

Then why is his scent all over you? I couldn't pick it up in my human form, but now it's distinct, and there is another scent I can't place. Maybe that's your wolf surfacing, though.

I frown. *It was a onetime thing with Corey. It won't happen again.*

Good, because we're supposed to be bonding and getting ready to be mates. You are betrothed to me, and you are mine. I don't want to force you to have sex with me, but if I need to claim you so others will leave you alone, I will.

I roll my eyes. *Would you really force yourself on me? I would like to see you try.*

No, I wouldn't, but I would also like you to work with me on this. You did agree, Ember.

I growl and surprise myself. I let instinct take over, and I move to attack him. He evades me and shifts back to his human form.

We continue to spar in silence this way for a good hour before taking a break. Then, instead of getting a drink, he plops down next to me and orders one of the other males to bring us water.

"Why don't you just go get us water?" I finally ask as the male with red hair brings us two bottles.

"Because I'm going to make it obvious that you're mine. I'm not leaving your side," he says, glaring at Corey across the practice area.

Corey looks at him curiously in return and then glances over at me. I shrug in response and understanding clouds his features. Then, finally, he turns back to his sparring partner, and they begin again.

I sigh. "Adam, you can chill out. I won't let it happen again."

"Quiet. We aren't going to talk about it in the open. Use our connection if you want to talk about it."

I roll my eyes again. "Fine. So, are you going to condition with me then, or are you going to do your own thing?"

"Conditioning. I'm not leaving your side," he grumbles and chugs some of his water.

I huff. "Territorial bastard."

"You will learn to love it," he says in response.

We spend the rest of the morning conditioning, and only when we break for the day does he give me some space.

"I'm coming by your house in an hour. That'll give you time to clean up. I want to spend the afternoon with my betrothed," he says, grabbing my hand as I go to leave.

"Okay. I'll see you in a little while then. Do I need to dress in anything special, or are we just going to hang?" I ask.

"Just dress comfortably. We may take a walk but nothing strenuous. I want to go over plans for tomorrow." He shrugs.

I nod and smile. I'm afraid to ask if anyone will be joining us, so instead, I say, "Okay."

We part ways, and I head off down the road toward my parents' home, only to be stopped a few minutes later by Corey.

"Hey, Em, hold up!"

I turn as he finishes sprinting to me. "Hey, Corey."

"Was he mad? I could tell he picked up on it when he shifted. His demeanor changed, and then the whole territorial show following confirmed it."

"He wasn't too mad. I think it pushed him to be more territorial than he has been, though. He's coming over this afternoon. It's going to mess up our practice time."

Corey frowns. "We'll figure it out. Zeke will kill me if I don't keep you on top of it. We may have to meet after dark."

"Let's just hope Adam doesn't stay over. I wouldn't put it past him at this point. Apparently, we have things to do as a couple tomorrow per Alpha's orders." I groan.

"Oh, I thought you knew about that already. He just told you?"

"Yes, he just told me! How long have you known about whatever it is?" Corey lifts his hands up as if I were going to attack.

"Calm down. I only learned about it yesterday. I thought you knew already. I'll be there with you. I have to be. I'll be his Beta and second in command."

"Well, let's hope he doesn't stay in super-territorial mode. I can't handle that and I'm trying to maintain appearances. I'm still looking to get out of this whole debacle." I sigh.

"We'll figure something out, Em. At least we can make the best of whatever we are given. If you can shoot me a text later, do it. I want to know if you'll be able to practice your magic today or if he plans on staying over."

"I will. I'll catch you later, Corey." I smile, and he jogs back toward the pack house. Once he's out of sight, I let my shoulders droop and head home.

Why does this all have to be complicated? Why can't I find my actual mate and live the life I want to lead?

CHAPTER EIGHT

Trudging through the front door of my house moments later, the smell of burgers cooking catches my attention. Carrying my empty thermos from this morning, I follow my nose as it leads me into the kitchen.

My family doesn't have a large kitchen. It's an open concept layout with a rectangular table for dining and a small area for cooking. A decent-sized island rests in the middle of it all with barstools, and the decor has always reminded me of one of those sixties diners you come across on family trips.

My mother picked out black-and-white tile for the floors with red accents throughout. She even went as far as to hang pictures of Elvis Presley and Marilyn Monroe on the walls. My mom swears it reminds her of her first job and where she met my dad. Well, my not-dad, I guess.

I push those thoughts from my mind regarding my dad situation. Even though my dad is not my dad, I still love him. A smile breaks out across my face as I walk through the entryway and find my sisters seated at the bar, watching my mother cook. Their long red hair is pulled back into matching braids, and they watch her at the stove eagerly. They must be hungry.

My stomach growls loudly, and both of them whip around to find where the noise came from. I offer them a sheepish smile in response. It's been a busy morning.

"Hey, what all are you cooking? It smells delightful in here." I move closer to my sisters as I speak to my mom and pull them into a hug.

"Mom is making us all burgers and fries. We weren't sure if you would be home for lunch or not," Tansy says, returning my hug.

Winnie hugs me from the other side as she adds, "Yeah, we thought you wouldn't be back until late again."

"Well, I'm glad you're home, sweetie. They must be working you hard. We've barely seen you this week. Is training going well?" my mom asks, angling away from the stove enough to see me but maintain an eye on the food.

"It hasn't been easy, that's for sure. I'm exhausted, and I can tell my body has been through the wringer. So, how are things for you two?" I ask my sisters.

Winnie groans. "I hate training. I feel like I'm always tired now."

"Oh, stop your complaining, Winnie. We're doing the easy stuff. You're just out of shape. I told you it was important to run and exercise with me. It'll help us when our wolves finally surface," Tansy adds, ever the active one.

"I didn't think we would be doing this, but they explained to us what happened with the demon and that there was another attack. Did you know anything about it? They were really vague," Winnie says, watching me eagerly.

I look at Mom as she begins to plate the food with a frown. "I told you that we would fill you in on things if needed."

"Yes, but they mentioned that Ember was there. Why don't you tell us about it? Was it scary?" Tansy watches me, and Winnie's brows shoot up into her hairline. Curiosity dances in their eyes.

"Yes, I was there, and so were Corey and Adam. We took them out. It was pretty scary. I hope you never have to face any, but the things they are teaching you now will come in handy if you do. I'm glad that they'll be teaching everyone now and not just those fated to be high-ranking Betas or a Luna." I move to an empty stool and sit.

Mom finishes up our plates and begins to pass them out. "Hopefully you girls will never have to face them. Let's stop this talk about the demons and attacks, though, and enjoy our lunch. Is there anything other than training going on, Ember?"

I sigh and pick up a fry. I stare at it and bite into it, groaning at the flavor. It tastes delicious, and it gives me time to organize my thoughts. "Yes and no. I'm supposed to go to some type of event tomorrow with Adam per the Alpha's orders. I don't have many details yet. Adam is supposed to come by later. He's having territorial issues right now."

"Territorial issues? Why would he be having that?" My mom stares at me, and I look at the ceiling, trying to figure out what to tell her.

I'm definitely not telling her about the thing with Zeke. That will stay a secret until I figure out how to get out of the Luna thing. "Oh, you know how males get when their female is around a lot of other males." I shrug.

"You are so lying," Winne says with a giggle and Tansy giggles as well.

I glare at them, and my mom says, "That doesn't make any sense. Did you and Corey get together again? I thought you were past that?"

I had just taken a sip of water she had put down with the plates, and now it spews from my mouth. "What?" I ask incredulously. I didn't think she knew about that.

"Oh, you think I was oblivious? I'm not stupid, Ember. I was young once too. I get why Adam is territorial. He is your betrothed, despite what you would like," she says with a brow lifted. She takes a sip of her own glass of water.

I stare at her in disbelief as my sisters laugh. I have no words. How do I respond to that? I pick up my burger and begin to eat in silence, and my sisters finally settle down. Several minutes go by, and we finish our meal.

My mom finally says, "So, should we expect Adam later?"

"Yes. He'll most likely come by. I plan to try and get some more conditioning in this evening after he leaves if I can. It may be a long night." I stand and gather my empty plate and cup.

"I'm glad you're taking this training seriously but don't overdo it, okay, Ember?" She seems to have something else she wants to say by the look on her face, but she doesn't say it. I know she's worried about me with all the demons hanging around, but we should be fine.

"I won't, Mom, don't worry. I'm going to head to my room for a bit. I'll check in with you all later."

A resounding bye from my sisters follows me out of the kitchen and down the hall.

Once I make it into my room, I grab my cell off my nightstand. Since I'm not able to leave the area, I haven't had much reason to carry it around with me. I know I'll take it with me when I go to Alaska, but maybe with Zeke gone, I need to keep it close. Especially if something happens that I have no control over in regard to my new power. He did tell me to keep it handy anyway.

I glance down at the screen and see a message from Zeke.

Zeke: Hey, hope all is going well. I hope to hear from you soon.

I smile and respond eagerly with a lengthy message telling him about training. I leave out the thing with Corey and mention that Adam is more territorial. I also mention that I have a decent aim with my flame now and that I can't wait until he gets back.

I set the phone down and busy myself with picking up my

room. I pick up dirty clothes and organize things on my dresser until my phone goes off. I'm surprised Zeke messaged back so quickly. We continue to message back and forth while I tidy up, and I faintly hear the front door open downstairs.

Seconds later, footsteps pause outside my door, and a knock echoes through the room. "Come in," I call out, and Adam pushes through the door.

"Hey, are you cleaning up for me?" he asks curiously.

"No, just doing a regular tidy-up. How was lunch?"

"It was good. Dad filled me in a bit more on what to expect tomorrow. He wants us to dress nicely for dinner. Apparently, we're going to meet the Alpha for the pack stationed in Alaska and learn a bit about the other shifters and tribes in the area."

"Oh, that sounds complicated. Is your dad sure he wants us to go help out? If there are that many in the area, why is there an issue with the Kushtaka?"

He shrugs. "I don't know. I think it's just a training thing for us. It will be good to learn about the different cultures because it'll be useful when we lead."

I sigh and plop down on the edge of the bed. He joins me a second later and grabs my hand. I look up at him as he traces circles with his thumb.

"I get you're still not on board with all this, Ember, but we have had years to come to terms with being pushed together. So please help me make the best of it," he says quietly, staring down at my hand.

"I'm trying, Adam, but I feel like I've lost all of my freedom now. I can't even leave the area. Is this what life as the future Luna will be like?" I ask, over the lump forming in my throat.

"No, it won't be. We'll change things. I promise that you won't feel like you're trapped much longer. I'll find a way to increase your freedom, but I will need time. I need you to work with me, and I also want to keep you safe. You'll get to take those classes you dropped and get any degree you'd like even.

It'll be on a different timeline, obviously, but just work with me."

"I get it. It's just difficult." I frown, and he lifts his gaze to mine.

"I brought you something, and I hope it will cheer you up," he says, changing the topic at hand. I watch in confusion as he drops to the floor and slips something out of his pocket. I stare in shock as he flips his hand over, and shows me the ring in it. "I know this isn't a traditional thing, but I wanted you to have this ring to show that you're mine since you aren't ready for me to leave a mark on you."

I blink and realize I can't say no because we aren't in a traditional relationship. We were thrown together via a contract by our parents, and he's trying to make it the best it can be. Frustration fills me, and I want to cry but not in a good way. I hate that we're both being denied the chance to find our true mates.

I hold my hand out, fighting back my tears, and he slips the ring on my finger. "Thank you, Ember. I promise I'll do my best to do right by you and make you happy."

I nod in agreement but stay silent as he moves back to sit next to me on the bed. He wraps me in a hug, and tears finally slide down my cheeks.

"I'm sorry. I don't mean to cry," I say.

"Don't apologize for how you feel. I want us to always be honest with each other. I hope one day, we can grow to love each other."

I nod, and he leans back away from me. I wipe my eyes. "So, tell me more about what to expect tomorrow."

CHAPTER NINE

I t's an hour before the party, and Adam should be here any minute to pick me up. He refused to let me walk to the pack house, even though doing so would help calm my nerves. I'm slightly thankful that we're driving because the shoes that best fit my dress are stilettos and walking in them for long distances would cause blisters on my feet.

My outfit for the evening is a black chiffon formal evening gown. It has a V-neck and ruffled lace for sleeves. My stilettos are shiny black, and I curled my hair in loose waves that fall down my back. I even went as far as to pull out my matching ruby jewelry set to wear with the dress. The red pops wonderfully with all the black, and I feel like a princess. This is the most I have dressed up since prom in high school.

Hearing a knock at the front of the house, I'm still listening to see if it's Adam. I relax as I hear my dad answer the door. Their words are too faint to make out, but it's Adam's voice. I apply another layer of gloss to my lips and double-check my appearance in the mirror. I want to look amazing and feel confident tonight. A lot is riding on the image of Adam and I being a unified pair. Despite my desire not to be tied to him, I do care about my pack.

I slowly make my way from my room and down the hall, following the sound of voices. Adam is keeping up a steady conversation from the sounds of it with my parents. When I enter the living room, though, everyone goes silent. You could easily hear a pin drop with the silence. Feeling nervous, I look at them all and notice how wide Adam's eyes are. His eyes then change and begin to glow faintly as his wolf surfaces. At least he likes how I look.

"Way to make it awkward. It's not like any of you haven't seen me dressed up before," I mumble and move toward Adam.

"Oh, honey, you look gorgeous," my mother whispers, grabbing me before I make it to Adam and giving me a tight hug.

My dad follows her move, and they wrap me in a group hug, murmuring words of how pretty I look. I gently shrug out of their embrace and look over at Adam, who looks on with wonder in his eyes. They glow faintly, and he shakes himself almost as if his wolf is arguing with him.

He steps forward as my parents finally step back to give me some space, and Adam takes my hand. "You look stunning. I'm not going to be able to leave your side tonight." I laugh, and he continues, "It's true! You're going to turn every head once we get there. Every male will drop to their knees, begging for you to leave me for them. My wolf wants to claim you now so there's no mistaking who you belong to."

I flush as memories of what Corey and Zeke did to me flit through my mind. I mentally chastise myself for bringing those thoughts up and offer Adam a smile. "I guess that's not a bad thing, right?"

"No, they'll envy us. Let them." He smiles wickedly and then laughs.

He maintains his hold on my hand as we finish our farewells and make our way outside. He leads me to the passenger side of his black Chevrolet pickup and helps me in. The truck is an average vehicle and one that is frequently seen in eastern Oklahoma.

I ease into my seat, and he gently closes the door. I situate my skirts around me as he walks to his side and climbs in.

"So, we talk with the Alpha from Alaska and fly out to his territory in two days? Are you sure we're ready for this?" I ask as he puts the truck into gear.

We pull out of my parent's driveway. "Yes, I think we're all ready. It'll also prove that we're ready to lead despite your wolf not showing yet. She will soon, though. I'm sure of it."

I frown and turn my attention to the window. I'm still not sure what will surface. Will it be a wolf or something else entirely?

"Everything will be fine, Ember. Don't worry." He reaches over and squeezes my hand, and I turn to offer him a smile in response.

We drive the remainder of the distance in silence, and Corey meets the truck as we park. He meets Adam at his door, and I wait as they both walk over to mine. This is how it will be now, the three of us, always together. Our protector and the Alpha and Luna. Joy.

Upon reaching my door, Corey breaks out into a huge smile, and he assists me as I slide gracefully out of the truck. "Wow, Ember, you look hot! Reminds me of prom!"

I laugh, and Adam growls in warning at Corey, which causes me to laugh even harder. "Chill out, Adam. You're going to drive me crazy if you do this all night. It's not my fault you asked someone else to prom. We have good memories of that night."

He groans. "Fine. You're right. Let's forget about my past stupidity. Plus, Corey is going to be with us all night, so I'll tone it down as best as I can. Just keep your hands to yourself, dude." Adam punches Corey in the arm playfully.

"I will try my best," Corey responds with a smirk as he rubs his arm.

"You two are insufferable. Can we go in and get this night over with?" I step toward the porch of the pack house, and it seems to snap them out of their thoughts.

"So impatient. Let's go through. We don't want my father upset with us early on. I also want to learn more about what we will face this week in Alaska," Adam says, grabbing my hand and pulling me to his side.

Corey follows close on our heels as we make our way into the house and toward the spacious dining room. We are to dine first and dance following.

I smile politely perched on Adam's arm as we enter the room. His grip tightens on me, and eyes follow us to our seats. Adam pauses, letting go of my hand, and pulls out my chair. I thank him as I sit, and both Adam and Corey sit on either side of me. We are positioned to the right of the Alpha, and we offer pleasant greetings as the rest of the partygoers find their seats.

As the seats continue to fill up, I let my gaze move along the table, taking in everyone joining us. Some of the other wolves I recognize from the pack and others I assume came with the group from Alaska. Seated next to who appears to be the Alpha of the Alaska pack are two huge males and a very tall woman. She is taller than any female I've ever seen.

The woman has platinum blond hair and a pleasant smile. Something about the trio seems off, though, and I can't put my finger on it. Their energy is different. I divert my attention away from the group as Alpha Gale begins to speak.

"Now that we're all here, allow me to make introductions. Alpha Turner, this is my son, Adam, and his mate, Ember. Seated with them is their main protector, Beta Corey." I fight a grimace at the use of the word mate in reference to my tie to Adam and nod accordingly.

Alpha Turner smiles. "It's a pleasure to meet you all. I look forward to you visiting my territory. I have with me my wife, Adeline, and several guests from neighboring territories. This is Zendaya, Ulric, and Prospero. They have been assisting with the Kushtaka issues."

The three guests nod their heads in greeting, but the final male holds my gaze. He watches me curiously, and something about him sends chills down my spine.

"Welcome, all. Now, let's eat, and then we'll join in on some dancing in the room down the hall in celebration of your visit, Alpha Turner." Alpha Gale claps his hands, and several butlers bring out trays covered with food. They place them in the middle of the table, and we wait for the Alphas to fix their plates before digging in.

The food is delicious and seems to melt in my mouth. The steak is a perfect medium-rare, and the asparagus tastes just right. I fight hard not to eat like a starved beast but my control slips.

"I love seeing a woman with an appetite," the man, Prospero, says with a wolfish grin.

I nod in acknowledgment as chills once again run down my spine, and I force myself to slow down. I keep my eyes down on my food and avoid looking at him, but a heavy weight seems to settle on me. I look up quickly and see Ulric, the other male, watching me. His gaze is different, soothing almost, and makes me fall into a sense of calm. It's strange, and I feel comfortable, so I look him over.

He is broad-shouldered and muscular, with his button-down shirt fitting firmly over his biceps. His shoulder-length black hair is styled loosely, and his eyes glow a beautiful shade of green. As we make eye contact, the room seems to spin, and his smile intensifies.

I blush and snap my gaze back down to my almost-empty plate again. Warmth spreads through my belly, and my magic stirs, setting me on edge. I don't need it to make a flaming appearance right now.

"You okay?" Adam asks in a whisper at my ear.

I look up into his eyes. "Yeah, I think I ate too fast."

"Do I need to get you anything? Tums?"

"Nah, I'll be fine in a little bit." I shrug.

He nods and turns his attention back to the Alphas who have been discussing the training plans. I haven't listened to a single bit of it, but I know Corey and Adam have been soaking it in.

A nudge to my right causes me to turn, and Corey is smiling at me mischievously. "Don't think I didn't see what just happened. Adam may have missed it, but I know that reaction," he whispers, and I turn scarlet.

I keep my gaze focused down as we finish our meal and take little slips from the water glass in front of me. I refuse to look across the table at Ulric. I don't understand what happened when our gazes met.

After several minutes, the Alphas finish their meals, and we all make our way out of the dining room. Loud music hits my ears as soon as we pass through the door and into the hall. It's curious that we couldn't hear it before with our hearing. I guess the dining hall is soundproof. The upbeat music makes me forget the awkward incident from earlier, and I tug at Adam, who has my hand, trying to get to the room faster. I love to dance.

As we enter the room, I dash past Alpha Gale with Adam in tow. I can't wait anymore, and his chuckles follow us out to the floor. Corey follows along, and we dance as a group in the middle of the room. Other members of the pack dance around us, and I let the music carry me away.

Colorful lights flash throughout the room, and I notice the chandeliers are dimmed. Streamers decorate the walls, and there are tables with appetizers and punch along one wall. It's simple but not too low-key that a visiting pack would see it as offensive.

Energy courses through my body as I laugh and sway my hips. I feel light and free. Corey moves off to dance with another pack member, and Adam spins me into him. I smile up at him, lost in the moment.

"Ember, your eyes are glowing. I think your wolf is trying to surface. Do we need to step out?" He quirks a brow up and speaks with concern.

I stop and stare at him as panic fills me. I let my guard down, and I do a quick assessment. I blink a few times, trying to clear my mind. "Maybe she's trying. I'm not sure. I'm going to grab a drink and cool down some. I'll find you when I'm ready to dance again." I dart away from him before he has a chance to speak and head straight for one of the punch bowls.

I grab one of the premade glasses from the table and toss it back like a shot. It gives me a moment to think, and I notice how hot I feel as it slides down. I look down at my fingers and see black sparks, so I reach for another glass.

I'm tossing it back when a male's voice startles me. "I wondered if you would ever leave that male's side. His scent doesn't mesh with yours, but the scents you carry have sparked my curiosity. Allow me to introduce myself formally. I'm Prospero."

I whip around and meet his gaze as he does a slight bow. The creepy vibes I got earlier across the table are worse as he stands before me. I arch my brow and cross my arms across my chest. "It's a pleasure to meet you. Adam and I are bound, despite what my scent tells you. What can I help you with?"

He smiles too cheerily. "You could help me with a lot of things, sweet treasure, but I'm afraid now's not the time. Tell me, though, who are you really? Is Ember even your real name? Is life in this pack a game to you?"

"What do you mean?" I ask, feeling confused. "I have lived here all of my life."

"Is my brother harassing you, little wolf?" the darker male says off to my left. "I'm Ulric, by the way, the better-looking brother." He chuckles.

"Why, brother, I'm not troubling our new friend at all. I'm just asking her basic questions. I'm on my best behavior tonight," Prospero says with a wink, and I frown.

Ulric offers me his hand. "I find that hard to believe, brother. Would you care to dance with me, Ember? You looked like you were having a lot of fun out there earlier."

I glance down at my fingers, noticing they're no longer sparking, and place my hand in his. "Sure," I say, and electrical pulses fly up my arm as our hands meet. Burning pain spirals down my back, and I hide my discomfort behind a smile as my eyes meet his. He seems surprised, and they faintly glow before he blinks it away.

He leads me out into the center of the room, and I glance around to find Adam. He might not like this, but he and Corey both are occupied at the rear of the room with their backs to the dance floor. They are deep in conversation with a few Betas.

"I apologize if my brother did anything to upset you. He can be a brute most of the time." Ulric twirls me around, and I feel as if we're floating.

"He didn't bother me too much." I shrug and lean into him as he spins us. His arms slide around me, and he gently holds me close as the music changes to something slower.

"You mentioned you have lived here your entire life as I arrived to rescue you from him. Do you like it here? You seem different from the other members. I can feel more power radiating off you than even the Alphas have."

"That's strange that you say that. I think my power is why I'm bound to Adam, but I have lived here since birth. My mother was a member of this pack from birth, and she met my father out of town," I say cautiously.

"I'm sorry if my question upset you. I didn't mean any offense. I'm just curious. There is something unique about you." Ulric gazes down at me.

"It's fine." I shrug. "How far apart in age are you and your brother? You don't look much alike."

He chuckles, then says, "We are only half-brothers, and we are only a year or so apart. It's a long story, but Zendaya is also a half-sister of ours. We have a crazy family."

"Oh, I guess that makes sense. Wow. None of you favor each other at all except maybe in height. Are all of your parents tall?"

"Yes, and I believe that explains our earlier interaction. You were checking me out at dinner." His tone is teasing, but I still blush.

"I was only making an observation. You're all larger than the wolves I grew up with. Plus, I can look, but I can't touch. I'm claimed, remember?" I blush again, realizing what I just said.

"So you say, but the one you say is your mate doesn't match the scent lingering around you. They tell me otherwise. I can't distinguish them all, but I can discern the scent belonging to the Beta that shadows you and your-to-be Alpha, who is currently glaring daggers at me."

I glance over my shoulder and see both Adam and Corey wearing murderous expressions on their faces. Ulric twirls me further away from them and pulls me closer.

"Did the Beta claim you, little wolf, and also a vampire? I didn't know there were any down this way."

"No one has officially claimed me. Are those the only scents you smell on me?" I ask perturbed, and I send up a silent prayer to the gods that no one heard him.

"There is another unique scent, but it's difficult to make out. I have been around for a long time, and I have only come across a scent similar to that a few times over the years. It was never by choice. Did a demon mark you as the others did? The scent reminds me of hellfire."

I cringe at his words, and panic rears its head. "No, I have been attacked by some recently, though. That's why we are to train in Alaska. But unfortunately, we have an Imp problem."

"That would make sense, I guess. Does your-to-be Alpha know about the others? I don't see that sitting well."

I open my mouth to make a retort when a hand lands on my shoulder. Ulric and I stop moving, and I glance over to find Corey. He glares at Ulric and then turns to me with a smile. "Can I cut in?"

I don't miss the smirk on Ulric's face as I respond, "Yes, you may. Thanks for the dance, Ulric. Maybe I'll see you around?"

"I hope you will, little wolf. Take care of her, Beta." He bows slightly, and Corey tugs me away.

"Did I hear him say what I thought I heard him say?" Corey asks, pulling me toward the opposite end of the room, closer to where Adam still stands, glaring at Ulric, who is now standing with his siblings across the room.

"What did you hear exactly?" I ask cautiously.

"Did you tell him about us?"

"No, he picked up on the scent. He was very curious, and I think he picked up on the other scent."

He looks at me with concern. "The other scent, as in the new scent you now have?"

"Yes, that one, but he couldn't identify it." I shrug and glance around. This conversation is making me nervous.

He runs a hand through his hair and spins me around, distracting me with dance moves.

"Why didn't Adam intervene if you guys were worried? He's supposed to be stepping up to the role and all."

He chuckles. "He and I thought it would cause less of a political stir if I stepped in. We aren't sure how those three guests tie into the Alaska pack yet, and they give us weird vibes. That male seemed way too comfortable with you."

I shrug, feeling strangely disoriented as if Ulric and I have some type of connection. "He was nice at least."

"Yes, but even though Adam didn't intervene, he struggled. His wolf wanted to tear free and claim you, while also murdering that male. He has territorial issues tonight, especially because of those two tall males. He didn't like how they were eyeing you at dinner or how they have watched you all evening on the dance floor."

I frown at his words and think back over the night. After that incident with Prospero and the food, I tried not to look at them. Did they really watch me, as he says?

"Oh, here he comes. I guess my time with you alone is over. I hope he'll let you out of his sight to practice some over the next few days," Corey says quietly.

"Ember, Corey, may I cut in?" Adam asks authoritatively, and we stop moving.

"You may. Have fun, you two!" Corey chirps as he places my hand in Adam's.

Adam smiles at me and pulls me close. He leans in to whisper into my ear. "Were you trying to drive me mad with jealousy earlier, dancing with that other male?"

I roll my eyes. "No, but it seems it did drive you a little crazy."

He tightens his hold on my arm, and it's almost painful as he says, "You are mine, Ember, remember that. Fuck, if you would let me claim you and complete the mating process, no male would dare step within a ten-foot radius of you. They wouldn't even think about it. It would strengthen us both and maybe finally unlock your wolf."

I look into his eyes as they glow, and I know his wolf is fighting for dominance. Adam's hands drop lower on my back, and I know where he's trying to go with this.

I growl in frustration, and his hands stop moving. "In time, Adam. I'm not ready yet, and you know that. We still have a long way to go."

He leans into my neck and begins to pepper kisses there. I can't help but fight the shiver of pleasure it causes, but it doesn't feel anything like what Zeke or Corey did. Instead, his kisses are possessive and aggressive. There is no electrical tingle like what I felt with Zeke, and we don't have a connection like Corey and I have. Nothing like what a real mate should feel like when they touch.

"Stop, Adam. We're in a room full of people." I try to pull away.

"I know, that's the point. Let them see and know who you belong to. You are mine."

I glare at him, and my magic swirls through my veins. I let it give me an extra boost as I break out of his hold and turn wordlessly away from him. Then, fuming, I push my way through the dancing bodies around us and out the door. I don't stop until the night air hits me as I lean against the railing on the front porch.

I stare out into the night, steaming and confused. How am I supposed to make this work between us and lead this pack? I can't do this. The territorial bastard needs to get it together. I need a connection with him unless I can find an out. Prick, he docs not own mc.

"Men can be a pain in the ass. You okay?" a melodious voice asks from the dark to my right. I turn and watch as Zendaya steps forward with a smile. She seems to glow against the night, and her platinum hair looks ghostly.

"Yeah, I'll be fine. Did you get tired of dancing?" I change subjects, and she leans against the rail next to me.

"Oh, no. I could dance all night, but that room seemed to get a bit stuffy. I needed some fresh air. It seems that you did too."

"Yeah."

"You know, you aren't meant to be with him. I can sense things, and you're different from these wolves. Your power is greater, but why are you here?"

I stare at her, trying to process her words, and frown. "I'm not sure what you mean."

She sighs and turns her gaze to the yard. "You will, one day, soon. Enjoy the fresh air, Ember." She turns and waltzes back into the pack house, leaving me staring after her and confused.

I rub my head as it begins to ache and turn my focus to the stars overhead. They are bright and endless, but I feel small standing beneath them. Suddenly, the urge to run fills me, and I slide out of my heels. I don't want to talk to Adam after what happened, and I don't want to be here anymore.

Carrying my heels, I sigh as the damp grass hits my feet, and I break out into a run. As I sprint down the road, my dress flows behind me, and the expulsion of energy seems to calm me.

By the time I reach the steps to my parents' front porch, I feel calm and focused. I let myself in and quickly move through my nightly routine. Sleep sounds lovely, and I know I only have a few days to prepare for the trip to Alaska. Let's see if I get an apology from Adam in the meantime.

CHAPTER TEN

I'm sandwiched between Adam and Corey a few days later as we fly on a private jet headed for Alaska. Only a handful of the Betas we have been training with are allowed to join us. We are basically to run the perimeter of the pack's territory and dispose of any violent individuals that cross our paths.

I got a message from Zeke a few days ago, letting me know he would join us by the end of the week, if not sooner. He has had luck rounding up some help to train us against other species to better prepare for demon attacks. I also hope that he's found a way to break me from this contract with Adam and his family. Unfortunately, my hope is starting to diminish. He is trying to make us more serious and has been pushing me to complete the mating bond with him. I'm not ready to do that unless there is zero chance to get out of it.

The ring he gave me rests on my hand like a weight. I thought it would appease him and not make him want to push things, but it only seems to have increased his determination.

I close my eyes as the plane begins its descent. My stomach rises and falls with the bumps. We are landing at the airport in Juneau, Alaska, and going into the airport to meet Alpha Turner's people. We are supposed to take vehicles from there and cross over to Douglas Island.

As the wheels make contact with the ground, my stomach jolts. We roll across the tarmac, and the tension in my shoulders finally begins to ease. Who knew how nerve-racking flying could be? This was only my first time, and once we reached a reasonable altitude, it wasn't as bad as I had predicted it would be. During takeoff, I felt like vomiting, though.

"Are you ready for this?" Adam asks as the plane coasts to a stop.

I sigh and push from my chair to stretch. "I'm as ready as I'll ever be."

"This will be a fun and easy trip. Don't you worry, Ember," Corey adds, standing next to me.

"I just hope we can explore in our downtime. I would love to see more of the area." I scratch at my head and resituate my hair in its ponytail.

"That would be nice, but I doubt we'll get to. Remember, this is an official mission, not just a training exercise, and definitely not a vacation," Adam says seriously, and I roll my eyes. He ushers us to follow him toward the front of the plane, and the three of us stick close. We are to work as a team after all.

On the flight, he made sure we had everything memorized regarding what our schedules would be like. We are to set an example for the rest of the pack members on this mission and focus on building our bonds. We are to follow orders given by Alpha Turner to a T. We are not to party, be mischievous in any way, and keep our hands to ourselves. Adam and I are to keep it PG-rated according to Alpha Gales' rules. I laughed hysterically at this, which seemed to offend Adam, but it gave me a new sense of hope that he may back off on the mate thing some during this trip.

As we step through the door on the plane to descend the metal steps, a blast of cool air hits me and causes me to freeze in place momentarily. They told us to dress warmly, but this is different. My magic responds to my momentary lapse in control, and my body tingles and heats. I shiver in response, but I let it spread through me, warming my chilled skin. I keep it in check enough not to let the flames burst free. I smile and startle as Corey nudges me from behind. I didn't think about my scent, but I'm sure he picked up on it.

"You okay?" he asks, and Adam turns his head to look at me curiously.

"Yeah, it's colder than I expected. The mountains are gorgeous! Do you see them?" I gesture away from us toward the snow-covered mountains. It pulls their focus away from me, and we continue our way down the steps.

"They are pretty, almost as beautiful as you are," Adam says, and I swear a melted cheese scent fills the air.

"Quit trying to flatter me. You know the rules for this trip. No funny business." I shrug.

Corey groans behind me, and Adam frowns as he says, "Will he know if we do anything?"

"We aren't going to test it, plus, you know I'm not ready." I cross my arms across my chest, and we fan out where we can see each other better.

"Not even if it's just sex for pleasure? I bet if Corey offered, you would jump right on it." Adam growls in frustration.

"Don't bring me into this, bro," Corey adds, lifting his hands in mock surrender.

I roll my eyes. "What you want from me, Adam, is different, and you know it is. It's not the same."

"Are you sure about that? Do you even know how I really feel?" he asks, giving me a serious look.

"Can we not have this conversation now? We need to look for Alpha Turner's men and set a good example for the pack, remember?"

"Fine, but we'll finish this later," he says with a grunt, and I roll my eyes once again. Adam is going to make me lose my shit on this trip.

"How long is this trip again?" I ask, trying to switch gears and lighten the mood.

"Two weeks unless otherwise told to stay longer by Alpha Turner," Corey says.

"It shouldn't be more than that. With us providing extra help with the Kushtaka issue, things should return to normal quickly. Then, when we get back, I'm taking you on a real date, outside pack territory, with the freedom to do whatever we want." Adam smiles.

I frown, but I also can't fight the excitement of going off pack land. It may be my last taste of freedom unless Zeke finds another way out.

"If Alpha Gale lets you. He doesn't want you two far from our protectors while so many demons are roaming." Corey ruins my train of thought with his negativity.

"I thought there weren't many attacks. Did he tell you two something different?"

Adam and Corey share a look. Their silence and their stare-off ends with Adam shrugging.

"There have been others in the area, yes, but I'm sure we can get cleared to go out."

"How many more attacks have there been?" I stop moving and force them to stop and look at me.

Corey frowns and looks troubled while running a hand through his hair. Adam seems confused about my concern.

"The Beta teams and boundary Sentinels have taken them out easily." Adam shrugs again.

I turn my gaze solely on Corey, and the air warms around us. He cringes, feeling the change, knowing it's coming from me. "How many?"

"There have been thirty different attacks since our first encounter," he answers quietly.

"Why is it important? You're safe with us, Ember. There isn't a need for you to worry," Adam says, pushing me gently to move forward.

"Because it matters to me," I respond and look over at Corey.

"You are safe. They can't get you, know that." He nods, trying to encourage me. His underlying meaning should be reassuring, but it's not.

I turn my gaze ahead of us and move with determined strides through the airport. We remain silent as we locate a man holding a sign bearing Adam's last name. *Courser and Group.* He leads our group out to waiting vehicles.

As we load our bags into the SUVs, he informs us that our luggage will be taken to our rooms while we are debriefed at the pack house. We will be given our designated patrol areas and any necessary information needed to perform our tasks. I nod, knowing that because I'm the future Luna, we will have more details of things than the rest of the group.

I toss my bags into the pile at the back of the SUV and climb in. The three of us have our own vehicle, but it doesn't keep the guys from sandwiching me between them. You would have thought one of them would have wanted to stretch out in their own seat, but no. The three of us sit squished together on the bench seat.

Thankfully, we ride in silence, giving me time to process what Corey revealed minutes earlier. There have been more attacks, and that can't be a coincidence, can it? Did the demons and Imps we have encountered somehow relay a message to their higher-ups, letting them know I exist? Do they know that I'm something special?

I try to push the worry from my mind and take in the scenery around me as we drive. Alaska is beautiful, and I wish I had more time to explore it. Juneau has gorgeous buildings that seem to take me back to a simpler time. The snow-capped mountains in the distance make it feel like a dream. I sigh sadly as we turn away from the shops to cross a bridge.

The water is dark beneath it as we move across but reflects the scenery around it. There are marinas filled with boats on either side of the waterway. I smile as I watch a few people move around on a fishing boat and ignore the few bumps as we make our way toward Douglas Island.

It's truly a wonderful sight to behold, but as we near the shore, something in me pulses. The sensation is strange, and I hold my breath, unsure of what will happen next. My magic swirls and tries to burst out of me, but I push it down and grab Corey's hand to anchor me.

He yelps and jerks his hand away before saying, "Jeez, Ember, you're on fire!"

I blink and take a deep breath, holding my magic down as best I can.

"Are you okay? You're a shifter, so you shouldn't be sick. Is it a fever from your wolf trying to come out?" Adam asks hopefully but concerned.

"I'm okay. It's probably just hormones or something. Maybe I'm a little car sick." I shrug and continue to take deep breaths.

"Do you think fresh air would help?" Corey reaches for my hand hesitantly this time.

"That might help. I'll take a short walk when we stop and see if it helps. I'm sure that'll be fine before we go to the debriefing, right?" I lift my brow and let my gaze meet our driver's.

"That should be acceptable. Just remember not to go too far and to meet in the main conference room," he says with a slight nod.

I slump back in my seat. "Thanks." I close my eyes as Corey begins to run his thumb in circles on my hand. It's soothing. I feel Adam grab my other hand and start to do the same with it.

"Your hands are warm. Wow," he murmurs and places a kiss on the hand he has.

I open my eyes and meet his gaze. He smiles at me, and I offer a small one in return before looking out the window behind him. The rocky shores pass by us in a blur, but I don't miss the small group of creatures swimming near them. They looked like otters but were they part of the Kushtaka or regular animals?

We follow a road as it curves its way closer inland. Trees surround us, and I can't help but admire how tall and beautiful they are. The sun shines high above them, casting dark shadows across the road, and it feels like I'm entering a new world. It's so different from the terrain of Oklahoma.

Soon, we're pulling to a stop in front of a large cabin with a wraparound porch. It looks more like a lodge than a simple cabin and has enormous skylight windows on its sloped roof. They look great for letting in natural light.

To the right of the lodge is a cluster of what looks like solar panels. They have their own area. I notice smaller tiny homes behind them tucked along the tree line. Everything else rests in the large clearing.

On the opposite side of the lodge is a large pond and training area. I can see a few individuals sparring and practicing there. Their movements are fluid, and I watch them as we begin climbing out of the SUV.

Corey lets me slide to the ground, catching me gracefully. I smile and quickly move toward the shade of the trees not far off from us. The open air does seem to calm me, and I feel my heart rate settle. I wish I knew what caused my magic to react as it did. What triggered it?

Suddenly, my magic stirs again, and my palms heat. My heart rate increases as a result, and I feel my flames trying to break free. I clench my eyes closed and kneel to the ground, pressing my hands into the dirt to ground myself.

"Em, you okay?" Corey's voice is hesitant, and I feel his hand rest on my shoulder.

I whip my eyes open, and flames erupt up my arm. He moves to block me from anyone that may still be lingering around the vehicles. I can faintly hear people talking and moving around as roaring fills my ears. "No, I don't think I am. I don't know what's going on. Something keeps triggering my magic, and I worry that it's not something good."

"Breathe. Focus on recalling your flames and slow your heart rate. Do you need to go for a run? Can you hold things at bay long enough to make it through the debriefing and get our orders? The run should help ease everything afterward."

"I think that would be good. I can't lose control here."

"We'll get this figured out. Call it back. You can do it. Zeke will be here in a few days, and maybe he can shed more light on things. He may be able to locate the trigger."

"I hope so." I close my eyes again and take deep breaths. My magic slowly recoils into a small ball as if it has been scolded. Then, finally, I feel my flames disappear and things cool around me.

"You two okay?" Adam's voice startles me, and I open my eyes as my magic tries to surge to life again. I clamp down on it with an iron fist as he nears.

I let out a breath as it settles once again. "Yeah, just a little nauseous. The curves made me car sick. The altitude difference may be messing with me too. I'll be fine in a bit."

Adam looks curiously between Corey and me as I push up from my kneeling position. "I bet they have some ginger ale inside. That's supposed to help with nausea and altitude issues from what I've heard." Corey drops his hand from my shoulder as we move closer to Adam and the three of us walk toward the front door of the pack house.

We take the front steps to the porch, and a man steps from the shadows. The guys move in closer to me as we take in whether he's a threat or not. Of course, he shouldn't be, but one can never be too cautious. He has short, cropped black hair and dark brown eyes. He's tall with broad shoulders and resembles Alpha Turner, somewhat.

"Hello, I'm James Turner. I wanted to introduce myself before you went to the debriefing. My father has told me great things about your pack, and I hope we can work together in the future." He lifts a hand to Adam and nods at us.

Adam reaches out to shake it. "It's a pleasure to meet you, James. Shall we head inside?"

James doesn't say anything to Corey and me as we all head into the pack house. I try not to let it bother me, but it does. It seems rude, and I get a feeling that I'm not going to like this guy.

We make our way down a hall lined with white shiplap and pictures of the pack. Many of the frames hold images of the Alpha and his family. It creates a homey feeling, and I feel myself relax. The hall leads us past several closed doors, and we take a few turns before we reach the room where the debriefing will occur.

We walk past one of the enforcers standing at the door offering him a nod and we take a seat at one of the tables in the front. James steers Adam to a seat for the two of them, forcing Corey and me to sit nearby. It's strange how Adam didn't protest, but I feel relieved. The only thing that bothers me is that we won't hear anything they discuss regarding the pack. Adam has included both Corey and me on all things related as of late.

I take a moment to glance around and notice the room is lined with whiteboards covered by different maps and other information. Tables are scattered throughout, covered with more paper, and a giant coffee pot rests at the front of the room next to a large sink. It's strangely cozy for being such a large meeting room. I love how different it is from what our pack does.

Silence descends upon the room, and I turn my sight to the back of the room as Alpha Turner enters, followed by a small group of Betas and protectors. He moves to the front of the room, where he proceeds to jump right into what he expects of us. First, he lists the rules and points out on each map what group will patrol where. He then pulls down a screen, giving us a presentation on the Kushtaka, their abilities, habitats, and other necessary information.

He explains that the Kushtaka are evil shape-shifting demons that can turn into sea otters. They use this disguise to appear harmless so animals and people will be comfortable around them. They then bring them to their deaths in various ways. Some of the younger ones lure people deep into the woods before killing them. They are strong and use dark magic to fight. They can be taken down, but it isn't very easy.

After the PowerPoint, we are handed packets with our information printed to avoid forgetting our orders, and we are dismissed. Alpha Turner makes sure to shake each of our hands as we leave, and I can't fight the urge I get to run as I make it out into the fresh air again. My magic stirs once again, and I know that not only do I want to run, but I also need to, so my magic will settle.

"I think I'm going to go for a run. Does anyone want to join me?" I ask Corey, Adam, and James as we stop at the bottom of the stairs.

"A run sounds nice, but I was hoping to give your future Alpha a tour of our place. We will be working closely together in the future," James says casually with a shrug.

Adam lifts a brow and looks at both Corey and me as if he's weighing his words. He and Corey do that silent conversation thing again, which drives me crazy, before he nods and turns to me. "You guys go. I'll see you at dinner. Stay close, though. Don't go too far."

I roll my eyes but nod as I say, "You got it, boss man." He frowns as I go to turn away, and I'm stopped as he grabs my hand.

He spins me around and pulls me into him roughly. I blink, and then his lips are on mine. It's demanding, and I know he's marking his territory with his display of affection. I'm his, and no one is to touch me. He breaks the kiss after a minute and rests his forehead against mine, breathing heavily as if he wants to do more. His eyes glow as his wolf hovers near the surface. "I need you to take this seriously, Ember. I need you safe. I want to be with you, but his tour will benefit our pack. Find me at dinner as soon as you return so that I know you're okay."

I stare at him, stunned by his intensity, and he turns to James with a smile. I miss what he says before the two walk away from us. I finally shake myself and turn to Corey. "Jeez, he can be so territorial."

He laughs as he says, "That he can. Let's go."

COREY AND I ARRIVE BACK AT THE PACK HOUSE THREE HOURS later, covered in dirt and sweat. Not only did we run, but we also did a bit of training. We sparred, and he helped me practice using my magic. I only did small things because it wanted to flair and explode at first, and I didn't want to draw attention to us. At one point, we thought we heard someone in the woods nearby, but upon further inspection, we didn't find a single track. It was weird. Everything we did, though, seemed to take the edge off. I feel much better.

"Wow, what happened to you two?" James quips as we sit down, and Adam growls.

"Chill, Adam, we only sparred and ran. Corey kicked my ass," I say, grabbing the pitcher of water from the middle of the table and filling my empty glass.

"I wouldn't say that. You bested me quite a bit. You can take her on tomorrow, Adam." Corey smirks and begins shoveling food on a plate from the platters resting in front of us.

I smile as I take in the various dishes lined up in the center of the table. They look fantastic, and my mouth waters. I need to refuel after burning so many calories during our practice session. I gulp down some of my water before eagerly filling my plate.

"I like that idea. You have been progressing well, Ember." Adam smiles mischievously.

"I'll join you all tomorrow if you don't mind? I would love to practice with someone new," James adds.

"Great. So while you guys were out, I got our rooms squared away. We're in one of the tiny houses, but it's larger than the others." Adam picks at his almost-empty plate of food while he talks, and I can't help but wonder what he's not telling us.

"Awesome," I say between bites and continue shoveling food into my mouth. I'm starving.

We finish eating, listening to Adam and James discuss training tactics and weapons. They also discuss territory and trivial matters between some of the other packs. The way James describes sharing their land with other supernatural beings is fascinating, and I can't help but wonder how they manage it without bloodshed. Wolves are naturally territorial.

I follow the guys out in a food haze as we make our way toward the tiny houses. The buildings are each unique and gorgeous. Ours has massive windows to let in natural light and a blue wooden exterior. A small porch wraps around it, and it has a slanted roof.

Adam pushes open the door, and I take in the small area. The room is toasty and smells of vanilla. There is a small kitchen area that opens up into the combined dining and living space. A cozy couch rests in the middle of the room with a small bookshelf across from it. A small bathroom is open down the hall, and a loft hangs above us. A bedroom rests across from the bathroom, and a small closet is open, revealing a washer and dryer.

"Are you and Corey taking the loft space?" I ask Adam, moving toward the bedroom.

"Corey is, but we're sharing the room," Adam says, and I turn, stopping to see Corey disappearing up the ladder to the loft.

"What?"

"What do you mean what? You are my mate, Ember, and we need to get used to sharing a bed. You can only put off my claim for so long."

"I get it, Adam. However, I wish we could have discussed this first."

"We probably should have, but as your future Alpha, there will be times we won't be able to discuss things, and you'll have to trust my decision. So here we are."

I huff and continue to walk toward the room. The bed is at least a king size which is surprising for a tiny house. It takes up most of the room. Testing in an empty corner are our bags.

"I'm going to take a shower." I walk over and dig my stuff out of my bag.

"Okay, I'll be right here when you get done. Then I'll take a turn."

With my items in hand, I quickly make my way out of the room and take my time getting ready for bed. I'm frustrated, and it causes my magic to stir. I turn the tap to cold and let my magic heat my skin in an effort to take the edge off. I feel blindsided by his decision, and I know that what he said about making decisions for both of us in the future isn't true. There is always time to discuss things unless it's an emergency situation which shouldn't happen for things such as this.

Entering the room after my freezing shower, I toss my stuff atop my bag and move to the bed. I offer Adam a tense smile as he leaves to shower and pull back the thick comforter. I slide into the silken sheets and burrow down into the soft mattress. The bed feels lovely, and I feel like I'm wrapped in a cloud.

I let out a contented sigh as I tighten the blankets around me and close my eyes. I send up a silent prayer that Adam will stay on his side of the bed, but something tells me he won't.

Nervous butterflies take flight in my stomach minutes later as I hear the shower cut off. What will he do? Will he insist on holding me, or will he let me have my space?

He enters the room, smelling of pine and wearing a loose pair of athletic shorts. They hug his hips and show off his six-pack. He's leaner than Corey but just as lethal, and I can't help but admire his figure.

I force myself to look out the window as the moonlight streams in, illuminating everything in its glow. The blue tint of its light makes the room seem magical. It feels surreal, and I almost pinch myself until I feel the bed dip.

"How is the bed?" he asks from behind me.

"Cozy and warm," I respond without looking at him.

I hear him peel the comforter back enough to slide in. The bed moves as he slides closer to me and wraps himself around me. He sighs into my hair as he says, "I think I'm falling for you, Ember."

I blink and turn my head slightly to give us some space and look him in the eyes. He seems to be searching mine, hoping for the same response, but I sigh. "I'm sorry, Adam, but I don't feel that way. I still need time to adjust to all of this. I'm trying, but don't forget that we have both fought against this our entire lives. It's not that easy for me to accept things like you have."

"I get that, and I don't expect you to say it unless you mean it. But I wanted you to know how I felt. I don't want to keep anything I feel from you, Ember. I want us to trust each other completely. We need to if we're going to lead our pack successfully."

I roll back to my comfortable position and close my eyes as he snuggles in closer.

"Are you going to sleep?" he asks.

"Yes, we have rounds to make tomorrow, and I'm exhausted from the events of the day. You should rest too."

"You're right. I thought maybe I could entice you into other things, though."

"We talked about that, Adam. You know it's not time."

"Fine. Goodnight, sweet." He leans over me and kisses my cheek before repositioning himself in the bed. He stays wrapped around me, and strangely enough, we fit together well.

"Goodnight, Adam," I respond, once he's quit moving.

After several minutes, his steady breathing lets me know he has fallen asleep. I lay awake and stare out the window at the moon, wishing life was different. I let myself get lost in the stars and how unreal they seem. Then, as my mind wanders, I slowly feel my eyes grow heavy, and sleep embraces me.

CHAPTER ELEVEN

The next three days rolled steadily by. Our patrol spans a large area on the southern end of Douglas Island. Instead of walking the path each time on foot, Adam insisted on carrying me. I sat astride his back as if he were a horse to make the rounds. It was weird at first, just like sharing a bed with him was that first night, but I have slowly adjusted to his presence.

His scent now coats my skin, but it's not the same as if we were a mated pair. It covers my own scent, and any left by those that have claimed me, but nothing will compare to when I complete the mating process. When that happens, both my scent and my mate's will become one and the same.

Despite his scent coating me, he has bugged me each night to finish things. I'm still holding out that there is a way to break the contract and find true love. I refuse to give up on that front.

As we pace along our path today, darting around the various trees and jumping over boulders, I bury myself down deeper into Adam's fur. The air is chillier today, and I can sense a storm on the horizon. James trots beside us in his arctic wolf form, and Corey follows along on the other side. We maintain a tight formation for each shift even though there haven't been any signs of attack.

James and I are getting along better now that he has determined how important I am to the two males with us. He isn't as much of a prick as I thought he was upon our first meeting. He's got a good sense of humor and genuinely cares about his pack. He will make a great Alpha when his father decides to step down.

I enjoy watching the guys in their wolf forms. Each is sleek, deadly, and beautiful. It makes me ache to join them, but I'm not sure what exactly will burst free when it's time. Their fluid motions make my muscles ache to run, but my inner beast has refused to show despite the increase in power and unpredictable bursts I've had this week.

I'm caught up dreaming about the guys running through the trees when Corey lets out a warning growl that causes me to open my eyes. I lift my head to peek over Adams's head as he comes to a stop. We are near a rocky outcrop near the ocean, where a group of harmless-looking sea otters stares back at us.

Unsure if they are Kushtaka or actual otters, I slide down from Adam's back and sniff the air. I frown as the smell of garbage hits my nostrils. It's similar to the way the Imps smelled. There is also the smell of murky, stagnant water mixed in with the rotting garbage stench. It confuses me.

I glance back at the otters as the males move to box me in, preparing for an attack. I'm currently the weakest link despite the number of weapons I have on me. Black magic swirls around the tiny creatures, and they're replaced with creatures that have faces like men but are covered in fur. They have webbed hands, and their eyes glow unnaturally silver.

"You're encroaching on our territory," the one in the front grunts out.

James lets out an ear-shattering roar before his voice fills the air. *This is my pack's land, and we offer refuge to many. Who are you to claim it as yours? Leave now, and there won't be any trouble.*

The Kushtaka in front laughs, and it sounds like gravel. "I don't think so, pup. We were told we could have this section by one of the fallen. He only asked for one thing in return." The being nods toward me.

I don't know this fallen you're talking about. They hold no claim to this land. Be gone before things get messy. James's voice is filled with the power of an Alpha as he speaks.

The males bristle, preparing to attack, but a plume of water shoots up from behind the otters, and we all watch as a being with black wings lands behind them. The Kushtaka don't even flinch as the water falls and reveals Zendaya in another form. She has a cold smile on her face as she takes us in. Her black wings fan out on either side of her as water drips from them.

The wolves bristle as James asks, *What is the meaning of this, Zendaya? We offered you refuge.*

She tilts her head to the side as if contemplating his question. "For some reason, my brother wants us to claim this territory. Since I owe him for several things, he roped me into assisting him in clearing your pack off of it. He also wants what doesn't belong in this world, which is Ember. She will be his new treasure."

I pale as her words register and the males growl. James asks with confusion lacing his words, *Why wouldn't she belong? She's to be Luna of her pack and mate to future Alpha Adam. Also, what use is this land to him?*

"This land hides one of the few access points that leads to the realm of Hell. That is why the Kushtaka have remained here all these years. It strengthens them, and he wants to control this access point. Ember knows why she doesn't belong. Ask her, and she will tell you what you have all chosen to ignore." Zendaya's musical voice sounds almost mocking.

Despite your claims, Zendaya, this land will remain in the hands of the Turner pack. Tell your brother to piss off. Take these beings with you and don't touch my mate. I move closer to Adam as he growls, his words laced with power at the dark angel.

"Oh, but you are wrong, little Alpha pup. This land has always belonged to us." Silver swirls around her, and armor covers her from head to toe. Gleaming swords form in her hands, and the magic moves over the Kushtaka, giving them metal-coated talons and armor. "Now we can do this the easy way, or we can do this the hard way. What's it going to be?"

You will not have this land! James roars and launches himself forward.

He meets one of the Kushtaka head-on as Zendaya says, "So be it."

The rest of the Kushtaka rush forward at her words, and we meet them head-on. Adam and Corey keep me behind them, and I launch daggers as best as I can around them. They herd me back, trying to keep me safe, but I know they need to focus on taking out the Kushtaka.

Roaring fills the air as Imps, and other flying demons burst from the trees and the water to join the attack. We are vastly outnumbered, but our fighting continues, nonetheless.

Ember, stay back. We will handle this. Adam glances over his shoulder briefly, and he and Corey rush a group of Imps.

A yelp comes from Corey as one of the Imp's talons breaks off in his side. It protrudes out as if it were a dagger, and I know I can't let this go on. My heart breaks as the idea of what I need to do forms in my head. In response, my magic rumbles to life, and this time, I let it sweep over me.

Black flames erupt out of me, knocking the demons closest to me to the ground, causing them to disintegrate. The ground rumbles beneath me, and I feel as if time has stopped. I blink and shoot flames toward the beings attacking the males, and they disintegrate, giving my guys time to recuperate, but they stare at me in shock.

Ember, no! Corey yells, but it's too late.

I feel my body begin to shift and change. It burns, and I feel my bones break as they realign. My flames turn to a burning red as my body continues morphing into its new form. I feel my face elongate, and sharp teeth burst through. Fur coats my body, and as the pain settles, I find myself towering above the wolves as I stare down Zendaya and her posse.

"There she is." Zendaya's words wash over me, and I growl, causing the ground to shake.

Instead of checking on the males, I launch myself at a group of Imps and bite through them as they scream. Then, I cast flames out from me and push the males back away from the attackers as I take them down.

"Oh, Ember, how sweet of you to try to keep your friends safe. Unfortunately, I have more than enough on my side to help me," Zendaya says, and I pause to watch as more sprout up from the depths of the ocean.

Ember, what is happening? Adam's voice bursts through my thoughts as I begin to assess the new number of enemies looming in the air behind Zendaya.

I'm sorry, Adam. We had to keep this from you because of the contract. I'm not a wolf but something else. I'll explain later. Zendaya, leave them be. It's me you want!

"It is you I need, but I can't leave them be. I also need this land. I won't harm them, though, if you come with me. I would rather not cause too much trouble in this world anyway. I have other concerns," she responds.

Please don't do this, Em. We'll find another way. Corey groans.

I can't take them all, Corey, and we're outnumbered. You all need to remain alive. Adam, you can find your true mate and live to tend to our pack if I go with her. Tell my family I love them. I step forward toward Zendaya, and she motions for her attackers to fall back.

"Now shift back, little hellhound dear, so we can go. It'll hurt if I have to force you too," she says, and I blink, having no idea how to do that.

You can't take her, Adam roars and goes to move forward before Zendaya flicks her wrist at him. Her magic swirls around him, and he howls in pain as his body returns to his human form.

Leave him alone, Zendaya! I roar. *James, Corey, stand back and get him to safety,* I say, and power laces through my words, causing them both to bow their heads. It's similar to that of an Alpha but different.

"Now, now, Ember, let's go," Zendaya says, and I take in the remaining Kushtaka as they fall into place around her.

I don't know how to shift back, I say sadly.

"I see. That is a problem. Well, this is going to hurt." She flicks her wrist, and her magic swallows me.

Pain rips through my body, burning and stinging. I feel like my insides are being ripped out and shoved back in after being melted. I drop to the ground, screaming as my body reforms. Without warning, she lifts me into the air and tosses me into the ocean behind her.

I land with a loud splash and take in mouthfuls of water as I fight to swim to the surface for air. Despite my kicking, something continues to pull me down into the dark depths below. As I'm pulled down, something solid and cold forms around my left wrist and blackness begins to edge in on my vision.

I fight, trying to break free but fail as my feet touch the sand, and then the sand comes up around me. I blink as my lungs burn, and the sand disappears as I drop soaked onto a concrete floor.

I vomit up water and cough as I take in air, but it's different. It's got a smoky taste, and I glance around, taking in the small cave I have landed in. I attempt to stand up when a heavy hand lands on my back, followed by the soft flutter of wings, and blackness swallows me.

CHAPTER TWELVE

E verything feels heavy as my body begins to wake from a deep sleep. As I force my eyes to open, I notice the comfortable surface beneath me. I can't recall getting into bed. My thoughts are foggy, and memories evade me as I push into sitting. I look around the room and take in the large canopy bed with mounds of pillows surrounding me, silk sheets, and one fluffy comforter that rests across my lower half.

The room I occupy is large with stone gray walls covered in various tapestries and old-fashioned paintings. The floor is covered in fancy rugs, and a small sitting area is near an arched wooden door. A wardrobe occupies one wall with a small vanity and a mirror. Behind it is a smaller archway with a thick door that appears to lead to a bathroom.

I glance down and gasp as I take in the silky gown I'm wearing and search my mind for where the hell it came from. I don't recall ever owning something like this. A thick gold bracelet rests on my left wrist, and a gorgeous diamond ring hangs around my wedding finger.

I'm so confused. Where am I? I slide off the bed to explore the bathroom and use it while there. I then rummage through the wardrobe and pull out a robe that I wrap myself in. I'm not sure whose clothes these are, but I don't think they're mine.

Memories of my childhood days surface, and I realize I've never been one for wearing dresses. Faces of family and friends in the memories are hazy, and I can't recall any names. *What is wrong with me?*

My stomach growls loudly, and I move toward the chairs as I spy a pitcher of what appears to be water. At least, I hope it is because I'm parched. I lift the pitcher and smell it just before pouring it into a glass. It cools everything in me as it slides down and makes me realize how warm I am.

I grab a chair and curl into myself as I glance around the room. I glance at the door, wondering if I should venture out when a loud knock sounds, and it's pushed open. A male with broad shoulders, sandy brown hair, and wings of the same color enters, wearing a fine suit. He appears out of place but holds himself confidently as if he owns the place. It confuses me, and he smiles as he meets my gaze.

"I'm glad you're awake. I was hoping you would wake soon. How are you feeling?" he asks, moving toward me and taking a seat across from me.

"I feel okay. Who are you?" I ask.

"Ah, you don't remember the love of your life? That accident was unfortunate. I'm glad Zendaya arrived in time to save you." His dark brown eyes sparkle, and I blink at him.

"Who is Zendaya? Where are we? What accident, and who are you again?"

"Oh right, sorry. I'm Prospero, son of fallen angel Greed. We are engaged to marry soon. Zendaya is your best friend and my half-sister. She rescued you from a terrible attack by a group of rogue demons and hellhounds. You were severely injured. We are in Hell, our home, specifically in Greed's region where he rules under Lucifer, King of Hell."

"Oh, why can't I remember any of that? Am I from here too? Part of me wants to believe I'm not. Am I dead?"

"You are from Earth, so you're right, and no, you aren't dead. We met and fell head over heels for each other, and I couldn't stay away. So, here we are. Would you like to get reacquainted with your surroundings? Zendaya is dying to see you, but she wanted me to check on you first. You've been asleep for days, and only the healers have been allowed in to see you."

"Why didn't they let you in?"

He shrugs. "They were worried I would remove your bandages. You were severely burned too. Their magic has done you well, though, because you can't tell you were injured at all."

I furrow my brow, and his smile gets bigger. "Can we eat first before you show me things? I woke up starving."

"I figured you would be. The servants should be here any moment with food." At that moment, the door opens softly, and two women with white hair and blue skin enter, holding large trays covered with silver tops. They set them before us on the small table and lift the lids.

The food looks odd but smells amazing, and I immediately dig in. I was quite a bit hungrier than I initially thought. I keep my eye on the women as they take up a spot near the wardrobe and watch us quietly.

"These ladies will attend to you whenever you need them. There is a small rope there by your bed that will signal them to appear. When you're done eating, they will help you dress, and we can take a walk. The healers told me I was to keep any activity you do to a minimum for at least a week."

"Did I like to do something strenuous before?" I ask between bites.

"Oh, yes. You have kept yourself to a strict training schedule, my love. You plan to help lead my army of shifters and hounds. It was a dream you had as a child that came true. You're a magnificent leader to the small group you preside over, but

Zendaya has led them in your absence. You'll get to return once the healers clear you," Prospero says, picking up some of the food for himself.

"Oh," I say, and we sit in silence as I continue to eat. "So, is this our room?" I finally ask, setting my fork down.

"Yes, but only yours. You thought it would be best to have separate rooms until after our wedding and mating. It hasn't kept us apart that much, but it appeases you. I never understood why you wanted us to be separate when no one cares about our activities behind closed doors," he says with a shrug, and I frown.

"I guess that is odd. Can you tell me more about my accident?" I ask, and the ladies flutter forward to collect our plates.

"Another time, dear. You need to get ready for our tour." He helps me stand, and I let him lead me over to the wardrobe.

The ladies rush from their cart to me at the wardrobe and begin pulling out dresses. They each have several in their hands for me to assess, and it makes me feel overwhelmed. The dresses have huge skirts and don't seem all that comfortable.

"Is there anything less poofy?" I frown at them, and they nod before turning back to the wardrobe and pulling two different dresses out. One is light silver and appears to glow, while the other is black with a straight skirt. "I'll try the black one." I nod, and they move forward.

It's an odd experience as they push my hands away and pull my clothes from me. I don't recall anything like this happening in my past. I blush when I catch Prospero eyeing me as he might devour me. Should I have asked him to leave?

Once the dress is on, the ladies quickly move to my hair and face, applying creams, powders, and jewelry. They huff at me when I sneeze but remain silent.

"You look, beautiful, darling. Ravishing!" Prospero says, pulling my attention to him as he moves past the ladies and takes my hand. "Thank you, ladies. We are off."

I let Prospero lead me out through the door and into a stone hallway. It makes me think of childhood stories of castles and knights. But wait, I remembered something! I look around, taking in the arched stonework on the doors, and Prospero leads me into a spacious hall with enormous windows looking out into a red-colored sky. It's odd and bothers me because it doesn't seem right. Shouldn't it be blue?

Strange lights dance in the sky as he asks, "It's beautiful, isn't it? You should see it when it's nighttime here. We don't have sunlight like the earth, but the red glow mimics it. It gets very black out when it sets. That's when the lights you see really begin to dance across the sky in a beautiful array of color."

I nod at his words, and he leads me on. Thoughts swirl in my mind, and images from my past trickle in. I'm not sure if looking at the lights caused it or just being out of the room, but flashes of faces move by, and I know that they're my family. I can't recall any names. Images of several attractive males move by, and one stands out briefly. Another one seems connected to the ring on my finger. I stare down at it in confusion. Didn't Prospero give me this?

I grimace as my head begins to throb, and Prospero leads me down a flight of stairs and into another hall. We follow it along for several minutes before it opens up into a room with a grand staircase. A tall woman with black wings and platinum blond hair stands, leaning against the bottom rail casually. She smiles as we approach.

"Ah, there she is!" she exclaims and moves to embrace me. I let her wrap her arms around me tightly, and she pulls away after a moment. Her touch seemed to ease the pain in my temples. "You look ten times better than the last time I saw you. Those healers are amazing! How are you feeling?"

I blink at her for a moment as I gather my thoughts. "I feel fine. You must be Zendaya, I take it? I'm sorry, but I don't remember you."

She looks sad as she glances over at Prospero. "I know. I hate that, but you were in a terrible accident. We'll get your memories back in no time. Are we going to tour the castle?"

"Yes, I believe we will." Prospero moves to lead us up the staircase when a flying creature darts down out of the air and lands on his shoulder. I step away from him, unsure of what it is, and he gives my hand a reassuring squeeze. "I believe I'll have to take a raincheck, ladies. It seems father needs me at the moment, but he wants to see both of you at dinner tonight. It'll be in his private dining hall. Zendaya, take care of my lady and show her around, would you?"

"I will, brother. We'll see you soon," she says, grabbing my hand from Prospero's.

"Will you truly be there until dinner?" I ask over my shoulder.

"Yes, dear, but time will move quickly. Go and enjoy yourself."

"Okay." I turn, and Zendaya pulls me close as she leads me up the stairs.

"I'll give you a brief tour of the inside and then show you the gardens. That was always your favorite place to go before the accident. It's a safe place, and not many of the others in the castle go there. Persephone planted it for us, but she quit visiting after an incident with Prospero. I'm not sure what happened, but it didn't end well."

"Oh, you'll have to tell me more sometime. But, for now, just show me around the castle. My head is throbbing a bit."

She frowns at me and then does something with her hand. "It should stop hurting soon. Just know that you're safe with me. Also, I'm sorry for the incident that caused this."

"Why should you be sorry? You didn't do anything. It was an accident."

"Yes, but in time, you'll remember it. I had to do what I had to do. Did you know that I have a daughter?"

"You do? Does she live here with you?"

"I do, and no. She's somewhere safe. It's a secret that I have only shared with two others. One has decided to use it against me while the other has kept it. So now, I'm trusting you to keep it. She has a lot of my abilities but she's different. I hope one day you get to meet her."

"I'm sure she's amazing." I smile, and she leads me on.

We spend the next two hours moving through the castle at what feels like a snail's pace. She shows me the kitchens, pantries, and many other rooms. One room was filled with women wearing silver bracelets on their wrists and ankles. They seemed content, but an air of sadness hung around each of them. It confounded me, but Zendaya told me not to worry too much about it right now.

Eventually, we meander to a door that's decorated in an array of colorful flowers on the top half. Vines creep up its sides and at the base of the door is an image depicting a pile of bones and skulls. There's a strange yet peaceful energy surrounding the door, and the flowers seem to wink at me. Some of the petals close, and others open as I continue to stare at the magical entry.

"Inspired by Persephone," Zendaya says and pulls me through the door. I can't help but wonder if she's leading me to my death or the garden she mentioned.

CHAPTER THIRTEEN

I stumble through the door as it slams shut behind us and glance around as evening sets in. The day seemed to slip away as I toured with Zendaya. It also appears we have entered some type of magical forest. Flowers bloom everywhere, and many plants glow. The light around us is a faded red, slowly giving way to black, but the garden remains bright.

Zendaya leads me down a winding path toward a bench that overlooks a small pond with fish and a giant field. There's training equipment set up in the area, and I glance at Zendaya as she smiles.

"You're not the only one who trains frequently. This will always be a safe place for you, Ember. Remember that," she says and pulls me to the bench.

"Should I worry about being safe? Does Prospero harm me?" I feel fear begin to sprout in my stomach.

"He hasn't, but I don't trust him at times. I think you'll understand why I'm telling this to you in time. Your memories will slowly begin to return. You have a place in our world here. You just haven't found it yet, but you will."

"Okay, why are you being so cryptic? Are you always like this?"

She laughs. "I guess so. Do you like this garden?"

"It's very pretty and unique. I don't know what any of these plants are."

"That's not surprising, not only because of your memory loss but also because these plants were grown to thrive in the underworld or, as others call it, Hell. Persephone created this garden for Greed as a gift for his hospitality."

"Oh, like from Greek mythology?" I ask and wonder how I remember that.

"Yes, exactly. You're remembering things, good. Prospero tried to start something with her while she was here, but she refused him and he, in turn, doesn't like the garden she left behind. He has tried to destroy it many times, but whatever magic she used lingers. Everything grows back every time. So, I thought it would be a great place to train, and so did Ulric."

"Who is that?"

"You'll meet him again in time. You, too, will enjoy training here. It's always peaceful, and no one bothers me when I'm here. If you want to meditate, it's excellent for that. Anyway, enough about that, how about I share some stories with you while we wait to attend dinner? It'll help calm my nerves. My father puts me on edge quite often."

"Sure," I respond with a smile.

Zendaya starts by telling me about her childhood. She didn't know she was Greed's daughter for a long time until he came for her with a group of men. Someone had reported a young angel child with amazing magic in a small town full of water demons on the outskirts of Hell. Apparently, angel wings aren't common for all demons in Hell.

Greed hauled her back to the castle and cut her off from her people for a long time. She was trained to fight, using many different techniques. She even had a fling with a hellhound which led to her daughter. However, he hid her away after she told him what happened to her as a child. She hasn't seen her daughter nor the man since, at least not up close.

After sitting for two hours, I stand and stretch. Zendaya leads me back into the castle. We wind our way back to the large staircase, ascend it, and follow a long hall to a fine banquet room. It's filled with many tables, but only one long table rests at the head of the room. Seated there are Prospero and a couple with dark hair. Steaming dishes sit before them, and servants hover off to the side.

"Ah, there they are!" Prospero announces, standing with a flourish and moving toward us. "I was beginning to worry. Ember, this is my father, Greed, and his wife, Alora."

"It's a pleasure to meet you both." I bow lightly, and they beam back at me. Prospero ushers me to a chair next to his.

"The pleasure is mine. I'm very excited to meet my son's latest treasure. You'll make a fine bride, my dear. Now let's eat. I'm quite hungry this evening. It's been a busy day," Greed says and reaches for one of the platters.

The servants move forward and remove the lids from the platters in one sweep to reveal strange-looking foods. I don't recognize any of them, but Prospero and Zendaya both pile food on their plates. I gently scoop up some of what they have and double up on the bread, which I do recognize.

I tentatively take a bite of the charred meat Zendaya is eating and moan at how delicious it is. It's smoky and tender, with a hint of garlic and butter.

"Does the roasted fire boar taste well?" Alora asks breathlessly, staring at me.

I blink and glance around, noticing Prospero adjusting himself, and widen my eyes as I meet Alora's gaze again. Did what I do have the same effect on her? Holy shit. "Yes, it's delicious."

She licks her lips, watching me again, and I drop my gaze to my plate, feeling uncomfortable.

Prospero clears his throat, and the tension in the air seems to shift as he says, "So, Father, our troops seem to be training well with our newest additions, wouldn't you say?"

"Yes, they are, thankfully. I do think we need more hell-hounds, though, don't you agree?" He looks at Prospero directly, and I glance at Zendaya out of the corner of my eye. She's frowning, and for some reason, it makes me nervous.

"Is there such a thing as too many?" Prospero responds, and Greed laughs.

"That a boy. I'm sure our darling Ember here will give us many generals. If only we could find a way to strengthen the others to her capacity. I can feel her magic, and I must say, it is addictive. Ember, who are your parents again?"

I blink at Greed, trying to recall, but Zendaya answers for me. "You know she can't remember things right now, Father."

"Oh, right, I forgot. Well, with the new shifters we have brought in over the last few months, we should be able to come up with something. Have you been working on that, son?" Greed has an evil grin on his face.

"I have, Father, and I have help. Don't you worry. We should have several babes soon," Prospero says, and I stare at his face in confusion.

Zendaya rests a hand on mine as they continue to talk, and I pick at my food. "So, you're saying we'll have some new hell-hounds with our blood? That's excellent. The girls are holding up well then?"

I blanch as I catch on to his meaning, and Zendaya squeezes my hand. I look over at her, and she shakes her head as if to tell me to hold my tongue. How is this okay, though? Has this gone on the whole time Prospero and I have been together? Have I been okay with this?

I drown out their words as thoughts of what horrible things

have been done to those girls I saw earlier go through my mind. No wonder there was an air of sadness lingering around them. They have been used by these beings and probably more for sex, all to build an army!

I push my plate away from me, drawing Prospero's attention to me. "Are you feeling unwell?" Zendaya lets go of my hand as he grabs the other.

"I think I need to lie down." I push away from the table, and he stands with me.

Greed frowns at us. "I hope you're not feeling ill, dear. Is there maybe a child on the way already?"

"Hopefully soon, Father. I'll get her to bed, and we can talk more over drinks later. Goodnight!" Prospero says over his shoulder as he leads me away.

We walk in silence back to our room, and I make my way to the bathroom. I turn the tap on and fill up the tub. "I'm going to soak and then turn in for the night."

Prospero looks at me with hungry eyes. "Do you want some company?"

I glance at him and don't miss the bulge in his pants. It doesn't do anything for me, though, so I say, "I just need some time to myself to process. I took in a lot of information today and still don't remember a lot from before."

"Okay, well then," he adjusts himself, "I'll be back later to join you in bed. I'm going to visit with my father some more. Ring one of the bells if you need anything, and one of the maids will be here. Good night, love." He places a kiss on top of my head and quickly leaves.

I undress after he leaves and wonder if he will visit that room with the women before speaking to his father. Is this the life I have to look forward to with him? Why can't I remember anything still?

I soak for an hour in the tub, but it does nothing for my frustration. I know that the healers told Prospero to keep me from training for a week, but something tells me I need to go for a run. I need space, so I grab a pair of shoes and make my way back to the garden.

Pushing through the door, I feel myself begin to calm. I walk past the various plants to the training area and take off on the small track surrounding it. The wind blowing through my hair feels good as I move, and I feel some of my magic spilling into the area around me. It causes the plants to glow brighter as if taking it all in.

After several laps, I pause to catch my breath and notice all the plants are blooming, and dancing lights float above them. I look at my hands and see black flames dancing on them and realize they are reacting to my magic even more than before. That's strange. Did they do that before?

I head over to a nearby bench to watch as the plants slowly lose some of their glow. That's when I look up and see the sky. It's incredible and reminds me of the northern lights. I have only seen pictures of those in books, growing up. I pause and admire them, and then it dawns on me that more of my memory has surfaced.

I reach for the tendril of thought as it tries to float away and growl in frustration. That's when I hear the flutter of wings. I whip my head around and spy a man moving toward me with a confused expression on his face. I don't recognize him, but something pulls me to him. He's like a magnet with his green eyes and black wings. He's sexy, and I can't help but admire him.

"Ember? What are you doing here? You're supposed to be back on Earth," he says, and I blink at him in confusion.

"I'm sorry, do we know each other?"

"Yes, we met several weeks ago at your pack house. Remember, your Alpha hosted a dinner, and we danced? Why don't you remember that?" He frowns and looks down at my wrist.

I follow his gaze and notice he's staring at my bracelet. "I don't remember any of that. So why do I feel like I can trust you if we've never met?"

He moves toward me, startling me, and grabs my wrist. The bracelet glows a bright white before dropping to the ground at my feet. Suddenly, pain blasts its way into my skull, and I scream. I feel as if I'm on fire, and I close my eyes as my power erupts around me. My back burns, and I hear the man gasp.

The pain subsides, and my memories swim in my mind. It's as if a sledgehammer has been taken to my skull. "What the hell is going on, Ulric?"

"There you are. I see my brother has been up to his tricks again. Nice wings, by the way."

"What?" I spin around like a dog chasing its tail, attempting to look at my back. Huge white wings extend from my shoulder blades and hang down my back. I reach around and finally grab one and gasp at the sensations that spiral through me. "Holy shit. What is going on?"

"I have no idea, and I'm not sure why you have wings. I thought you were a wolf shifter?" He pulls me by the hand toward the bench I sat on earlier with Zendaya and forces me to sit. Tingles run up and down my arms at his touch, and my wings quiver. Weird.

"Well, it turns out I'm not. It turns out I'm a hellhound from what I've heard here. Why do I have wings, though? Is that normal?"

He frowns. "Usually, hellhounds don't inherit the wings from the angelic blood that helped create them. However, on rare occasions, I have seen one with wings. That usually means they are related to one of the strongest fallen angels. Not many fallen have white wings, though, except those who are related to Lucifer, ruler over us all."

"Well shit. I wish someone would have told me that. Wouldn't they have popped out after my first shift?"

"Wait a second. I'm extremely confused. Are you related to

Lucifer? I'm not sure if they would have, honestly. But, as I said, it's rare for hellhounds to have them."

"Are you sure only Lucifer's line has white wings? Is there a way to hide them?" I feel overwhelmed now, because if that's true, then I may be screwed.

"Yes, it's true. How are you related to him if you have been on Earth this whole time? Ember, what are you not telling me? You can trust me."

"How do I know that? It was your siblings that drug me down here in the first place. Zendaya said she owed Prospero a favor. Oh shit! Did he threaten her about her daughter? Is that why she did that?" I try to stand to pace, but Ulric grabs me and makes me meet his gaze.

"How are you related to Lucifer?" His grip is firm, and I know I have to tell him.

"I'm his daughter. He and my mother had a one-night stand, and she hid me away."

He runs his hand through his hair as if stressed. "Fuck, we need to get you out of here. Does anyone here know that?"

"I have no idea. Zendaya knew more about me than I knew about myself. Do you think Prospero threatened her daughter? I thought she liked me when we first met."

"I did like you and still do. You're a terrible secret keeper, Ember, but I see my other brother found you," Zendaya announces, startling us both.

Flames shoot to my hands, and my magic is ready for an attack. "Why are you here?" I ask.

Zendaya glances at Ulric before she says, "I had a feeling that my brother would find you. Not Prospero. I wanted you two to find each other."

"Sister, is he using your daughter against you? Is that why Ember is here?" Ulric asks, pulling me behind him. I let my flames die out and watch on curiously.

"He did. She is safe, though, because she is now training with

Lucifer's hellhounds. Ember was supposed to come to our world at some point. She is his heir, and she can help bring balance back to us all. Father has gotten carried away, and you know it. What he is doing with those women is terrible, but I know with Ember's help, we can set them free." Zendaya's eyes glow with anger.

"He is out of control with it, I agree, which is why I have refused to assist in his plans. Prospero and some of our other brothers have enjoyed it too much. Helping them escape will put targets on our backs, though." Ulric runs another hand through his hair.

"Where would we take them?" I ask.

"That's the part we need to figure out. I think we can hide them on your pack's land. It's going to be risky getting them there, though. We need more help." Zendaya shrugs.

"Are you saying we take them through the hell gate in Texas? That's the closest one to Ember's territory," Ulric questions.

"Are they even all shifters?" I add.

This time Zendaya rubs her head. "I believe they are. Some of them are with child though, so it may be challenging. But we need to get them out of here before they start testing new things on them."

I stare at the two angels as they're quiet for a moment.

"There is a ball coming up in a few weeks that we could utilize as a distraction. I know many other groups from reigning regions will be there, so maybe we can get them to aid us. Ember, you did smell like a vampire when I met you. Is your vampire friend here in Hell, now?" Ulric asks, and I cringe.

"Shit, Zeke. God, I hope he hasn't killed Corey for letting me get kidnapped. I don't know. I don't know much about the vampires in Hell."

"Hm, we may be able to reach out to them. Let's plan on using the ball as our cover. We can take the women out to the gate that will lead them to Texas, and then they can be brought to Ember's pack's lands for safety. Should we reach out for help from Lucifer?" Ulric stands and begins to pace.

"That may not be a bad idea. If we send a message to Kai to let him in on what's going on, I think we can get someone to meet the girls and assure their safety. I know the two of you don't always see eye to eye, Ulric, but getting them to help may be the best solution." Zendaya frowns. "Although, it will bring Vixie way too close to this for my comfort."

"Who are you guys talking about? Can we trust these people with this information? What if they realize who I am? I'm not ready to deal with that whole daddy issue yet," I say in a rush, and Zendaya laughs.

"You'll be safe. I can teach you how to hide your wings tonight before you go. We'll need you to keep up the appearance that your memories are still missing for the time being. On the matter of who they are, Vixie is Zendaya's daughter. Kai is Lucifer's top general and one of the strongest hellhounds in existence. Somehow, he is related to Cerberus, but no one knows how."

"Holy shit, he's real too? Oh my God, my head is hurting. Okay, so if we can trust these guys, let's see if they will help. So how do I keep up appearances as Prospero's betrothed? I don't want him to touch me. Wouldn't that look odd?" I place my hands on my hips.

"You're just going to have to suck it up for a bit, girl. There are more important things at stake here. We need to get those girls out, and then you're going to help us balance Hell." Zendaya growls, and it scares me.

"How do I do that without letting Lucifer know who I am?"

"We'll figure that out. Let's call it a night, and we can meet again to train tomorrow. We'll both work with you, Ember, to teach you how to use your divine gifts. Zendaya, we'll see you tomorrow," Ulric declares and bends down to pick up the bracelet I was wearing earlier.

"Mhm, okay, brother. See you at breakfast in your room, bright and early, Ember!" She blinks and then pushes off the ground into the air. Her wings fan out, and she flaps them to gain height before flying toward the top of the stone castle.

"I need to learn how to do that," I say, while watching her fly away, in awe.

"I'll teach you, but not tonight. Tonight, I'm going to teach you how to hide your wings when needed." He places a hand on my shoulder, and fiery tingles dance across my skin.

Before realizing what I'm doing, I pull him to me and plant my lips on his. He hesitates for only a fraction of a second before responding. Air moves around us, and I feel him set me gently on the bench we were seated on earlier.

Fire erupts in my belly, and my sex clenches as he moans. Something forms between us, and I feel it in my mind. It's almost like a glowing chain has formed, and I can sense his emotions. He and I are connected somehow.

I pull back. "What is that? Do you feel it?"

He's breathless as he says, "Yes, I do. I think you're meant to be my mate, Ember."

"How is that possible, though?"

He sits back and pulls me onto his lap. "I have no idea, but I thought I felt it when we met. Why is it confusing you? Do you have a mate already?"

I stare at him and think back to the sensations I felt with Zeke. They were almost exactly the same but not. "I felt something similar with Zeke, my vampire friend."

He frowns and wraps his arms around me. He nuzzles my neck as he says, "Sometimes we can have more than one mate. Maybe you do? We can explore it at a later date. But, right now, it's just you and me."

I smile at him as he pulls back to meet my gaze. I rub a hand over his cheek. "Okay. What do you want to do right now?"

He smiles mischievously and chuckles. "I think we both

know what I want to do, but because we're trying to keep your cover, I'm going to restrain myself. So instead, I'm going to teach you how to hide your wings."

"Fine." I roll my eyes, and he begins to teach me how to focus my magic on cloaking my new feathery appendages.

The process is simple and easy. He explains that if I picture my wings being hidden by a curtain, they will be cloaked from everyone's eyes. I'll still feel them, but they won't be visible. I close my eyes, and the charm works. I feel something like velvet slide down over my wings. I open my eyes to find Ulric smiling at me, and we practice it a few more times before I head back to my room. I'm thankful to find Prospero not present as he said he would be. I have a lot to process from today, and I need to prepare for tomorrow.

I throw myself into bed, still smelling of Ulric, and fall quickly into a dreamless slumber.

CHAPTER FOURTEEN

As morning arrives, I wake feeling refreshed. Memories from the last day float through my head, and I smile at how the day ended. I have a mate. It's not Adam but a freaking angel. So what if he's a fallen angel? He's mine.

"Would you quit daydreaming and get up already?" Zendaya's voice startles me, and I sit up quickly.

"What are you doing here?" I ask, taking in the table before her filled with food.

"Breakfast, remember? Get up. We have stuff to do today. I need to give you a better tour of the castle, so you know where to go when it's time for you to leave."

"We didn't talk about that last night. What about Ulric? How will he explain his absence?"

"What are you talking about?" She looks at me confused, and I can't help but blush. "Oh, so it's true then? He's your mate? I thought so."

I toss a pillow at her, and she deflects it. "How did you know?"

"I have certain gifts where I can see things. Not all things, just some. It's weird and only works part of the time. He'll find a way to cover his absence. It may be slightly more difficult for him, but he'll figure it out. He's sending a message to the vampires this morning to inquire about your friend and see if they will help."

"I hope they can help. We'll need some backup for this. What about a message to that Kai guy?"

"Oh, I've already taken care of that. If Ulric were to send it, he wouldn't even open it to read it. Kai and Ulric can be stubborn as mules. Isn't that the saying they use on Earth?"

I laugh. "Yes, that is the saying."

I climb out of bed and move to the table next to her. As I plop down, the smell of coffee hits me. "Where did you get coffee?"

"There is always coffee in the pantry. Don't let anyone tell you otherwise. The kitchen staff runs on it. One of the perks of living in Hell is that there is always coffee. They didn't have it in Heaven, only tea. Sometimes that isn't strong enough."

I quickly fill a cup with the black liquid and add some milk and sugar. It tastes magnificent as it goes down, and I instantly feel more awake. "So, after exploring the secret passages are we going to train some? I would love to do that. I feel like a newborn, and I want to learn how to fly with these babies." I point my thumb over my shoulder to my invisible wings.

"I think we can manage that. Ulric and I will help teach you some angelic tricks. I'm interested to see what gifts you have." She lifts her cup of coffee to her lips and takes a sip.

A knock on my door draws our attention, and we stiffen. We both silently listen and watch as it opens to reveal Prospero carrying a tray of food.

"Good morning. Oh, Zendaya, what are you doing up here so early?" He looks confused as he glances between us.

She smiles wickedly. "I'm just spending time with my best friend. We have plans for the day. I didn't realize you were bringing us food. The servants provided us with plenty, after all."

He sets the tray down and walks to me, planting a kiss on my head. I fight the urge to flinch, and he sits beside me in another chair. "My, you smell wonderful this morning, Ember. Did you use a new bath soap? I'm sorry I didn't make it up here last night as I told you I would. I was tied up."

I frown and look at Zendaya's eyes. It dawns on me that I am now linked to Ulric. Shit. I didn't think it would change my scent, but I know nothing about having an angel as a mate. I guess it's similar to having a wolf mate, and your scents become one, but does that also mean Zeke's is mine now too? Is that why Corey worked so hard to hide the scent?

"Yes, actually I did! I added some petals from this gorgeous flower I found in the garden to some of the bath salts. I'm glad you like it!" I say and beam at him, hoping he doesn't catch the lie.

"Hm, we may have to have some of those plants moved to your room. It smells delightful. Zendaya, you wouldn't mind leaving while I ravish my future wife, would you?" he asks over my shoulder, pulling me toward him.

I lean back and stammer out, "But we have plans to explore more of the castle! There is so much I don't remember, love. Maybe later?"

He glares over my shoulder at his sister, then turns a softer eye to me. "Fine, dear. If that's what you wish. I think we need to have some time to ourselves soon. Have you had any luck with your memories?"

His concern makes me almost laugh, but I plaster on a defeated expression. "No, but I'm enjoying making new memories and learning about our home. It's so beautiful."

Zendaya snorts behind me. "I'm glad someone thinks so."

"Our home is gorgeous, sister. What's not to like? Well, I

guess I can share you today. Do you mind if I enjoy breakfast with you?"

I smile up at him and nod as another knock sounds at the door. What the hell? Is this grand central station or something? Who else could show up?

I glance over at Zendaya as the door once again pushes open, and Ulric walks in. Shit.

"Brother, what are you doing up here?" Prospero asks on a growl, and I can sense that this may go sideways.

"Oh, I didn't mean to interrupt! Our lovely sister asked me to prepare one of the small boats for the lake this morning. She wanted to show your betrothed the view on the water. I just wanted to let her know that everything would be ready for her this afternoon if they still planned to go. Oh, is that breakfast food? Care if I join?" Ulric strides forward, and I can feel his irritation toward Prospero through our bond.

I frown but add, "Oh, I didn't know you were going to surprise me with that! That'll be such a wonderful treat, Zendaya." I feel like I'm laying it on thick, but it seems to work as Prospero groans beside me, and Ulric laughs.

"It seems you have a lot of plans for the two of you, sister. Are you trying to steal my betrothed?" Prospero asks her, pulling me completely into his chest.

I see Ulric stiffen out of the corner of my eye, and I send a silent *I'm fine* out toward him.

He blinks in surprise and then looks at me before looking back to Zendaya. *How the hell did you just do that? Can you hear me?*

Yes, I can hear you. Isn't that what mates do, communicate telepathically?

But we haven't completed it yet.

Eh, well, this is different, right?

I mean, yeah, I've never had a mate before, and angels don't talk about this kind of stuff. So maybe it's unique to hellhounds.

Shifters do it, so maybe not? We can wait and see.

"No, brother, just reminding my best friend how great our friendship is. Don't be so territorial," Zendaya says.

"Fine, I'll tone it down a bit. But, darling, you do need to discuss with your maids what type of dress you would prefer for the ball. We have a huge ball coming up soon, and you'll be the center of attention. I can't wait to introduce you to some of our family friends," Prospero says, taking a bite of some of the bread on the table.

Ulric sits down across from me and grabs some food as well. He winks at me as he takes a bite, and I try not to blush.

"Have I not met these friends before?" I ask, turning my gaze back to Prospero.

"Well, yes, some of them, but there will be so many more there you have yet to meet. It'll be a wonderful night."

"Hmm, okay," I say and sip at my cooling cup of coffee. "So, Zendaya, are you about done? It'll take me no time at all to dress, and we can explore some more."

"I'm ready when you are, sister." She smiles, and I laugh.

"Gentlemen, if you don't mind, I have things to get ready for. So, can you leave?" I ask, and Prospero frowns at me while Ulric laughs.

"If you ladies need anything, seek me out. I'll gladly help in any way I can. Have fun!" *Find me later in the garden, and I can teach you some things. Watch Prospero. I don't think I can hold back if he tries anything, especially in front of me. Gods, I can't wait until I can have you to myself.*

"Thanks, Ulric!" I say at the same time Zendaya does. We watch as he leaves quietly with a mischievous smile.

Prospero stands next with a frown. "Well, I guess I'll go busy myself. Find me this evening when you're done, Ember. I would like to have dinner with you. Hopefully, Father won't insist we all join him tonight as he did previously."

I nod as he leans in to kiss me. I let him and do my best not to cringe at his touch against my lips. I'm successful, and he leaves with a smile. As the door closes, I deflate in my chair. "Oh God, could that have been any more challenging?"

"I feel like we covered well, although Ulric showing up almost put us in a bind. Get ready, so we can get to exploring and have you memorize the layout of this castle. There are more halls and tunnels than you realize. We'll need to find the easiest and quickest route to get those girls out. Your path may be a bit more challenging."

"I'm sure it will be if I'm to be the center of attention at this ball. Ulric said he would meet us later in the garden, by the way. I hope you can teach me to fly today."

"When did he say that?" she asks, standing from her chair.

I stand myself and move to the closet, digging for something resembling pants. All I come up with is a short dress. I toss it on and hope for the best as I respond, "We communicated telepathically. Can angels not do that?"

"Well, yes, but only after the mating bond is sealed. So I guess you're more unique than we originally thought." She shrugs.

"Interesting. Well, I guess we'll learn more about what else is different about me as we train. Shall we?" I smile, and she frowns at me as she takes in my appearance.

"What are you wearing?"

"This was the only thing that didn't have extremely long skirts. I don't have any pants in that thing. Hell, I don't even know who picked all those outfits out, but they aren't what I would wear, ever."

She rolls her eyes. "Come on, let's go get you clothes that fit and cover more than that dress does. There is a group of seamstresses that live on the bottom floor that make all of our clothes. They have pants for me that may fit you. We can request more be made to fit you in whatever style you prefer.

We can tell them to toss what's in your wardrobe now and replace everything."

"Isn't that wasteful, though? Can we not repurpose the clothes or something?"

"I haven't ever thought of doing that. What would you do with them?"

"I don't know. Is there a demon orphanage or something we can give them to? I'm sure they could use clothes."

Zendaya looks at me like I have grown a second head. "Well, there is an orphanage. No one has ever done that before. We'll have the ladies send the old clothes there. I guess that's better than throwing them out."

"How have you never thought of that before? People on Earth are always donating things."

She shrugs. "I mean, this is Hell, but then again, that may be something to lead to better balance. Things like that aren't common here, even though we have many things similar to how the earth runs. See, you're already beginning to start the balancing process."

I roll my eyes. "Whatever, let's go see these ladies about some proper clothes."

We stroll out of my room and into the hall. I take everything in with a new eye as we walk. Zendaya leads me down the hall to a small stairwell tucked behind a large tapestry that leads down. The stairwell is warm, and the scent of baked bread lingers in the air.

Reaching the bottom, I notice it opens up to a large kitchen, and different types of demons—Imps, and some that look part angel, move around, busying themselves at the counters. Some of them are covered with flour, leaving tiny white dust clouds behind them as they move.

"Wow, I didn't realize how close my room was to the kitchen!" I exclaim and spy a rack of cookies cooling that look delicious. It makes my mouth water as I imagine the sugar resting on my tongue.

"Yes. Your room is technically one of the old guest rooms. Father wanted all guests to have fresh food and drink as quickly as possible when he built the castle. Now, there is a completely new building set apart from the castle for guests. He worried about prying eyes, and none of the guests questioned why he built it. They assumed that he just wanted more space because he's greedy, and well, that's what he does. He has a never-ending desire to have more, more, more," Zendaya says nonchalantly.

"That sounds pleasant, I guess. So, there is no one else staying on my floor? I honestly haven't paid much attention."

"No, there aren't. If your friend comes with the vampires, I'm sure that will change."

"Yeah, for sure. He'll probably try to stay in the same room with me, knowing him." I roll my eyes, imagining how Zeke will react. I also can't help but wonder what the rest of the vampires will be like.

"Oh, why do you say that? Are you with him as well?" Zendaya quirks her brow up and smirks at me.

"Yes, I am. I think he's also my mate. I get the same tingling sensation and whatnot as I do with Ulric. It's difficult to explain, but there isn't much difference between the sensations."

"You have quite the entourage, sister. I'm jealous. I have yet to find the one meant for me. I hope I will one day. I mean, I have been around for a long time, but Fate is a mysterious bitch sometimes. I've met her, and she can be quite cryptic. Apparently, she and I are related somehow." She shrugs and leads me out of the kitchen, down a small hall crowded with large fabric containers filled with clothes.

"How in the world did you happen to meet her? I must hear this story," I eagerly ask, following her and taking in the dark hall around us. The scent of lemon hangs in the air, and the humidity is ridiculous.

"Well, it was actually at one of Lucifer's balls many years ago. But, of course, he doesn't hold them near as often these days, with there being unrest in several areas of the realm. Anyway, she was seated at the back of the room, watching everyone on the floor with a strange look on her face. I felt drawn to her as if my blood recognized hers." She pauses as she pushes open a large wooden door, and I look in to see several groups of various beings working on creating outfits.

"She eyed me as I moved closer to her, and I asked her if we had met before. She said no that we hadn't, but that her blood was in my veins—like calls to like. She didn't explain how but told me who she was and that I would be helping her with something big later on in my life span. I have only run into her a few times since that first meeting, but that's when I received my gift of foresight. She touched my forehead and bam. I had the worst headache I've ever had for a month following that night."

"Wow, what a meeting. So, this is where I need to come if I need anything made for me?" I ask, gesturing to the group in the room.

"Yes, here, let me introduce you to some of them. They can take your measurements and whip up a pants suit now if needed. If not, I'm sure something of mine they have made will fit. Let's go."

She grabs my hand and pulls me to a group of green-skinned demons sitting around a table with red-skinned demons and one with green-and-black spotted skin. They pause and look up at us as we stop, and the green-and-black spotted one smiles. She has sharp pointed teeth, and even her eyes are a green color.

"Hello, Madam Zendaya. Are you here to order new clothing?"

"No, Salandra, I'm here to have my soon-to-be sister-in-law fitted for new clothes. This is Ember." She pulls me in front of her, and I offer a small wave.

"Oh, I thought Lord Prospero wanted Amillia, specifically, to create things for her." Salandra glances past us, and I follow her gaze to a tiny pixie watching us curiously. Her purple hair hangs down to a bob, and she has glowing silver wings. She flits toward us.

"Oh, I didn't know he planned for such a thing. Hello, Amillia, you and Salandra can both work on this. Ember needs new outfits. She isn't pleased with her wardrobe."

"Oh, I would love to help. Salandra and I can have outfits whipped up for you today. It would be our pleasure!" Amillia says cheerily.

"What styles do you prefer?" Salandra asks me, smiling.

"I would love some pants, honestly. I mean, the dresses hanging in my wardrobe are nice, but they aren't me. I want simple things that are soft and breathable. I also need training clothes and something for a ball." I look over at Zendaya for help on the ball issue.

"Her ball gown will need to have pants beneath the skirts. Make her outfits like you do mine where she can hide weapons if needed. We'll have guests soon, and she needs to be able to protect herself," Zendaya orders, but pleasantly.

"We can do that. We'll begin work on your order immediately," Salandra says, and the group begins to busy themselves.

"Will you fit one of my pants suits to her for now, please?" Zendaya adds.

"I can take care of that, madams." Amillia flutters over to a rack of black outfits. "This one should do fine. It's made of dragon leather and lined with silk. You can put all kinds of things in the hidden compartments." She flutters to me and gestures for me to strip.

I slip the small dress off, and she helps me into the new item of clothing. It slides on like a glove, and I love the way it feels against my skin. "Wow, this feels amazing!"

"It fits well too. The legs are a little long on you, though.

Amillia, will you take that in?" Zendaya asks, gesturing to my legs.

"Yes, I will." Amillia flits around my legs, and a purple glowing mist hovers around them. As it clears, the fabric shrinks to fit around me better.

"That's nifty," I say and turn from side to side.

"Yes, it fits you much better now, Madame Ember. We will have your clothes in your wardrobe this afternoon," Amillia says with a head bow.

"Thank you. Zendaya, are we ready for that tour now?"

"Yes, we'll go out through the kitchen, and you can see the halls and exits that lead from there. Fire up that brain and get ready to retain as much as you can. There will be a quiz later."

"You're joking, right?" I ask, following her back toward the large wooden door.

"Not at all. Memorizing the layout could play a key role in a life-and-death situation. We must be prepared."

"Great," I groan, and she leads me back into the kitchen, where we begin our lesson of memorization.

CHAPTER FIFTEEN

Hours later, with a minor headache, Zendaya and I sit on the grass in the garden. She continues to quiz me on the different routes we can take to get out of the ballroom and all the possible scenarios that could happen. We made a headcount of the women we need to escort out when doing our walk-through. It was strange that none of them paid us any mind as we sat watching them. Then again, they too had bracelets similar to what I had on. Zendaya tinkered with mine to weaken it so it would let my memories through when I met Ulric. They can't have their memories unless the bracelets are removed or broken by another.

"Can we take a break from going over all this information and maybe do something active for a while?" I ask, stretching back in the grass and staring up at the strange sky.

"Only if you're positive that you'll remember everything." Zendaya looks at me sternly.

"I'm positive that if I try to take in anything more right now, my head is going to explode."

"You are quite a nuisance at times, aren't you? Fine, we can work on something active. Did you have something in mind?"

"Well, I would love to learn how to fly like you."

She smiles at me wickedly. "We can start working on that. But first, we have to strengthen your wings. Can you make them visible?"

"I think I can. Ulric walked me through it briefly." I close my eyes and picture my wings. "Did it work?"

"Hm, yes. Why did you close your eyes, though?"

"I guess for concentration? I don't know." I shrug.

"Well, we need to work on that too. I want you to hide your wings but keep your eyes open. We're going to do it ten times successfully with your eyes open before we start the strengthening exercises."

"Okay," I say and drop my gaze to the ground.

"Now, hide them."

"I'm trying. It's not that easy, you know."

"It should be. You are part angel and all. Come on, try harder!"

I growl at Zendaya and sweat beads on my brow. I feel a light tickle at my back, and I move my gaze to Zendaya, who smiles at me.

"You did it. See, it wasn't that hard. Now do it again."

I growl at her again and continue with my focus. We spend thirty minutes doing this before I call it quits. I only manage to hide my wings five times successfully.

"You need to work on that more on your own time. You have to be able to do that with your eyes open. Oh, look, here comes lover boy."

I whip my aching head around and smile as I spy Ulric coming through the door. As he nears, I feel a tickle at my back again, and Zendaya laughs loudly.

"Well, I see someone's happy to see me. We need to work on controlling your emotions, so your wings don't pop out like that." He pulls me into him, and I frown.

"It's not easy, jeez. You and Zendaya are going to make my

head explode with all this. We've been practicing just that for the last half hour."

Zendaya smirks as Ulric speaks, "Well, then you need to keep with it. Are you taking a break then? What else are you ladies planning to work on?"

"I was getting ready to teach her some wing exercises to strengthen them up. She wants to fly like us, but her wings are weak." Zendaya steps up beside me and pulls me out of Ulric's arm.

"How about we work on that and see how you feel afterward? I want to see you practice in your hellhound form. You haven't been in it much, right?"

Ulric crosses his arms and looks at me contemplatively as I frown again. "No, I had just attained that form when crazy chick over here dragged me down to hell. However, I only fought a little bit, so it would be fun to work in my beast form."

"I'm only crazy when I want to be. I had my motives, you know." Zendaya shrugs.

"Well, let's do a few wing exercises to warm up, and then we can move forward. Zendaya, do you want to show her the few exercises you were going to teach her?" Ulric plops down on the ground before us in the grass.

"Absolutely. Okay, little wolf, I want you to practice extending your wings out and then pulling them in tight to your back." She smiles wickedly.

"That should be easy enough," I say and try to extend my wings out. But instead, one wing wobbles erratically while the other doesn't move. "Shit."

"You can do it. Just focus, love," Ulric encourages. "I had the same issues when I first started learning how to use mine, but I was also a lot younger than you."

"Thanks for the confidence boost, I guess." I grunt and fight with my wings to get them to extend, and they finally do after several minutes. Pulling them back in seems to be easier than extending them. "Okay, so how many times am I supposed to do this?"

"As many times as you can, sister, but just do ten for now, then I'll show you a few more." Zendaya twirls around me.

"Fine, but then we move on to my new form for practice, right?"

"Correct, but don't expect it to be any easier," she playfully admonishes.

I roll my eyes and follow her lead as she guides me through several more exercises for my wings. My desire to fly deflates slightly because I'm a long way off yet, due to the fact that my wings are weaker than a newborn kitten.

"Okay, enough of the wing stuff, Ember, let's see you shift," Ulric declares, placing a hand on my shoulder.

I stiffen and smile at him warily as my brain tries to process how to shift. I was worried and extremely emotional last time and in danger.

Zendaya tosses me a knowing smile, and I know she senses my hesitance and understands why. Taking a deep breath, I channel down into my magic as I have before to throw fireballs and let it consume me. My leap of faith takes me where I hoped to be, and I feel my body begin to change. It burns, and black flames dance around me as my limbs elongate and my head changes. Finally, I stand tall on all fours, staring Zendaya down. I growl as she laughs.

"I was beginning to worry, Ember," she says after cackling for a moment.

"Why were you worrying, sister?" Ulric asks in confusion.

"The only time she's managed to shift was when she was in danger. I thought I was going to have to throw something at her." Her smile is radiant as I growl in response.

At least I managed it without too much of a hassle this time. This form is comfortable. I shake my black fur and sit on my haunches as I speak to them telepathically where only they can hear me.

"Don't get too comfortable there, little wolf. We're going to run you through some drills. Show us what you can do in this form." Ulric eyes me with wonder, and I roll my eyes.

Stop staring at me. Have you not seen a hellhound before?

"I have, actually, but you're larger than most. It must be because of your bloodline. Can you call your wings to this form too?" He places his hand under his chin, looking me over.

I tilt my head to the side and think about my wings. I try to coax my magic into letting them sprout from my back, but nothing happens. *I don't think I can.*

"Maybe if we practice with your wings more, you can eventually do it?" Zendaya suggests, and I shrug in response.

"We'll come back to that thought then. Okay, let's get to work!"

My training starts with running, which isn't as bad with four legs. Next, Ulric and Zendaya create an obstacle course to have me practice quick turns, jumps, and pivots. It's exhausting, but I know it'll benefit me in the long run. I'll need these skills and more to take out my enemies and protect those I love.

My paws dig into the earth with each step, and I feel my power race through me, energizing me. I feel unstoppable until I'm hit in the face with a mound of dirt. It causes me to trip over my front feet, and I land in a heap. Growling, I shake myself off and look around to find Ulric doubled over, laughing. I stalk toward him with a glare as he continues to laugh.

What was that for?

"You weren't paying attention. It was quite comical. But seriously, no matter how much you're enjoying your run, you need to always be aware of your surroundings." He pulls himself together and looks at me with his hands on his hips.

Noted, so can we get back to practice?

"Actually, we need to call it a day and get cleaned up. It's almost dinner time, and we said we would meet Prospero, remember?" Zendaya says from behind me, and I turn to face her.

I shift back and return to my human body with hidden wings. "Ugh, do we have to?"

"Yes, you have to." Ulric places a hand on my shoulder. "You have to keep up the ruse that you have no idea what's going on and that you're madly in love with my brother."

I frown once again. "Fine, but I may need to work some steam off later. I'm going to come back to train this evening."

"Understandable. I'll meet you here," Ulric says as Zendaya arches a brow at us.

"I'll pass on tonight, but I'll help you get ready. Let's go before we're late. I'm sure there are new outfits in your wardrobe now." Zendaya smiles and grabs my hand.

"Oh! I forgot about the outfits. That'll cause a stir, I'm sure. Let's see what I've got. Will you be at dinner, Ulric?" I step toward Zendaya but look over my shoulder hopefully, at my mate.

"I'll be there. Just don't wear anything too provocative. It might cause issues." He frowns, and I light up. This could be fun.

"Okay." I offer him a saccharine smile. "See you later!"

I hear him grumble something unintelligible as I move away, and I have a feeling he knows what I'm up to.

When Zendaya and I reach my door, my heart sinks a little at the note left there. We're to dine once again with Greed and Alora, but this time it'll be in the formal dining hall rather than Greed's private one. I only hope that tonight's events won't be too stressful.

CHAPTER SIXTEEN

L ater, Zendaya and I stroll toward the dining hall. I know that what I'm wearing will stir up some trouble, but I welcome it tonight. Ulric is going to be beside himself. I chose to wear a scandalous pantsuit with an open back and a low-cut V in the front that stops a little above my navel. It's a dark maroon color and feels like silk against my skin.

I left my hair down and straight and found a few cosmetics to use that the seamstresses brought up with my outfits. I guess they thought I needed that as well. Zendaya laughed and said they always bring her new colors with her outfits. I shrugged, and we played around with the different items they left in a small bag while she shared more of what everyone's lives have been like living in Hell.

Zendaya pushes the door to the dining hall open, and I follow behind her, listening as the men continue their conversation. I smile as the conversation stops and all eyes swing to me. Zendaya chuckles softly in front of me, and we continue moving to our chairs. Another gentleman sits next to Ulric this evening. He resembles Ulric some, with cropped dark hair and green eyes.

I scan the room with a smile as I take my seat and notice the heat in Prospero's and Ulric's eyes. Even Greed gives me a heated look. It worries me, but Ulric's gaze keeps me grounded and excites me.

"You look rather astonishing tonight, my dear," Prospero says, staring at me from where he sits next to Greed.

"Thank you. I thought I would try out some of my new outfits. Are we early, or is the food running late?" I boldly ask, changing the topic. I get a smile from Alora. She, too, has a heated gaze, and I can only imagine what's on her mind.

"We wanted to make sure you were all present before they served." She snaps her fingers, and servers burst through the doors, carrying platters.

I nod and watch as they begin placing plates in front of us. I cast a glance toward the other male sitting with us and catch Ulric's eye.

"This is our older brother, Edsel. He and I share a mother, in case you were wondering why we appear so similar." Ulric smiles and nods to his brother.

"Hello, Ember, future sister. It's a pleasure to meet you." Edsel bows slightly.

"Yes, you as well." I turn my gaze away from them toward Prospero, who shrugs.

"I forget you can't remember some people still. Apologies, brother." He tilts his head, and I look back to see Edsel frown.

Ulric leans in to whisper something into his ear, and his frown deepens before he looks back at me. Edsel's posture changes, and he becomes more guarded as Ulric sits up and begins to eat.

I let him know what's been going on. He's trustworthy. Ulric's voice enters my mind, and I try my best to keep my gaze away from him. The food on my plate becomes very interesting, partially because I have no idea what it is.

I trust your judgment. Do you like my outfit? I tease and swirl my fork around on my plate, gathering my courage to taste the strange meat. What kind of meat is purple, anyway?

"How was your day, ladies?" Prospero's voice draws my attention, and I risk a bite of the food. Thankfully, it's not terrible.

That outfit is exactly what I didn't want you to wear tonight. It's pretty distracting. It makes me think of all the things I want to do to you.

Hmm, like what? I take a bite off my fork again.

"Oh, we had a lot of fun today on the water. It was beautiful. Ember, wouldn't you agree?" Zendaya pulls me into the conversation, reminding me that we have an image to maintain. I'm glad we planned it out during the memorization task this morning. I still have somewhat of a headache from that.

"Yes, it was lovely and a great change in scenery." I smile encouragingly.

First, I think I would kiss every bare inch of your skin before slowly pulling everything off of you. Then, that silk would easily slide down those gorgeous shoulders of yours, and then that outfit would pool at your feet. Finally, it'll leave me to gaze at your glorious body.

I fight the images making their way into my head as Prospero says, "Well, I sure missed spending time with you, Ember. I had planned to show you some things myself today. Maybe tomorrow?"

I blush as Ulric pushes an image of him kissing his way down my skin into my mind as he holds me against the wall in nothing but my bra and panties. "I'm sure we can. What were your plans?"

I fire back an image of what I want to do to Ulric through our connection. It involves me in a particular position between his legs and my hands doing something as I kneel before him with nothing on while removing his pants. I show him how I'll slide my hands up his muscled thighs to cup him while I use my tongue to explore.

A loud bang echoes through the room as someone's knee hits the bottom of the table, and Ulric spews his drink everywhere as he breaks into a coughing fit, while Prospero speaks with a raised brow. "I had planned to fly you over to the lava mountains to picnic. Brother, are you okay?"

I turn my gaze to meet Ulric's with a wicked smile on my face as Ulric responds. He's wiping wine from his lips as he speaks roughly. "Yes, brother, my drink went down the wrong pipe."

I softly chuckle as he fires back, *I'm going to hold you to that one. What else do you have in mind, mate?*

"Son, you know better than to drink that fast. Have some manners," Greed says, and Edsel throws me a knowing look. Does he have a mate? Does he know what's transpiring between his brother and me?

I'll definitely do that and maybe let you tie me to the bed. I do know a thing or two when it comes to sex.

"I guess I couldn't help myself, Father. Some things are just too tempting, as you well know." He shrugs. *As much as that excites me, it also riles my blood to imagine another man's hands on you that aren't mine. Of course, if it's another of your mates, I might work past that, but anyone else touches you in that way again, they'll die.*

"I can't deny that claim. I'm Greed after all." Greed places a hand on Alora's leg, and both of their gazes heat as they meet. The temperature in the room seems to spike as well, and I turn my gaze down to my plate. Please don't let this turn into some strange orgy fest.

As we eat, the sexual tension between Alora and Greed seems to dissipate, and the rest of dinner goes by with a generic conversation about the castle. We talk about things that need to be redone or things Alora wants to change in preparation for the ball. I try my hardest not to look over at Ulric as we continue to send each other scandalous thoughts. Ulric occasionally grunts in response to an image and has to adjust himself in his seat. Edsel shakes his head at us a few times, but thankfully, Prospero is oblivious to it all. Instead, he's wrapped up in the conversation of whatever Greed is going on about with Alora.

I think we need to meet in the garden later, when you can get away from Prospero. You know he's going to try something after seeing you like this tonight. I don't want him touching you. I'm going to mark every piece of your skin, my scent be damned. If he hasn't caught the change in it yet, I doubt he'll notice if we make love. Ulric's voice caresses my mind like the silk I'm currently wearing.

I maintain a bored expression as I pretend to listen to Prospero and Greed. *Why must we meet in the garden? Do you not own a bed?*

Woman, we risk a lot going to my room. Are you sure you want to do that?

How will anyone know it's me? Does Prospero not visit the chamber with all the shifters, regularly? Do they not carry your brother's offspring and maybe even your father's?

His growl reverberates in my mind, but he controls it enough that it only stays in our telepathic conversation. *Yes, they do. Are you saying that we could play your visit off as me having a tryst with one of them?*

It would work, wouldn't it?

He's quiet for a few minutes, and I offer a smile to Zendaya beside me as she looks at me suspiciously. "I think I'm getting tired. How about you?"

Zendaya smirks and flicks her hair over her shoulder. "I guess. Do you want to walk with me up to our rooms?"

This gets Prospero's attention. "I'll escort her, Zendaya. I didn't realize that today wore you out so much, my love. Shall we go?"

Don't let him touch you. I would hate to have to attack him prematurely before you have a chance to escape from here.

I won't let him. Calm down. Send me an image of how to find your room. "Yes, I think that would be nice. I'll see you all tomorrow." I nod and offer a slight bow to Greed and Alora as both Prospero and Zendaya move to leave with me.

Better yet, use your nose and follow my scent. "Have a good night, ladies, brother," Ulric says.

"Yes, what he said." Edsel nods.

Are you seriously turning this into a training situation? Don't I get enough of that during the day? I rest my hand on Prospero's arm as he quietly guides me out.

It's never too much training if it'll help you stay alive later on. I'll see you soon. Ulric's voice sends shivers down my spine and causes my core to tighten.

"Are you cold?" Prospero moves his arm to wrap it around me. He pulls me closer, and I force myself not to stiffen.

"I guess, a little. It's been a busy day, so maybe it's just fatigue." I shrug as he maintains me in his hold.

"Well, I hope you're not too tired. You can't just come to dinner dressed like that. I thought Alora was going to ask for a threesome for a moment during dinner. Not that I would complain, but I know you're not ready for that. I think we need some bonding time first."

I stay quiet for a moment as we walk awkwardly with me in his arms. "I'm pretty tired, Prospero. Maybe another night?"

He's quiet as we walk the remainder of the distance to my door. He opens it like a gentleman and follows me in. I turn to face him as he moves quickly to me and pulls me against him. "I think I can change your mind. Let me, love. I've missed our time together. I'm ready to have an heir that's of our blood."

I frown. "Not tonight. Don't I need to clear it with the healers first?"

"Screw the healers. I think you'll be fine." He pushes himself into me and leans in to kiss my neck. "Let me show you what you've been missing."

He backs me toward the bed, and my mind starts to scramble on how to get out of this situation. I feel my knees hit the edge, and I try to stop him. "Prospero, love, what are you doing?"

"I'm trying to convince you. Why are you holding out?" He pushes me roughly onto the bed, and anger flares in me. He crawls atop of me and pins my hands to the bed with one hand as he pushes my top away from my breasts. The fabric barely covers them as it is.

I glare at him and pull my arms free of his grasp. "Prospero, I'm saying no. Don't force the issue. Have you always been like this?"

He looks at me with what I assume is something similar to a puppy dog pout. "I'd never force you. I'm sorry, love." He sits back, still straddling my body, and runs his hands through his hair in frustration. I pull my top across my exposed breasts and prop up on my elbows. "I'll let you rest. Tomorrow, we're spending some much-needed time together whether you let me make love to you or not."

He growls and slides off the bed, giving me room to breathe. Tension drops from my shoulders, and I push up off my elbows and return to standing. I move to him and wrap my arms around him. "Thank you for being patient with me. I'm still recovering, after all. Goodnight."

He places a soft kiss on my lips before he responds, "Goodnight."

He releases me, and I move back to the bed. Once he's out of my door, I flop back onto the bed and stare at the ceiling. How the hell am I going to keep this from going somewhere I don't want it to? He won't become violent if I continue to refuse, will he? Tonight could have gone very badly had he forced himself on me.

Feeling frustrated, I quickly strip out of my outfit and move to the bathroom to shower. I don't want his scent lingering on me if I'm going to make my way to find Ulric.

I spend a little extra time scrubbing and using the scented soaps. It also gives me time to focus my thoughts and prepare to use my senses to locate his room. This may not be an easy task since I've never tried something like it before. I'm willing to try, though, and in the worst-case scenario, I'll just flip it around and make him find me. It'll be like a game of hide and seek if it comes to that.

Slipping into a thin gown, I wrap a long robe around me to keep out the chill before poking my head into the hall. It's dimly lit and thankfully empty. I let out a breath before I leave my room and stand in the middle of the hall. I close my eyes and concentrate on the smells around me. Something like the scent of sea salt catches my attention first, and I recognize that as Zendaya. It's one of the strongest scents next to something akin to burned hair. I wrinkle my nose at that scent before a softer smell of fresh morning dew on flowers hits me. That has to be Ulric's.

I open my eyes and keep my nose homed in on the scent as I tread lightly down the hall. It leads me down several other halls, stairways, and even through a large library before I end up on the other side of the castle. The hall here is decorated in lighter shades of blue. A picture of a gorgeous woman and two boys hangs at the end of the hall. I recognize the boys as Ulric and Edsel and assume the woman must be their mother. I wonder what happened to her.

I pause as I take in the doors surrounding me, trying to distinguish the difference in scents. The floral scent is mixed with a citrus scent here. I let them lead me to one of the doors and push it open without knocking. Ulric is expecting me, so why knock?

The door swings open, and both Ulric and Edsel look at me. Ulric smirks while Edsel glowers.

"Are you two seriously doing this? Aren't you supposed to be pretending to be betrothed to your kidnapper?" Edsel lifts his brow, changing his glower to a look of disapproval. "How do you expect to hide your scents from Prospero exactly?"

"You and I both know he isn't the most observant when it comes to scents. He always has lingering scents of those other female shifters on him, so why would he notice ours?" Ulric shrugs and moves from the chair he was sitting in toward me.

"How will he distinguish my scent from another shifter anyway?" I ask, wrapping my arms around Ulric.

"For one, Ember, you're not a shifter but a hellhound. Your scent is unique. Even though we have a few female hellhounds that live in a small village on the outskirts of our territory, your scent is unique. My brother tells me you're Lucifer's daughter. That makes a huge difference," Edsel says in a big-brother voice.

"Yes, brother, it does, but Prospero doesn't know that about her, remember?" Ulric pulls me into his lap as he returns to his chair.

"You're playing a dangerous game here, but I get it. When you find your mate, it's special, and you need to treasure every moment with them." Edsel's gaze goes distant as if he's lost in a memory.

"Did something happen to yours?" I ask curiously, and he shakes his head, coming back to the present.

"Sort of, but that's a story for another time. So, I'll leave you two to it. I'll see you both tomorrow." He bows his head and leaves the room quietly.

I turn to Ulric. "So I passed my scent training?"

He laughs and places a kiss on my forehead. "That you did. Now where to start?"

He stands us and guides me over to the bed. Then, snapping his fingers, the fire dims in the room and casts everything into shadow.

"That was fancy," I say as I pull my robe off my shoulders and let it drop to the floor.

"If you think so. I like that gown you're wearing, but I think I'd like it better off of you. Let me help you with that." He steps forward and gently pulls it off me. He drops it to the floor to mingle with my robe as I stand before him bare.

A rumble echoes through his chest, causing shivers of desire to course down my spine. In a blink, he has me on the bed with my legs spread, running his hands across my skin.

"Your skin is as soft as I imagined it would be. The things you make me want to do, Ember." He growls and places kisses along the inside of my legs.

"I think your clothes need to go as well, mate." I pout and point to his shirt.

He smirks as he bites my inner thigh playfully before removing everything he's wearing. I stare in awe at how large he is, before he distracts me with a lick across my sex.

"Oh," I say breathlessly, and he continues to devour me. I squirm and moan as he brings me closer to my climax.

I try to reach around to grab him, but he pushes me back on the bed. "You'll have your turn soon. We do have all night."

I whimper as he plunges a finger into me, pumping it in and out. "Oh, God, Ulric!" He pumps his hand faster until it pushes me over the edge. I scream his name as I plummet, and he presses his mouth to mine, quieting me. I taste myself on his lips and use that moment to wrap my hand around his member.

He moans into my mouth as we roll over. I then slowly make my way down toward his groin area. Smiling up at him, I continue to use my hand to pleasure him before leaning in and sliding my tongue across the edge of his head. I lower my lips down and over it until I have taken him as far as I can. I tease and suck until he suddenly flips us over.

Once again, he's on top, and I'm stunned by how quickly we moved. "I don't want to come in your mouth, love. I want to coat your insides and claim you as mine. Everyone will know you belong to me. Screw it if my brother picks up the scent. No one but those meant for you will have you."

I smile at his words and then gasp as he plunges into me. A strange sensation pulses through me that feels like lightning, and I feel everything he feels. We're connected through our bond as well as our bodies. The sensations are heightened as he pumps in and out of me, harder and faster, bringing us closer to a massive climax. I clamp my teeth down on his shoulder as I begin to plummet once again, and he returns the bite. I know we'll leave a physical mark with our teeth, but neither of us mind as we climax together.

The fire surges in the hearth as our bond seals and then sputters out. Finally, we release our hold on each other, leaving trickles of blood to dry from our bites.

"Wow," I sputter out.

"Yes, wow indeed." Ulric smiles down at me from where he hovers atop of me. It's then that I notice my wings are spread out beside me as his wrap around us.

"So, what now?" I ask hesitantly.

"Now, we do that again."

CHAPTER SEVENTEEN

A fter I sneak back to my room before dawn to shower, Zendaya lets herself into my room and smirks at me as I dress.

"So, did you have fun last night?" She plops down onto one of my chairs, and minutes later, my maids bring in food and coffee.

"I did. Why do you ask?"

"Well, you have a glow about you, and your wings are still visible."

"Shit." I stand still and focus on hiding them. "Do you think the maids will say anything?"

"No, they despise Prospero. They also know better than to share things like that. You would be surprised by what they know. They're good with secrets."

"I hope so." I sit in a chair next to her and grab the coffee. "Did you convince them to bring this up with breakfast?"

"I did. I told them how much you loved the stuff, and they were more than eager to share it." She shrugs, and the door swings open, letting Prospero in.

He frowns as he takes us in. "What are you doing here, Zendaya? Can you two not ever be separated?"

I laugh as Zendaya gives him a pointed look. "I'm having morning coffee with my best friend, thank you. Of course, we could ask what you're doing here, but I remember you saying you wanted to spend today with your betrothed."

I stop laughing as I remember his comment at dinner last night. Shit.

"I do have plans for us today. It won't be anything too strenuous because we have guests arriving much earlier than expected for the ball. I guess they wanted to visit or something. It's odd." Prospero's jaw twitches.

"Why is it odd? Do we not regularly have guests? This is a fine castle after all." I tilt my head to the side, fishing for more information.

"We do on occasion but not normally. They have requested to stay in the old guest quarters, which is this hall. It has been a long time since their kind have visited. I hope to convince them to stay in the new guests' suites. I don't like that they will be so close to you." He frowns again, glancing around the room.

"I'm sure I'll be fine. Who is it that will be arriving?" I look at Zendaya, who shows no sign of knowing. I have a feeling she does, though.

"Oh, it's the vampire princes and their entourage." He finally sits in one of the few chairs remaining empty. The other has my robe thrown across it. Hopefully, he won't notice Ulric's scent on it.

"Are the vampires not kind? Why are you so worried?" I ask lightly.

"They are. They just don't always agree to our terms here. We have changed things a lot over the years, and many have opposed our decisions. We also don't wish them to discover our secret about the shifters and hellhound army we're trying to build."

I look at Zendaya as her mouth forms a firm straight line, and then I frown at Prospero. "I see. Well, I guess we just won't mention anything around them then?"

"If only it were that simple. The walls have ears here. Anyway, finish up your food, love. I'm taking you to our art gallery. I had planned to picnic with you, as previously mentioned, but I don't want to be too far off when or if our guests arrive today." He nods at the food, and I offer him a kind smile.

"I'm sure it'll be lovely to see so many creations. It should put us both in a relaxed mood." Zendaya smirks at me.

"I'll let you finish your coffee and catch up with you later, Ember. I hope you'll find me when you're free." She winks, and I try not to laugh.

"Thank you, sister. We'll see if I let her out of my sight today," Prospero adds, and I roll my eyes. Thankfully, he doesn't see it as he watches his sister leave.

I sip on my coffee and eat some of the fruit the maids brought in as he watches me. It makes me nervous how he looks at me, but I remind myself that he won't hurt me, at least as long as I pretend to be clueless.

"I'm happy you're enjoying being here, my love, despite not remembering things. You seem to have fallen into a new routine that suits you." He runs his hand along my arm as I hold my coffee cup.

I force a smile. "Yes, if only I had those memories back. Where did I spend most of my time? Did I not have favorite things I did? I would love to know what those were."

"Do you not enjoy the things you're doing now? Why do those old things matter?"

I frown at him, but of course, he wouldn't know. We don't have history, and he kidnapped me. "I guess you're right. Let's go see that art you mentioned." I return to finishing my coffee.

"That's better, love. You will love the pieces we have. My

father has collected some of the best art from around the world. He has the biggest gallery in Hell." He beams with pride.

I nod and stand from my chair to walk over to my wardrobe. Knowing Prospero is in the room, I take my clothes to the bathroom to get ready quickly. I hear him voice his complaint as I stand behind the small door, changing. He can get over it.

"I'm ready," I proclaim, stepping from the bathroom.

"You didn't have to go into the bathroom, you know." He pouts, and I roll my eyes.

"You'll be fine. Now, shall we?" I smile and grab his hand.

He pulls it to his lips and places a kiss on my wrist. "We shall."

He guides me out into the hall, and we head toward the central part of the castle. I pull up the layout of things from my task yesterday and double-check things as we make our way to the art room on the opposite side. It has several doors leading down to the servants' lower levels and can provide an escape out of the castle if needed. It is also closest to the room where the ball will be held, according to Zendaya. The ball is always held in the room opposite the art gallery and only has one small stairwell leading to the servants' halls below it.

I maintain a sweet smile as we walk, listening to Prospero go on about the history of each hall and part of the castle. He shares many things similar to Zendaya's, but some of his stories predate her appearance at the castle. They fascinate me, and I find myself enjoying listening to him.

When we enter the gallery, I glance around at the artwork. Finally, I will have time to pause and look over things today instead of being quizzed about halls and escape routes. Prospero leads me to an image of all the fallen angels, hanging on the wall closest to us.

"This is the first painting completed after the arrival of the fallen in Hell." His voice is soft and filled with awe.

I look closer at the picture and spy, who I assume is Lucifer standing in the middle of the group. He is a broad-shouldered man with a scar across his right eye. His long black hair is pulled back over his shoulder, and his massive white wings flare out behind him. I recognize Greed standing beside him, but I don't recognize any of the others.

"Can you tell me who these angels are?"

Prospero smiles. "Absolutely! The man in the front is Lucifer. My father is on his left, and Pride is on his right. The woman next to Pride is Lust and next to her is her sister Envy. Next to my dad is Wrath, then Sloth, and Gluttony. You don't ever want to get on Wrath's bad side. She is vicious. Both Sloth and Gluttony are males that are pretty laid back. You would like them."

"Oh, wow, so you know them all?"

"Well, yes, I do. They used to visit my father a lot when I was younger. They only come around now, on occasion. Anyway, let's move on." He tugs on my hand, and we move down toward the next painting. It's a large painting of a massive tree.

"That is gorgeous. Do you know who painted it?"

"I don't, but I agree with you. See how it supports different parts of the universe? This is the tree, Yggdrasil, mentioned in Norse mythology. We have many paintings from different beings in this gallery that didn't sign things. This is one of them, but it's very realistic."

"Wait, you mean that this is real?" I point at the tree, and he nods. My mouth drops open, and he taps it with his hand to close it.

"If you keep your mouth open like that, I may have to put something in it. Are you trying to tease me, Ember? I'll take you here, right now, if you wish." He pulls me closer to him, and I place my hands on his chest to stop him.

"I don't think that's a good idea. What if someone were to walk in?"

He leans in and nips my ear as he whispers, "I'd like to see them try." He slides his hands to my waist.

"Still, no. I want to see the rest of the pieces in this gallery." I grab his hands and push him away lightly.

He huffs and pulls back. "Fine. I'm beginning to get impatient, love."

I roll my eyes in response, and we begin to walk slowly through the room again. He shares bits and pieces about each painting as we stroll along hand in hand. I'm thankful he doesn't push things anymore, but I worry just how much more he'll take before he snaps.

I do my best to play the head over heels in love fiancée that I'm supposed to be, but my mind keeps drifting back to last night with Ulric.

I can sense your thoughts, mate. Is everything okay?

I blush and play it off as if it were something Prospero said, and he continues to elaborate about the painting of the naked couple before us.

I'm just daydreaming about your bed. Nothing too crazy besides listening to your brother talk about paintings.

Well, maybe we should do it again tonight?

I would enjoy that immensely, but there was mention that the vampires are arriving early?

Yes, but no worries. You can easily get to my room. I doubt they'll arrive today. Will you be training again today?

Of course, I have to be ready, and I still have a lot to learn. We're only what, a week away from the ball now?

Yes, we are. Just remember not to overdo it.

Please, like that could happen.

"Are you listening, Ember? You appear lost in your head." Prospero halts us, looking at me in concern.

"Hm? Oh, sorry. I was lost in thought. What did I miss?" I blink rapidly as Ulric's words spill through.

You could easily overdo it.

"I asked if you were hungry. Would you like to dine with me for lunch? I can have it brought to your room if you're more comfortable there, or we could go to mine?" He looks at me eagerly, and I know right where his thoughts go.

"Let's dine in my room. Zendaya and I are supposed to train together this afternoon, so she should be coming by to get me shortly after lunch. I'm getting a lot stronger." I smile sweetly at him.

"That's excellent news, my love. Let's head toward your room then. I think I hear your stomach growling." He turns us, and I spy a servant standing near the door. "Archibald, will you have a meal prepared for us right away and sent up to Ember's room?"

"Yes, sir, I'll get right on that." The butler performs a slight bow before exiting the room.

"Now, let's take our time heading to your room."

I smile as Prospero leads me back down the hall, telling me about his childhood and playing with his brothers. He mentions that he trained from an early age to be the warrior he is today. He doesn't mention anything about his mother as we walk but elaborates on practicing with Ulric and several other brothers.

When we arrive at my door, he pushes it open for me, and I'm shocked at the spread of food on the table. I forget how quickly the servants can move in the lower halls to prepare things ahead of time.

Prospero leads me to a chair, and I sit. He takes the one next to me, and I'm thankful he doesn't push things as we eat. It leaves me somewhat relaxed, and as I leave later to train in the garden, he escorts me to the door and leaves me with a sweet kiss. For once, I think he could possibly be a decent friend, but I know that's something that will never happen after my secret gets out. Once it's out that I've had my memories back this entire time and that I'm also mated to his brother, the betrayal will run deep.

CHAPTER EIGHTEEN

Several days later, I find myself making my way back to my room, sore from the night spent with Ulric. The morning shines bright, and it impresses me how much stamina he has. I arrive in my room and throw myself on the bed for a moment, stretching out. I still feel tired, but I want to spend as much time training today as I can. If the vampires are to arrive today, there is no telling if I'll be able to train with them around. Hell, Prospero may camp outside my door for all I know since they're all staying in this part of the castle.

I roll over and push up to head into the bathroom. I hear the door open as I step into the water, and the scent of fresh pancakes and coffee wafts through the open door. I quickly finish my morning routine and step out to find the table covered in fruit, pancakes, and a large pot of coffee.

I fix a plate and begin to inhale the food as my door opens, allowing Zendaya entrance. "Ah, starting without me? How dare you."

I chuckle around my food. "Are you going to eat with me every morning? Not that I'm complaining or anything, but I'm curious."

"Well, I did plan on it. It also lets me keep an eye on things in this area of the castle. I know you can handle yourself and all, but I hope my presence will make Prospero back off on pushing you. I don't want to see him and Ulric get into it before the ball. He'll at least have an option of escape at that point." She shrugs and slides into the chair opposite of me and begins to fill her plate.

"You have a good point. I just wish we could get everything over with. No offense to you all, but I miss home. I think everything will be different now that my secret is out. I'll hopefully have more freedom and won't be tied to Adam anymore." I grab an apple and take a large bite.

"I hope you're right. But unfortunately, it also may make the current Alpha hungrier for power. I don't think he's a good man. He has deceived a lot of people." She sips at her cup of coffee as my brows shoot into my hair.

"What? I've never seen him be anything but good."

"Oh, he has done a lot to increase his own power and place in your world. He did sacrifice his wife for power granted from Greed himself. I thought you knew that."

I stare at her, horrified at the information she just shared. "He sacrificed her? How would I know that? Does anyone in my pack know?"

She stares at me as if to discern that I'm joking. "You really don't know? I'm not sure if there are others in the pack that know, but he did have a Beta with him when he did it. He worked with a witch that knew how to travel through the realms to attain it. He wears a good mask if his secret has remained with him."

"Poor Adam. Oh, God, is it Corey's dad?"

She shrugs. "I don't know, Ember, but watch yourself when you go back."

"Wait, are you saying you won't be going with me?"

"I won't. Not that I wouldn't love to, but I have to find a way to keep Greed and Prospero from trying to take more girls after you escape. That won't be an easy feat. Prospero will be enraged that you're gone."

"He can get over it. I don't belong with him anyway. I don't like that you'll remain here. Won't they know you helped me escape?"

"I don't think they will, and if they do, I have a charm that I can use on them. I have been working on it for some time in case I need it. I can do a few other things with magic than what you've seen. I did create that memory-loss charm for your bracelet, after all. It helps me keep the image that I'm on Prospero's side. Also, I know it won't be long until we see each other again. Your life span is different from the shifters you live with. Because you're Lucifer's daughter, you'll live as long or longer than any of us."

I blink, trying to process her words. "Am I immortal?"

"Yes, I guess you are. That doesn't mean you can't be killed, though. We can all very much be killed."

"So why hasn't anyone killed Greed yet?" I ask in astonishment. "If he's caused so many issues, wouldn't someone have just taken him out?"

"It's a bit more complicated than that. He's not easy to kill for one, and only one with Lucifer's blood can kill any of the original fallen. So, it would have to be someone like you, but Ulric or I won't let you risk that. It's too dangerous."

I frown and stare down at my cup. "If he were gone, who would take his place?"

I glance up as Zendaya frowns. "Right now, it would be Prospero."

We sit in silence, and it gives me time to think over everything she just shared with me. Could I kill both of them for things to be righted here? Would it even fix anything?

The door swings open, and I paste on a smile, as does Zendaya as Prospero makes his way toward us. "You two are inseparable. What am I to do with you ladies? Are you truly making every morning a habit of eating together? Will I ever have you to myself for breakfast, my love?"

I laugh at his words, and he frowns in response. "Oh, silly, do you not enjoy the fact that I'm having fun with your sister? Is that jealousy?"

"I guess it is. Fine, if I must share you, at least it's not with another male." He smiles, and Zendaya chuckles mischievously.

"How are you this morning, brother?" she asks, finally getting her giggles under control.

"I'm doing well, I guess. It could be better, and you, sister?" He smiles warmly at her.

"I'm just peachy." She offers him a smile in return.

I watch the two interact as I go back to sipping my coffee. This is one of those times I think Prospero could be a good person, but other times, I see the darkness within his heart shine through. It's sad.

Are you and Zendaya alone? Ulric's voice startles me as it flows through my mind.

I hide my surprise by taking a sip of coffee. *No, why?*

I wanted to check before I showed up. The vampires are arriving shortly. Maybe I should send in one of the servants to deliver the message. It may seem odd that I'm sharing.

Okay. So that's a good thing, right?

Yes, but Prospero and my father will want to show dominance, making it known that they are better than the vampires. It's always been something they do when guests arrive. I'll send a servant in to announce it, and I'll see you shortly.

Okay. I roll my eyes and set my cup down. I recline back in my chair as a knock on the door sounds, and both my companions go silent as a servant enters.

"Sorry to interrupt, I was sent to inform you that the vampires are arriving soon." He bows slightly before backing out and closing the door.

"I guess this was to be expected. Ladies, I'll see you in the grand hall shortly. Would you please wear something appropriate to greet them? You know the drill, Zendaya. Help my love find something." Prospero stands from his chair and moves to place a kiss on my forehead.

"I'm sure I can dress myself, thank you," I say snarkily as he pulls back from kissing me.

"I don't doubt that, love, but I don't want you wearing something too revealing. Zendaya will make sure you have dressed accordingly. I'll see you soon." He backs away with a smile and turns to leave.

Zendaya moves to my side as he exits and sits on the arm of my chair. "You wear whatever you want."

I laugh. "You know I will. Why are we meeting in the grand hall?"

"Greed likes to put on a show of superiority. It's nothing. You remember where that is?"

"How could I forget? You did make me memorize all the exits and rooms in this place."

"I was checking to see if you need a refresher. Let's get ready. This may be eventful."

"Why do you say that?"

"If they brought your other mate, it will be." She stands from her chair and moves to the wardrobe. "Now, get over here and get dressed."

CHAPTER NINETEEN

An hour later, I stand in the great hall next to Zendaya with Prospero in front of us and Ulric behind us. We are to the right of where Greed and Alora rest in oversized chairs resembling thrones. There is a long red carpet spanning to the door at the opposite end of the hall. I now get why Ulric said it was ridiculous.

Greed and Alora are dressed extravagantly, and so is Prospero, while Zendaya, Ulric, and I wear something simple yet flattering. A servant announced earlier that the group would be arriving in five minutes, so we were all rushed into place. Prospero informed me to follow his lead, but we'll see how that goes. I would say I only trust him as far as I can throw him, but it's even less than that. I can lift heavier things now and toss them further than before my powers started showing themselves.

A loud bell sounds outside the door as the servants announce the arrival of the vampire royals. I expect finery similar to what Alora and Greed wear but fight the urge to laugh as the group enters the room. Instead, they are all wearing relaxed clothes that you would find on anyone walking the streets.

The group is large, and the outside vamps look like some type of guard for the royals. They keep stern expressions and a tight circle around whoever is in the middle. They're tall and elegant and seem to glide across the floor as they stop before Greed and Alora.

A pressure pushes on my head as the group stops, and I can't figure out why. I watch as the group opens, and one of them, who I assume to be the royals, steps forward and performs a light bow.

"Ah, Prince Zuko, it's a pleasure to see you and have you in our home. I see you brought your entourage," Greed says pompously.

Zuko stands from his bow. "Why yes, I have. My brother Ezekiel is here as well. We both look forward to the ball. Thank you for inviting us."

He ushers his hand behind him, and the guards part. My mouth drops. I fight the urge to ignite into flames as none other than Zeke steps forward and bows.

Sensing my distress, Ulric asks, *Are you okay? Your wings are shimmering, trying to break out of the concealing charm.*

I'm fine, just slightly pissed. That is my friend, possibly my other mate. Never has he mentioned being a royal or that his full name is Ezekiel.

Well, calm down, please, before you blow everyone's cover.

I let out a deep sigh and stare at Zeke, who refuses to look at me. It angers me even more, but I hold my tongue as I stand behind Prospero.

"Prince Ezekiel, it's been a long time since you've graced us with your presence. I do hope you both enjoy your stay. I'll bring the servants in to show you to your rooms and help you with any items you may have brought." Greed snaps his fingers, and a line of servants streams through the door.

The room is silent as the vampires turn and leave. It confuses me that we weren't introduced to them, or maybe they already know the names of everyone except me. I mean, I'm the youngest here by far.

"Now that that is done, you all are dismissed. I'll see everyone at dinner tonight to dine with our guests." Greed addresses us all, and we slightly bow our heads in return.

I follow Prospero as he leads us into the hall but once free of the great room, I part from the group and head for the garden. I need to get some fresh air and possibly exert some of my frustration.

"Where are you going, love?" Prospero stops me with a hand on my shoulder, and I growl. He pulls it back, staring at me in shock.

"I need some fresh air. I'll see you later." I don't give him any time to respond as I stride away. I don't even go to my room to change. Instead, I walk quickly through the decorative garden door and out into the middle of the garden, where I let everything drop.

Flames burst up my arms, and my wings break free as I stare at the strange sky. I feel as if everything between Zeke and me has been a lie. Did my mother know who he was?

I shake my head and take off at a sprint and begin to do laps around the track. I let my wings stream behind me as I run, enjoying the feel of the wind moving through them. I haven't gotten them strong enough to lift me yet, but I hope to get there, eventually.

Once my legs begin to ache and my breath is labored, I move to the grass and collapse on my back. I close my eyes, letting everything settle around me. That's when I register Ulric nearby.

How long have you been watching me?

Long enough. It distresses you that he didn't acknowledge you? I'm sure there is a reason. I hear his steps near but keep my eyes closed. I feel him lay in the grass beside me and pull me into his arms.

It does bother me. I don't understand, but then again, I guess if he were to acknowledge me, it would have put me in danger because then Prospero would suspect I have broken through the memory charms.

He places a kiss on my temple, and I open my eyes to look at him. *It would have, but I get it, love. We need to talk to them soon to get our plan in motion. Can you handle that?*

I sigh and lean my head against his chest as we continue to lie in the grass. *Yes. I guess I need to face him sooner rather than later to confront him about all this. Maybe he won't be like that in private?*

Don't get your hopes up, love, just in case he is. This is a different world than where you are from, and they may not know if we can be trusted.

When do we have to meet them?

Zendaya is preparing a room for us, or she was starting to about an hour and a half ago. They may all be there by now.

Was I running that long?

Yes, love, you were. How soon will you be ready?

I guess now. I sit up, and he does the same. "Should I change before we go?"

"Well, you do smell sweaty, gorgeous, but that's up to you. I may have brought you some clothes, though." He shrugs, and I laugh as I playfully slap his arm.

"I guess that's a gentle way of letting me know. I'm nervous about this, Ulric. Very nervous."

"It'll all be fine. Let's get you cleaned up and take care of this. We need to focus on getting you and the girls out of here over anything else. If he chooses to be an ass about you and your ties to him, he can kick rocks. You will always have others who care about you." We stand, and he pulls me into a reassuring hug.

"Thank you, Ulric. You've become my rock. I'm glad you're my mate." I kiss him softly.

He pulls away after a moment, "Me too. Now let's go before you start something that will really make us late."

I give him a mischievous smile, but instead of starting something, I let him lead me to the pile of clothes on the grass. I quickly change before we head back through the artistic masterpiece that is the door to the garden and head toward my hall.

"Zendaya has set up a small refreshment area for us down the hall from your room, closer to where the vampires are staying. Prospero is trying to have a guard posted outside your door, but I think I have him convinced that you'll be fine. I thought it was hilarious how you snapped at him earlier, by the way. The look on his face was priceless."

"I take it he's not used to something like that?"

"Not exactly, at least not when it comes to females. Zendaya is the only other one who will put him in his place."

"Will he be poking around while we talk with our guests?" Butterflies blossom in my stomach, imagining him catching us in our scheming.

"I doubt it. He said something about going to the barracks to make sure his new recruits stayed hidden. He does have a few male hellhounds he wishes to keep from prying eyes. They are unfortunately loyal to him for some reason. It makes no sense to me." He shrugs, and I squeeze his hand.

He leads me to a door that is only two doors down from mine and pushes it open. I keep a straight face as we enter, and he leads me to a seat next to Zendaya. I fall into it. He takes the one on my other side, and I glance over at our guests. Zeke and his brother Zuko sit watching us. Two females stand behind them at the back of the room. I can't help but glare at Zeke, who blinks at me before a smile spreads across his face.

Zuko clears his throat. "I'm sorry, but I don't know you, female. I also don't appreciate you glaring at my brother. It's quite rude, you know."

Ulric nudges me, and I drop the glare as I respond, "I don't mean any offense, but if you ask your brother, I'm sure he will tell you why I'm glaring. Won't you, Zeke?" I cross my arms across my chest as he bursts into laughter, and Zuko turns to stare at him in confusion.

"What the hell is going on, brother? How does she know you by that name?" Zuko finally gets his words out, and I feel Ulric stiffen next to me.

I blink, and then both Ulric and Zeke are in front of me. Ulric has a hand on Zeke's chest, stopping him from approaching. They growl at each other, and this time it's my turn to laugh.

Zendaya snickers beside me before she adds, "Zuko, Ember is your brother's mate. My brother, Ulric's, as well."

I tilt my head and look at both of my mates standing and still growling at each other.

"What?" Zeke finally asks.

"Ulric, let him go, please," I say and stand from my chair. "You and Ulric are both my mates, so you both need to get along. I'm not sure how this will work exactly, but Ulric has become my rock, especially since I was dragged down here unwillingly." I turn and glance at Zendaya.

"Hey, don't look at me. You said you would come if we left your friends alone. I told you my reasons for it." She shrugs.

"So you've been okay then? No one has harmed you?" He looks back and forth between Ulric and me, confused. "Will someone please tell me what the hell is going on?"

Everyone turns to stare at Zuko, who stands with his hands on his hips, glaring at us all.

"Brother, Ember is my mate. She is Kyra's daughter, my shifter friend who I have been visiting for the past several years. I've always felt drawn to Ember, but she was tied to the Alpha's son via a contract. After she discovered her Hell-linked powers, I could no longer resist. Then she was taken here while I was still trying to meet her in Alaska. I agreed to help her pack train against vampires and other Hell creatures because they have been having issues with rogues and demons." Zeke smiles at his brother. "Now that we have found her, I won't let her out of my sight again."

"Actually, you're going to have to. I'm technically betrothed to Prospero, who still thinks my mind is wiped, and I have no idea who I am."

"That asshole. I always knew he was up to no good. He must be hiding more than we thought," Zuko says.

"He is, unfortunately, and that's why we reached out to you. He is working hard to build an army of hellhounds to rival Lucifer's. He kidnapped several young women from the different packs of shifters on the earth plane to create this army. We have to get them out of here. We need you all to help us move them during the ball." Ulric grunts as he finishes, and I look at him curiously.

"We have a route planned to take them to the gate that leads to northeast Texas and then take them into Oklahoma where Ember's pack resides. We have also reached out for some extra hands on that side," Zendaya adds, looking at Ulric, who bristles.

"Who did you ask?" Zeke questions.

"We reached out to Kai." Zendaya smiles.

"Okay, that should work. I've worked with him before, and so has Zuko. It's been years, but he should see them safely to their destination. Will it be safe for Ember, though, to travel with him?" Zeke asks.

"Why do you worry about her traveling with Lucifer's best general? I'm sure he'll keep her safe, and then you can join them as well.

"You know?" Ulric asks, and Zeke nods.

"It's Ember's decision whether we share that now or not." Zeke looks at me, and I swallow.

"It's a concern. Zuko, because…" I pause and let my wings fan out, no longer hidden. All the vampires in the room go utterly still, and their eyes widen. "I'm Lucifer's daughter, and he doesn't know I exist."

"Holy shit, you have wings now? Wow, they're gorgeous," Zeke reaches out, staring at me in awe.

"How does Lucifer not know you exist?" Zuko asks. "I'm sorry, but I don't want to go into this blind."

I sigh. "He and my mother had a one-night stand, and he never returned to see that she was pregnant with me. My parents, not my real dad but the man who has raised me as my dad, married shortly after they found out they were mates. The secret was hidden from me until the demon attacks picked up, and I had a run-in with hellfire. It turned my world upside down, basically."

"Damn. That sounds like a hot mess. It makes perfect sense that Zeke would be mixed up in that. We only use his formal name in formal situations, by the way." Zuko smirks at his brother, who rolls his eyes.

Zeke turns back to me and then looks at Ulric. "May I hold our mate?"

Ulric growls but steps aside, and Zeke rushes to me. He pushes me back until I hit the wall and kisses me hard. His kiss is filled with need and longing, and I give in, letting him reassure himself that I'm his.

After a minute, we come up for air, and I spy Zendaya fanning herself while Ulric stands with his arms crossed, glaring. Zuko and the guards all wear smiles, and I blush at all the attention.

"I've been dying to do that. God, when I found that you'd been taken, I wanted to rip every shifter's head off. You don't understand the joy I feel having you back." He strokes my cheek, and I smile up at him.

"I missed you too, Zeke. Now can we move back to my chair, please? Also, you and Ulric are going to have to figure this shit out with me. I don't want the other glaring when one of my mates kisses me." I look pointedly at Ulric, who rolls his eyes.

Give me a break. It's not like I've had another mate before. He visually shrugs.

Can I get in on this conversation now? Zeke's words intrude, and both Ulric and I stare at him.

"You can do that too?" I ask with my mouth agape.

"Uh, yeah, I'm your mate too. Your special ability does extend to me, and it lets all three of us talk. We can work on shielding to have a more private conversation with each other if you'd like?" Zeke suggests, looking at Ulric.

"We can teach you, Ember. I know how to shield, but I didn't know I needed to with our bond. I mean, I guess I don't have to unless you feel threatened by him." He looks at Zeke questioningly.

"Okay, stop, both of you. We'll worry about it later. Can we get back to the topic we need to focus on? We need to discuss the plans to get the girls and me out of here." I place my hands on my hips and look both my mates in the eye.

"We should get some popcorn for this show, don't you think, Zendaya?" Zuko asks playfully.

"I agree, but seriously, let's discuss these plans." Zendaya snaps her fingers, and my ladies' maids materialize. "Girls, can you make sure to keep an eye out for Prospero or any other lingerers while we talk? I don't want us to be discovered."

"We will, madame," they say in unison and bow before disappearing again.

"I had no idea they could do that," I say, staring at where they were previously.

Zendaya shrugs. "They are handy now. I'll start."

Zendaya moves to grab a large piece of paper which she quickly scribbles out a layout of the castle. Next, she labels the hidden passages which she showed me on our tour.

"Being that you are guests, we can't exactly parade you

around the castle, so a map will have to do. However, if you can manage it with your speed, maybe you can find them yourself if you need to see them beforehand." She shrugs and speedily labels them.

"We reached out for your help because we need to get a group of female shifters—some who are pregnant—out of this realm and somewhere safe. Ember will be following them out as soon as they're free. The ball will be the distraction we need to accomplish this. You all, as well as a few trusted friends of mine, will get them to the gate that comes out in northeast Texas. From there, they will be escorted to Oklahoma by Kai and his group of hellhounds until they reach Ember's pack's land." Ulric nods at each of the princes.

"How will we keep them from realizing Ember is Lucifer's daughter if we aren't with them?" Zeke crosses his arms across his chest.

"I plan to follow, and I assume you will as well, Zeke. She is our mate, after all," Ulric declares with a firm expression.

Resting a hand under his chin, Zuko looks at the group curiously. "Of course, but won't it be obvious we're all missing from the ball? How are we to get her away from Prospero?"

Ulric smiles at the princes. "Leave that up to me. You and Zeke will go with her while Zendaya and I cause a distraction. There is an old love interest of his we have invited to the ball that should help with that."

I laugh loudly before I speak. "Oh Lord, why do I have to miss that? I can imagine what that's going to be like. Hell hath no fury like a woman scorned. I just know he did something to hurt her, especially with the way he is with me at times."

Both Ulric and Zeke bristle. Ulric's wings flare out a little as he looks me seriously in the eye. "I thought he hadn't touched you."

I tilt my head. "Well, yes, but that doesn't mean he hasn't

tried to. I can only do so much to fight him off when he gets in a possessive mood, but no, we have not had sex."

Zeke looks at me with a frown. "But you didn't deny that he hasn't exactly touched things that don't belong to him. So what did he do, Ember?"

Placing my hands on my hips, I ask, "Do we have to talk about this right now?"

Zendaya rolls her eyes. "Guys, let's focus on what's important right now. Neither one of you can attack him until we get everyone safe and where they need to be. The time to deal with Prospero will come in time. Trust me."

"I have to agree with the lovely angel. Focus, men, let's get this stuff straight," Zuko adds.

"You're all right. I'll try to rein it in. I may sneak a punch in at some point if I can." Ulric smiles mischievously, and Zeke nods in agreement.

I drop my hands to my sides. "What am I going to do with you two?"

They laugh, and we continue the conversation for another hour until one of my maids appears.

"This is the warning you suggested. Prospero is on his way to this area of the castle." She nods and disappears again.

"Well, I guess I better go pretend that I've been in my room this entire time. See you all at dinner later?"

Everyone nods in agreement, and I quickly sprint from the room and down the hall. I briefly remember to hide my wings with my charm spell before entering my room and throwing myself on the bed. There is a light knock at the door in no time, and I know he has entered a moment later.

CHAPTER TWENTY

"Are you sleeping, my love?" His voice is sweet as honey, and I stretch, pretending that I had been sleeping.

I sit up and blink at him. "I guess I dozed off. Have I missed anything?"

He walks to my bed and climbs up next to me, making himself comfortable against my pillows. "It seems that you did, although you weren't here when I came by earlier. Where did you go?"

I smile at him and flip my hair over my shoulder. "I went for a run in the garden. My hormones are acting up. I believe my monthly is to start soon."

He leans slightly away from me. "Well, do you need items for that?"

"I believe they're already in my bathroom. I'll check again and let you know. Were you worried about me?"

"Well, yes, I was, that's why I'm here again to check on you. I thought one of the princes had offended you. Do you feel able to attend dinner in a few hours?"

"Of course, I feel much better now. I think I needed some extra rest. Will we be having anything special tonight?"

"I have no idea. Alora handles the menu. Why do you ask?"

"Oh, no reason. I was curious is all. I guess I should start getting ready for dinner, huh? I probably smell atrocious after my run."

He pretends to sniff me, "Nah, you still smell sweet to me."

I roll my eyes. "I feel gross, so I'm going to take a shower. You can hang out if you'd like, but you're not joining me."

He pouts as I stand from the bed. "I get it. Fine, I'll wait while you shower."

I smile sweetly at him as I move toward the bathroom. I feel his eyes follow me as I pause at the door. I push into it and let it close gently behind me. Once the door clicks into place, I rest my back against it and take several deep breaths.

How am I going to finish playing this off? Both of my mates are here, and I'm supposed to pretend to be engaged to someone who only wants me so I can better his army. How am I going to keep them from killing Prospero if he puts a hand on me?

I let out a deep sigh of frustration and finally move to the shower to turn on the hot water. I quickly move through a routine to clean up, but I take my time as I get dressed. Thankfully, my maids put an outfit for me to wear for dinner in the bathroom. They had better foresight regarding the situation between Prospero and me than I did. I never thought I would be able to trust them as I do now, knowing that they're on our side.

I flip my hair and finish applying a fine layer of gloss to my lips an hour later and walk out to find Prospero sprawled out, sleeping on my bed. It cracks me up how loud his snores are, and I let him sleep as I move to the door. I pause, though, thinking how rude it would seem in his father's eyes if I were to show up at dinner without him. I plan to keep things settled tonight rather than stirring the pot, especially with my mates lingering in the room.

Turning around, I walk back to the bed and gently nudge his

shoulder. He snorts and opens his eyes, blinking rapidly as if to remember where he is.

"Wake up, Prospero. We need to go. It's almost time for dinner."

He snorts and pushes up from the bed, rubbing his eyes. "You took longer in the shower than I thought you would. Did I sleep the entire time you dressed? Why didn't you wake me when you came out?"

I smile at how flustered he seems. "My maids had a dress prepared for me in the bathroom. I didn't need to come out to get one. Are you not ready? Do we need to wait and give you more time before we leave for dinner? I'm sure it will be fine if we arrive late, right?"

He stretches. "I'm ready. I wouldn't dare give anyone a sign of weakness to use against us in the future, never. We'll be on time."

I roll my eyes. "Whatever you say, I just hope the food's good tonight."

"Have you not enjoyed the food? I'm sure we could talk with Alora about the menu. Is there something else you would prefer?"

I shake my head, ignoring the thought about cheese fries that comes to mind or even bacon. I feel lucky that there's coffee here, honestly. "No, but I don't know what to expect with the vampires at dinner. I've enjoyed everything that's been served."

"Oh, I see."

"Will you be civil tonight with our guest, or should I be worried that a fight will break out?"

"I'll be on my best behavior. I promise, cross my heart and hope to die." He smiles and crosses his heart with his hand.

I give him a side-eye but nod. He stands from the bed and offers me his arm, and I gracefully take it.

We take our time making our way down to the dining hall.

Everything in the castle seems to sparkle and shine. I guess the servants were told to scrub the castle. It's impressive and makes me realize how thick of a layer of dust previously covered everything, especially closer to my room. I'm surprised that we are the first to arrive at the great hall for dinner. Not even Greed and Alora are present yet. The table is covered in clean white linen, and silver plates and cutlery line it. Pitchers of water and crystal glasses rest in clusters down the table. Fresh flowers even rest in vases along the room. It's a huge change from what it's usually like.

I take my usual seat where Zendaya and I usually sit together; however, Prospero frowns at me and, instead of taking his usual place, sits in Zendaya's spot.

I frown and cock my head to the side. "What are you doing?"

"I'm sitting next to my betrothed." He tilts his head, mimicking me.

"You never sit next to me. Why sit next to me now? Zendaya always sits next to me."

"Well, tonight is different. We have guests, and I don't trust them. I've been trying to find someone to post as a guard outside your door, but apparently, Ulric has already covered that. Sometimes he can be such a great brother. It's nice that he already considers you one of the family."

I cross my arms across my chest. "Are you really you're going to be territorial tonight? I thought you were going to be civil and not cause any trouble with the guests?"

He shares a wolfish smile. "You're mine, not anyone else's. I'm making it clear to them that I'm not to be trifled with when it comes to you."

"Do you feel threatened by our guests that they will steal me away?"

"No, but one can never be too cautious." He grabs my hand and places a kiss on it.

I roll my eyes. Greed and Alora finally walk through the door. We offer pleasant greetings, and the rest of the party joins us shortly after. The entire entourage of vampires fills the room, and I try not to make eye contact with any of them.

After everyone is seated, an awkward silence hangs in the air. Greed smiles intimidatingly at the vampires while we wait for the food. The vampires appear bored. It seems like a game which irks me. Must things be like this? Finally, the servants bring out large platters and even larger pitchers of blood. Everyone begins fixing plates as soon as Greed starts filling his.

After we eat for several minutes, Alora breaks the silence. "How is the food tonight?"

Prince Zuko nods his head before responding. "It's delicious. Am I right in guessing that this is fire bore?"

Alora beams. "It is! I'm pleased you're enjoying it. Is the blood wine to your liking as well?"

Zeke says quietly, bowing his head, "It is my lady. Very flavorful."

The rest of us nod gently, and silence returns. I look around, willing someone to talk, but no one takes a hint. Feeling awkward, I take a deep breath and break the silence. "So, what's it like in vampire territory?"

I feel tension spiral out around me from the fallen who sit at the table, but both princes smile at me, and Zeke even winks.

"It's quite beautiful. Hela has kept it vibrant with various types of plants. It's very similar to the rain forests of Earth, wouldn't you agree, brother?" Zuko nods toward Zeke with a smile.

Zeke smiles in return, and I sense trouble brewing. "Yes, brother, it is. Although, having visited said place, I must admit that our territory is prettier. The humans have lain waste to much of the rainforest after all. Such a pity, honestly, how much they have damaged Earth with pollution and brought on climate change."

I'm surprised and lose my filter somewhat, asking, "Oh, is it truly that gorgeous? How would it compare to the garden here? Persephone created it herself."

Prospero whips his head around to me. "Who told you that?"

Oops. "That was part of the information in the tour Zendaya gave me. Was I not to know she visited here once?"

He looks over at his sister and glares before turning back to me. "Did she mention anything else?"

I tilt my head to the side. "No, should she have?"

Greed snorts and begins to laugh, only collecting himself momentarily to ask, "Are you worried, my boy, that your failed tryst with the goddess will get loose and embarrass you?"

Alora blushes, and Prospero goes deadly still. He looks around the table to assess what the vampires are doing, only to find them both looking on curiously. Zendaya and Ulric both fight to school their features, and I pretend to be clueless. I've strangely gotten good at it.

"No, it doesn't matter. I'm going to marry Ember. Why would it?" He picks up his fork and returns to his meal.

"Oh, but it was quite eventful, son. Tell them how you followed her around like a lost hellhound pup. I don't normally use this term, but adorable seems fitting. She hated to break his sweet heart, but she is married to Hades after all. They were made for each other." Greed chuckles before he sips his wine, and Prospero slams his fist down on the table.

"I'm a much finer male than he, and she knows it. Now, if you'll excuse me, my appetite has been ruined." He pushes away from the table and stands. He walks quickly from the room with a red face. At least he won't try to coerce me to have sex with him tonight.

I turn my gaze back to everyone at the table as the door slams upon his departure. Everyone seems amused but doesn't say a word. I shrug a shoulder and return to my dinner. No sense in letting good food go to waste.

Did you plan that? Ulric's words slip into my thoughts.

No, I did not. I was honestly curious. Zeke has never mentioned anything like that about his home. I smile down at my food.

You never asked, love, but then again, I never gave you the option to ask. Zeke's words make me jump a bit in my chair, but thankfully, it's missed.

I forget you can join in the conversation now. I need more education on this type of thing.

Oh, we'll give you more than that, love. Zeke's words are seductive, and I instantly feel myself clench at the thought.

Not tonight, Zeke. It's too risky for either of us to be with her, let alone together right now. Soon though. Ulric is the voice of reason, and I can't help but frown.

But that sounds fun. Fine. After we get away from here, we'll spend some alone time together—just the three of us.

I do like the sound of that, love. Zeke smiles at me from across the table, and I blush.

Dinner is finished in silence, and I make my way back to my room, escorted by Ulric, Zeke, and Zuko. We share pleasant goodnights, and Ulric gives me a pointed look before leaving. I can't help but ask, "What?"

"Don't come to my room tonight. I fear you'll be caught if you do, especially after how earlier went. I'll see you tomorrow afternoon for training. Zeke will be joining us." He grabs my hand and squeezes it.

I frown, wishing for a kiss but knowing it's not safe to do so out in the hall where anyone could walk up on us, "Okay, I'll stay put. See you tomorrow."

I watch him walk away and turn to enter my room quietly. So much tension hangs in the air in the castle now, and soon, even more guests will arrive. I can't help but wish that the ball and my escape were over with already but then again, what will my new life look like once I return home? How will my mates and I adjust while remaining under the radar from Lucifer's eyes?

I push my troubled thoughts to the back of my mind. No sense in worrying about it right now; it's not like I can control it. I'll revisit those thoughts when we are free from here.

CHAPTER TWENTY-ONE

I'm thankful my hair is pulled back into a braid this afternoon as sweat pours down my neck to my back. Why I thought Zendaya's idea of sparring with both my mates was a good idea is beyond me because I'm regretting it one hundred percent right now.

We spent the first part of this training session, teaching me how to block thoughts and also prepare for mental attacks. I didn't realize that was a huge thing, but I guess being a creature from Hell means more things will come at me in the future. Yay.

I dodge another punch from Ulric and jump, performing a cartwheel as Zeke sweeps his leg in an attempt to knock me to the ground. My wings are out and give me another form of balance as I move. It's different fighting with them in general. I've had to adapt my stances to accompany the new weight.

I maneuver around and use my wings to block Zeke as he attacks from my right, pushing him back. Somehow, a small force of power pulses out toward him when I do it, and he tumbles to the ground. I laugh, but it costs me as Ulric catches me in the side of the face. It knocks me to the ground, and I look up at him with a pout.

"That hurt."

He places his hands on his hips. "Of course it did. Do you expect your enemy to give you slack when you're distracted?"

Zeke laughs, and I glare up at Ulric from the ground as he offers me his hand. "You're my mate. That should count for something, shouldn't it?"

He smiles as I take his hand. "It should, but then I wouldn't be helping you be the best you can be. I want you to be able to defend yourself, little wolf. I don't want anyone to be able to get a hit in on you."

Zeke places a hand on my shoulder after Ulric pulls me to my feet. I'm not sure when he picked himself up off the ground, but I was a bit distracted. "You did good, pulsing that invisible power out at me. When did you learn to do that?"

I tilt my head to the side and think over the last few minutes. "I guess, now? I haven't managed to do that before. Is that another ability surfacing, pertaining to my hellhound?"

Ulric reaches over and taps my wing. "That, love, is an angelic power. I'm impressed that you're getting them so quickly. But, of course, you'll have to work on them more once you're away from here."

I frown at his words because it almost sounds like he won't be there to help me, but he will, right?

Zendaya approaches with a soft smile on her face. "You've come a long way, Ember. I look forward to seeing what the final version of you will end up being once you've mastered all your power. Would you like to go a round with me, now?"

I put my hands on my hips. "Really? I'm exhausted."

"You are, but it would be good for you, Ember. Let's go." Zendaya playfully punches my arm.

"Fine." I drop my shoulders and step into position. My mates step back to watch, but we jump as my ladies' maids appear next to us.

"Sorry to startle you, missus, but Prospero is making his way here as we speak. He is determined to come to the garden to speak with you, Ember," one of them says.

"Shit, seriously? I thought he never came out here. Ulric, you and Zeke need to disappear like ten seconds ago." I glance around as they quickly dive into the foliage around us. I'm not sure if they're hanging around or if they left completely, but I look at Zendaya and hide my wings.

She shrugs. "Let's continue with what we were planning to do. I'll leave only when he has shown his face, and I know things are okay. He hasn't been in here since Persephone left. Maybe that's what this is about? Father did embarrass him last night, which isn't a usual occurrence."

"Great," I grumble out, and we begin to spar gently. Each of us only halfheartedly swings at each other as we wait for Prospero to appear. The garden is my place of safety, but if he begins to come here, that may be gone.

He steps from the darkness of shade covering the path leading to the practice field two minutes later. He's wide-eyed as he takes everything in around him. It reminds me of a newborn seeing the world for the first time.

He spots us and makes his way toward Zendaya and me. We stop and look at him in confusion.

"Brother, what are you doing out here?" Zendaya frowns, and her words seem cautious.

Prospero meets her gaze and then looks at me. "I came to speak with Ember regarding last night's conversation. I also wanted to apologize, love, for my abrupt departure. I hope you'll accept my apology."

I look at him and cross my arms, feigning offense. "I guess I can accept your apology. I thought you didn't like to come to this garden?"

He looks down at his hands. "I'm a little uncomfortable at the moment about being here, but to have a future with you, I need to come clean and get past this. I thought I was in love with Persephone and she with me, but I was wrong. Unfortunately, I didn't realize it until too late, and now my father uses it against me when he sees fit.

"Last night was the first time he has done so in front of guests. He usually is more cautious, but I don't want anyone to find a weakness in me or those close to me. Storming out was not the best decision, but I couldn't control my emotions, for the first time in a long time. I blame that on you, Ember, but it may not be a bad thing. I think you're strengthening me. I can only hope that you'll understand that I don't harbor a flame for her any longer. I wanted to prove that by entering the garden, proving to myself that it's in the past."

I stare at him, bewildered and shocked. His confession has caught me off guard, and he seems genuine. What the hell?

"Okay," I say hesitantly. "I'm not sure what you want me to say."

He grabs my hand and drops to his knees. "Just say that you forgive me so that we can move forward together."

I look down at him even more confused, but I know I need to keep up the ruse. Thank God, the ball is only a couple of days off now. "Okay, I forgive you."

He rushes to his feet and pulls me into a hug. "Thank you. Now, can I join you, ladies, on your training?"

I look over at Zendaya, and she shrugs. "Sure, brother. How about we go first? Ember is a little tired from our round."

I roll my eyes but step back to give them space. I am tired, but she didn't have to point it out.

"Okay, watch how we fight, my love, and take note of my form. I'm one of our best fighters." Prospero seems confident, almost too confident, and Zendaya smiles eagerly. If he's one of the best, I can't help but wonder who is the best.

They both tuck their massive wings in close to their body right before they launch toward each other. Watching them move is impressive. They duck, swing, dodge, and roll as fast as

Zeke moves. I can't help but wonder if I look like that when I fight. Am I that fast now? How does that compare to normal shifters?

Zendaya seems somewhat cheery as she spars with Prospero. It's odd, and I forget for a moment that he is one of the bad guys regarding the situation I'm in. What happened to him in his past to make him the way he is?

It's okay to feel conflicted after his apology. He did, once upon a time, walk a different path. The way Greed handled his mother later in his life is part of why he is the way he is. It affected him more than it did Edsel and me when Greed killed all our mothers.

I startle at Ulric's words as they whisper through my mind. *He killed them?*

Yes. Did you not wonder where they were?

I mean, yes, I did, but I assumed they were somewhere else. So why did he do that?

Ulric's silent for a moment, almost as if he's thinking back. *They conspired to bring him down. Greed has never treated women well, and he has always collected them as if they were trophies. They wanted to put a stop to it, but someone reported their plans. He publicly humiliated them and then ordered them burned. He made us all watch.*

I drop to the grass, watching the fallen angels spar before me, and let Ulric's words swim through my mind.

After that day, Prospero changed, and Greed pushed him to be more like him. But unfortunately, he assumed his mother was the one that corrupted mine. They were in it together, though. We tried to keep him from the path he chose but failed.

My heart started to ache for them all as I imagined what Greed did to push Prospero. It couldn't have been good. He wouldn't be who he is now if it had been.

"What did you think?" I blink, coming out of my thoughts as Prospero and Zendaya stand before me breathless.

"You were both very fast." I smile up at them.

"Thank you. It felt good to spar. I haven't sparred with my sister in years. Let me help you up." He offers me his hand, and I grab it, letting him pull me to standing.

Zendaya remains quiet as she stands close by, and I glance at her. She smiles as she tilts her head, and I look back at Prospero.

"So, love, would you like to spar now?"

"Are you not too tired now?" *Hey, Ulric, Zeke, if I spar with him, do I hold back?*

"Of course not? I'm no weakling, love. I have quite the stamina level."

I roll my eyes at his words and take my time to respond.

No, love, you give him hell. Zeke's words move through my mind.

Just keep your wings hidden. I'm glad we stayed in the bushes. This will be fun to watch, Ulric chimes in.

Yes, it will be fun. Zeke chuckles, and it reverberates down the connection.

"Okay, I'll spar with you." I smile at Prospero and drop his hand that I've still been holding.

"I promise to take it easy on you so that you won't get hurt, love."

"What's the point of sparring if you're going to take it easy on me. No, don't hold back. I can handle it."

Zendaya laughs loudly, then says, "This is going to be fun."

"Am I missing something?" Prospero pauses and looks between the two of us.

I get in position and face him. "Not at all."

He moves into position and looks at me with worry. "If you say so."

I smile but remain in position as our eyes lock. I refuse to move first. Let him come to me.

He shrugs, and I remain still as he sprints toward me. He moves to swing at me with a right-handed punch, but I step to the side, and he breezes past me. I sweep my leg out, and it trips him, but he catches himself. He spins, swinging at me again, and I block his punch.

He steps back, assessing me. "You're much faster than I thought, love."

"I've been practicing." I shrug, and my magic courses through me, heating me.

This time when he moves, I form a shield of fire around me. It causes him to pause, but he amazes me by punching through it. I barely dodge his fist as it sails for me. It lands on my shoulder, and I notice a shimmery appearance around it and determine that he's using his power to coat himself. Impressive.

"That's an impressive trick! It burst through my shield easily," I say, and this time, I go on the offensive. I swing, and he quickly brushes it away, so I amp it up.

Flames burst from me, and I pick up my speed. He responds just as I had hoped, and we meet each other hit for hit. We move around the open space, and I can see he's getting winded. My flames urge me on, and I can hear my mates chuckling in the background of my mind. I will not let him defeat me.

We transition into using our legs to fight each other off and finally use our magic. He launches his mostly invisible magic at me in a wave to push me back, but I don't miss the slight shimmer it causes, and I push back with my flames. It meets his magic, and I amp it up a little, turning the fire black. It causes his magic to disintegrate, and he ducks to the ground to avoid it.

As he lands, I move, pinning him to the ground, and shout, "Game over!"

He stares up at me from the ground. "Holy hell, woman. I didn't know you could use hellfire. Have you always been this strong?"

I move my foot, letting him up, and shrug. "I don't know."

He stands, dusting himself off. "Right. Well, it makes me even happier to know that I'll have you at my side. I think I'm all sparred out now, though."

"I have to agree. You both look worn out." Zendaya takes that moment to walk up to us and hands us both a large cup of water. We take it and eagerly drink it.

"I think I need a shower now." I hand Zendaya my cup. "I'll see you both at dinner later?"

"Yes. I'll go shower as well before then. See you then, love." Prospero returns to sipping on his water, and I nod before taking my leave.

CHAPTER TWENTY-TWO

I leave my clothes in a pile by the bed and move to the bathroom in my room. I smell of smoke and lavender as well as sweat. I turn the water on and twist as I feel a slight breeze move around me. I smile as I find Zeke leaning against the vanity.

"You are sneaky, aren't you?"

He smiles and moves toward me. He grabs me and pulls me into him. "I am. What better time to make love to my mate, though, than in the shower? It'll cover our scent, mostly. Plus, you have me all worked up after kicking that fallen's ass."

I laugh at his words, and he silences me with a kiss. It's deep and passionate, and I bring my hands up to begin to remove his shirt.

Don't get caught, you two. I'm tempted to join.

Ulric's words cause me to laugh, and I sassily respond, *What's stopping you?*

I get Zeke's shirt off, and he helps me with his pants. We're in the steamy water in seconds, and then a gruff, "Make room," is said outside the shower.

I lift my head, and Zeke pauses. We watch as Ulric enters the shower too.

"Holy hell, are we really doing this?"

"Yes, love, I think we are. Don't be shy. We are both yours," Zeke encourages as he turns and presses me into Ulric.

He wraps his arms around me before kissing my neck and playing with my nipples. I moan, and then I feel light kisses on my thighs. Having closed them on the moan, I force my eyes open and see Zeke kneeling between my knees. I know exactly what he's going to do next, and I feel eager for it.

I watch as he makes his way up while Ulric continues to tease my nipples. My body feels like it's on fire, but there are no flames. When Zeke finds my sex, my knees try to buckle, but Ulric catches me. He bites into my shoulder, and the pain brings me to the edge. I moan as Zeke laps at me with his tongue and drags his pointed canines across my sensitive area. Ulric sucks and licks where he bit me, sending small pulses of pleasure down my spine.

"Oh God!" My knees try to give again.

"I think she's enjoying this," Zeke says from between my legs, and the vibrations cause me to moan again.

"Yes, she is," Ulric says behind my ear.

"I think it's time, love," Zeke says, and his fingers begin to work their magic while he sucks.

I can't hold back anymore, and I plummet off the edge as I climax. I scream, and my body goes slack, but I don't fall. Instead, Ulric turns me and pushes me against the shower wall before quickly inserting himself into me.

He pushes, and I moan as he seats himself deeply and begins to pump in and out. The shower is exceptionally steamy, and I realize my magic is coursing through my veins, heating it even more. Finally, we plummet together, and I cry out his name loudly. I'm startled as he passes me to Zeke's arms.

"I hope you can handle one more round, love." He leans into

me and bites down on my shoulder hard. I feel his teeth sink in and note that it's on the opposite shoulder of where Ulric bit me. I feel him sheath himself into my slick folds. I moan, "Zeke."

"Yes, love, say my name." He begins his own method and rhythmically pumps in and out.

Somehow, we climax together, and this time he rests us on the shower bench as we fall from our high. I sit utterly exhausted and watch as both of my mates wash themselves and me. How they have the energy is beyond me, but seeing their magnificent naked bodies makes my day. I feel myself begin to regain my energy as they finish washing.

"Holy shit, I can't believe we just did that. I've never done something like that before."

"Well, I hope you haven't. I might have to hurt someone if you did. We're your mates," Ulric grumbles as he washes his hair with my shampoo.

"I think we'll be doing more of this again soon. I loved watching you climax," Zeke says and pulls me from the bench.

Ulric turns the water off, and I'm guided out of the shower to stand on the soft bathmat. Both of my mates wrap me in towels and begin to dry me off. I stand there, letting them, unsure of what to do. I've never had anyone do this for me before, but it feels good. I feel adored, and I can tell they enjoy expressing their love this way via our connection.

"I feel sleepy now. How frowned upon would it be if I skipped dinner tonight?" I yawn and step away from them as I move toward the main part of my room to the wardrobe.

I hear them slide back into their clothes, and soon they stand beside me as I dress. They both appear relaxed and at ease after our lovemaking.

"I don't think it will bother anyone if you choose to stay here. I can make sure that food is sent to your room." Ulric's voice sounds deeper as it floats to my ears.

After I pull my top over my head, Ulric wraps his arms around me, and Zeke rests his chin on my shoulder.

"That sounds wonderful. Will you both stay or go?" I turn my head and place a light kiss on Zeke's cheek.

"I think it would be suspicious if I were missing, seeing as I'm a guest here," Zeke says softly.

"I could miss, but if you're not there, Prospero may come looking. Getting caught lying in bed with you might not be good, especially after that apology he gave you earlier. We're almost to the time for escape. We have to be very cautious for the next few days." Ulric places a kiss on my head and then releases me.

"Ugh, can't we just be past it so I can have you both with me all the time?" I grumble and step away from them, feeling fatigue weigh on me heavily.

Zeke chuckles as he says, "Soon, love. It's coming soon. Have patience."

I move toward my bed and throw back the blankets. I crawl in as I say, "I know but ugh. Okay, I'm going to call it a day. Would you mind letting my maids know to send in dinner? I'll see you all tomorrow. Oh, and tell them I don't want to be disturbed. Maybe that will keep Prospero from bothering me."

"I'll see what I can do, little wolf." Ulric moves toward the door, and I smile at him and Zeke sleepily. I watch them leave before lying back on the pillows and closing my eyes. I'm content and relaxed, perfect for sleeping.

CHAPTER TWENTY-THREE

I sit at my mirror days later, letting my maids style my hair and apply my makeup. It's finally the day of the ball, and thankfully, they have let no one disturb me. My nerves have been a mess. So much is riding on things going smoothly tonight, and I fear that something will happen to send everything off track. It's a feeling deep in my gut.

My dress hangs on my wardrobe nearby, and the weapons I have for tonight rest behind it. Ulric made sure to grab a slender sword that I have had little practice with, but he said it might come in handy. I hope I don't have to use it. I also have a few daggers that will be hidden on my person.

The dress I'm to wear is deep red. It's showy and flattering but also has pants beneath its billowing skirts. The skirt is made to be torn away, if necessary, which Zendaya specifically requested of the seamstresses. They didn't question why. I guess fights break out at balls here when they happen. With what I've learned of Greed's attitude, it doesn't surprise me.

My maids style my hair into a gorgeous updo with curls and small diamonds nestled into it. The room smells of hairspray, and I swear a thick layer rests across my bare arms. My ladies' maids use so much that nothing should move unless water is poured atop my head.

They choose to do my eyes elegantly with shades of browns and a black eyeliner that makes them pop. I smile in the mirror as they hand me a tube of lipstick to let me apply. "Thank you both so very much. I hate that I've never taken the time to ask your names. Will you forgive me for asking now?"

"It's fine, miss. We don't take offense. Our names are Janine and Jainee. Let's finish getting you ready for tonight. A lot is riding on you being ready. We have our own part to play in aiding you tonight," Janine says, and Jainee nods in agreement.

"Right. I know I should be focusing on what to do tonight, but I'm extremely nervous. I'm going to miss you both as well as a few of the others here. I hope one day, we can see each other again but under different circumstances."

Jainee nods. "I'm sure we will. Let's get you into your dress. It's almost time to meet Prospero for your last night of the false engagement. You can do this."

I nod in agreement and push from the chair. My body feels stiff from sitting for so long, but it takes time to be gorgeous for something like this, and I can't let my role fall short because I'm anxious to be home.

I move with them toward my dress, and they hold it out for me to step into. Once on, they hand me my weapons and help me place them in the correct spots. I run through the exits I'll need to take and when, as they grab my shoes. Thankfully, I'm not wearing heels tonight but flats that hug my feet. It'll be much easier to maneuver around in them than heels, especially if I need to run. Then again, if I need to go a great distance, I may just shift.

I finish adjusting a few of the daggers hidden within my dress and stand to look at myself in the mirror. Everything is hidden, and I look stunning. I touch my left diamond earring and finger it for a brief moment before letting out a sigh. I hope

I don't lose any of the jewels they put on me. I would love to keep them. I know it's a silly thought and not necessary, but it gives me something else to focus on.

"Okay, I'm ready." I smile, and my maids walk with me to the door.

As I open it, I'm not surprised to see the group standing in the hall. Zeke approaches me and takes my hand. He bends down to kiss it, holding my gaze.

"You look stunning, love. Like a bright star shining in the sky, you are radiant." He releases my hand, and Ulric grabs it, pulling me toward him gently.

"You're absolutely gorgeous, little wolf." He, too, kisses my hand.

Zuko bows his head as he says, "You're lovely tonight, dear. Are you ready for the events?"

I nod and let Ulric keep my hand as Zeke steps back to play the part of a prince again. "I'm nervous, but we'll do what needs to be done. But, Ulric, will Prospero not question why you're escorting me?"

"No, because I'm escorting them." He uses his free hand to point at the vampire princes. "We just happened to walk by your door when you came out, and you joined us." He shrugs.

"I guess that'll work. You all look very nice," I say as I take in their black tuxes. The three of them alone could easily steal the show with their good looks. They seem to radiate power and strength, which will draw many toward them. It pulls at me even now, but I'm confident of my connection to them. Ladies will be throwing themselves at their feet tonight.

"I do believe we should be on our way," Zuko drawls out, pulling our attention to him. "We need to make sure that we hold up appearances while my guards begin leading the girls out. I believe your maids will be helping them, Ember."

I turn to look over my shoulder at the door to my room and find it empty. I didn't hear them when they popped away, but

I'm thankful they are loyal to us. It's going to make a tremendous difference, especially if the women find it challenging to trust vampires.

"How long do you think it'll take for them to get all of the women to safety?"

Ulric places his hand underneath his chin, "It shouldn't take too long. They will be quick, I'm sure, especially with your maids being able to pop from one place to another. Their power is uniquely handy, being able to move through space like that. They should be able to take some of the girls directly to the gate and out."

My lips form a firm line, and I ask, "Are Kai and the others prepared and at the gate on the other side? Has someone made sure they're ready?"

Ulric smirks and takes a second to think it over. "I believe they are. We will have to double-check with Zendaya. Either way, they will be safe because the guards will not leave them if Kai or their people are not there yet. They'll move them as far away from the gate as possible while also keeping them safe."

I frown. "How long will it be until I can leave for the gate? Do you have a distraction and a backup plan? What if it doesn't work?"

"Don't doubt us, love. We have everything under control." Zeke grabs my other hand and plants a kiss on it again. It's comforting.

"Have faith, little wolf." Ulric beams at me.

"I think we should go now," Zuko chimes in.

"You're right. Let's do this and get the show on the road." I drop both of my mates' hands and make my way down the hall ahead of them. "Let's be prepared in case we run into Prospero before we arrive at the ballroom. He doesn't need to think we're together."

I feel a calm descend upon me as I take step after step down the hall. I let my magic course through my veins, and it reassures me that things will be okay. But the outcome of tonight is crucial, and I fear that we will not all make it out alive.

Moving through the halls, I notice things look different. Torches are brighter and more flowers rest in vases. Even garlands of flowers hang on the walls, creating a pleasant floral scent. It makes me wonder if Alora gathers things from Persephone's garden or if she has them brought in. I've never seen her there.

Minutes later, we stand outside the great doors to the ballroom. Prospero and Zendaya both stand, waiting for us in front of the doors. Two servants stand at the door, waiting for us to enter.

"My, you look ravishing," Prospero declares, walking toward me. He takes both of my hands and pulls me into a passionate kiss. It sends chills down my spine but not the good kind, and I fight stiffening in his embrace. I remind myself that I will no longer have to keep up this appearance just a few hours from now.

"Thank you. You're handsome yourself." I step back from his embrace and offer him a smile. It seems to appease him.

Zendaya approaches with a smile on her face. "You all look excellent. I love the outfit you're wearing, Ember."

I give her an award-winning smile, knowing that she hand-picked it for me. "Thank you! You look gorgeous as well, my friend. My outfit fits well, and I love the way it feels. I do have great help when it comes to picking them, you know." I wink, and she laughs.

"Stop fishing for compliments, Zendaya. We all know you helped her with her choice," Prospero grumbles, making us laugh even more.

Getting it together, Zendaya says, "It still looks amazing on her. You guys can't deny that. I mean, just look at her! Twirl for us, Ember."

I frown, but I do as she asks, and I can't help but admire the smiling faces around me as I do it. It makes me feel like a princess, but then again, I guess I am a princess if I'm Lucifer's daughter, not that I'll ever claim it.

Prospero reaches for my hand, holding it gently. "Shall we enter the ball?"

Feeling better after my twirl, I nod eagerly. "Yes."

He squeezes my hand, and we enter through the doors. I'm amazed at how the room has transformed. Where there were once open floors with nothing but paintings hanging on the walls, there now rests food tables and an open dance floor. The enormous chandeliers are lit with bright candles, and other candles are scattered throughout the room. It appears very old-fashioned, but it's also comforting. I especially love the warm light it creates.

I turn my attention to the tables covered in food. Alora chose black tablecloths, which causes the food to stand out against the dark color. People are scattered throughout the room standing and chatting as well as moving on the dance floor, dancing a waltz of some type.

I frown and turn toward Prospero and glance behind me at my mates. "I don't know how to dance like that."

Prospero chuckles. "Don't worry, I'll take care of you. If we dance, just follow my lead."

"Are you sure we can't just skip the dancing?" I turn back to look at the dancers on the floor as they move gracefully. It's evident that dancing comes second nature to them with how fluid they are with each move.

"Yes, we have to dance. My father is the host. He won't allow us to skip out. All his children must dance at least once." He squeezes my hand. "How about we dance now and then you can mingle? I have a lot of people for you to meet."

I gulp and feel my palms begin to sweat. How am I going to do this? This is nothing like what I know. "Okay, I guess."

"Be confident, Ember. It'll be fine." He leads me to the floor, and I paste on a smile as eyes follow our movements.

He gently spins me closer into his arms and adjusts my hands as the next song begins to play. Now that I'm in the center of the room, I can see a small band or an orchestra playing in a corner tucked at the back of the room. It's made up of various types of demons.

I force myself to relax as Prospero guides me through the dance, and thankfully, I don't step on his toes or trip as we move. I glance out of the side of my eye as we move at the different angels around us. Their wings are of various shades, but none of them are white. It makes me feel slightly better, knowing Lucifer isn't here.

As the dance finally ends, I let my shoulders sag, and Prospero leads me from the floor toward one of the tables. "You did well, Ember."

"Thanks, I guess. You did all the work."

He chuckles. "I can't make your feet move. However, I think you could easily master these dances with some practice. You're quite graceful."

I roll my eyes. "Thanks for the confidence boost. I think it'll take longer than you think."

"We have plenty of time. Oh, look, here come some of my old friends." He nods his head at a small group of males and one female. The males are all angels with dark black wings and dark brown hair. Their features are similar, and I assume they are brothers.

CHAPTER TWENTY-FOUR

The group of partygoers stops before us and bow lightly to Prospero, and my attention lands on the young female who doesn't have wings. Her hair is a long sandy blond and styled in curls that drop to her hips. There is a small bump at her stomach, and I realize she's carrying a child and isn't that far along. I let my gaze meet her green-eyed one, and I pale. I know her.

She blinks as she realizes who I am and goes to say something but stops as I shake my head. *Can you hear me?* I ask her through the telepathic connection our pack uses.

Yes! Oh my God, Ember, they got you too? How?

I sacrificed myself so they wouldn't hurt Adam or Corey. Don't worry, though. I'll get you out of here.

How will you get us out of here?

"Ember, this is Konrad, Magi, and Stole. My father trained the four of us together years ago. They are triplets and some of the best warriors in our army. This is their shifter my father gifted to them. Magi, what is her name again?" Prospero interrupts my conversation with my old friend.

"This is Amber. She is mine and is carrying my first child.

Isn't she gorgeous?" Magi pulls her before us, and I cringe at how roughly he pushes her.

I paste on a smile, hiding the anger simmering beneath my skin. "It's a pleasure to meet you all."

"Ember is my betrothed. We'll be planning our wedding soon. We hope to see you there," Prospero declares with a massive grin.

"We absolutely will be, won't we, brothers? Magi and Stole may steal the show, though. You know how they get." Konrad chuckles.

"You're not any better Konrad. Maybe Magi's son will be here by then." Stole looks pointedly at Amber's belly. "I wanted her for myself, but Magi defeated us in our challenge to have her. You think your father will give us another?"

"Why don't you all go make yourselves comfortable while I chat with Amber here?" I add to the conversation without thinking, and they all look at me confused.

"Why would we do that?" Stole asks, eyeing me.

"To catch up, of course! How long has it been since you all relaxed? It is a ball after all, isn't it?" I smile and reach for Amber's hand, gently pulling her toward me.

"I like her, Prospero. She'll be excellent for you. Come on. Amber will be fine with her, Magi. She may be our future queen after all, if things go according to plans and Greed passes on his title to our man here." Konrad shrugs and looks over at the table with the alcohol across the room.

Magi looks me over and then looks at Amber. "Fine. I'll come to find you when Lucifer arrives."

"What? Lucifer is coming?" I ask aloud and blanch, not intending to voice my thoughts.

"Of course he is, love. Did you miss the other fallen leaders in the room? I would introduce you to them, but it's not proper to approach them unless they allow it. Usually, that doesn't happen until Lucifer appears. They wouldn't be here if he weren't coming. I thought you knew that." Prospero frowns.

"I guess, I forgot. I'm sorry. You all go. Amber will be fine with me." I shake my head and smile at them all convincingly.

Prospero leans in to kiss my cheek. "Okay, I'll be back soon."

As they move away, talking animatedly, I pull Amber closer to my side. "How far along are you?"

"I think four months. Why?" She looks at me, concerned.

I lean in and whisper, "Because I'm getting you out of here tonight. Do you know if they gave other girls to any other warriors?"

She shakes her head. "As far as I know, I'm the only one, but there could have been others before me. They won't tell me why they kidnapped us."

"They're building an army to take on Lucifer, and they need hellhounds. Apparently, only shifters and hellhounds can produce hellhounds. Nonetheless, I'm getting you home."

"I would love that more than anything, Ember, but how are we going to do that? We're in Hell." She glances around the room, noting where the males she came with are.

I let out a sigh. "I have a way, Amber, but you're going to have to trust me." I take a moment to narrow my communication channel and put my blocks up as I reach out to my mates. *Can you two come here?*

Ulric responds, *Yes, is everything okay?*

I look around and spot Zeke and Zuko moving toward us, slowly grinning and greeting guests as they move, fulfilling the appearance of vampire royals. I can't spot Ulric, though. *Ulric, where are you?*

A tap on my shoulder has me turning around to his smiling face. "I'm right here. What's going on?" He glances over at Amber, who pales.

"It's okay, Amber," I whisper. "This is my mate, Ulric, and you remember Zeke?"

"Oh, and yes, why?" She looks around, and her eyes widen as he approaches with Zuko.

Zeke frowns as he glances between us. "I thought you were dead, Amber?"

"I thought I would be too," she states quietly, looking at us all.

"Amber, this is Ulric and Zuko. We're all going to work to get you out of here with the rest of the girls." I look pointedly at Ulric and spot Zendaya watching us closely from across the room.

"How are we going to get her to the others without her being missed? She's with someone if she's here. Who are you with?" Ulric asks softly, and she glances across the room to where Magi appears to be watching us.

Ulric follows her gaze. "He brought me," she gets out, barely audible.

"Shit, that's not going to be easy," Ulric says under his breath.

"We'll make it happen," Zeke adds.

At that moment, a horn blares, and everyone turns to the door. It opens, and a tall male with white wings steps through, followed by a mixed group of individuals—some with wings and some without. I stare in awe and immediately see similarities between him and me

"Shit," I say aloud, and Amber turns to me, trying to figure out what's wrong.

"It'll be okay, Ember. Keep your distance and don't draw attention. That distraction we discussed is going to happen soon. You and Amber will go with Zeke at that point and escape," Ulric says quietly as the room is still quiet, watching the king of Hell as he makes his way toward Greed and the group of fallen across the room. I recognize them from the picture but didn't see them before as I danced.

"What exactly is the distraction?" I continue to watch

Lucifer's group and then glance over at Prospero, who has a pained expression on his face.

"Persephone came with Lucifer." Zuko's voice snaps my attention to him, and I look back to the group to see a beautiful woman walking hand in hand with another male several steps behind Lucifer. She has long dark hair and striking green eyes. She's curvy, and her dress hugs her body like a fitted glove. Hades, the man with her, is dressed just as nice and has a pleasant smile on his face. His black hair and tan skin resemble Lucifer some, and I can't help but wonder if they're related.

"Oh shit." I look back at Prospero, whose eyes are glued to the woman. He seems to fight moving as the group with Lucifer stops.

"It's time," Ulric says and nudges me toward Zeke. "Zeke, remember to go to the gate and get her to Kai before you come back here."

"Wait, you're not coming?" I turn to him.

"I can't. If we are to keep their eyes away from you and on the distraction, I have to stay. Otherwise, who else is going to enrage Prospero so much that he forgets you're not in the room?" Ulric grabs my hand and squeezes.

"I don't like that idea, Ulric. I wish you had told me beforehand. We could have come up with something else." I cross my arms.

"It'll be okay, little wolf. Now go with Zeke," he urges, and I grab Amber's hand.

The sound of greetings fills the air as Lucifer's party stands before the rest of the fallen leaders. It gives a great cover for us as we quickly follow Zeke through the crowd toward the servants' entrance. Zuko follows behind us, watching our backs as we move.

We quickly move behind the tapestry and down the corridor. It's much darker than the room we were just in and smells musty, but I push all this to the back of my mind as I keep my grip on Amber's hand. I'm not leaving her here. My childhood best friend is not dead like I initially thought, and I'm making sure she gets home.

Zeke tries to take a turn to the right up ahead, and I stop him, pulling him the other way. There is a faster way to get us where we need to be.

Do you know if the rest of the girls are at the gate, Zeke? I reach out through our bond as we continue to move. Amber stumbles, but I help her regain her footing. I don't want her falling and injuring herself or the baby.

I believe so. I didn't have time to check before we had to leave. I thought we had more time. I wish Ulric had shared that tidbit about the distraction. Do you think it'll work?

I hope it does. After what Prospero said to me the other day, I have my doubts. I'm choosing to ignore them, though.

Amber tugs on my arm. "Ember, can we slow down? I can't keep up with you all. I'm extremely out of shape, and you all move faster than normal shifters. Why is that? I know Zeke is a vampire, and I assume he is too, but you didn't have this before. What happened to you?"

I slow our pace but keep us moving. "I'm not a shifter, Amber. I'm a hellhound. I found that out after we discovered demons had attacked your home."

She sucks in a breath. "My parents?"

"They weren't there, Amber. I can only assume that they were killed or taken like you were. A demon was masking itself as your mother and attacked me as I tried to help. That's what released my magic. After that, a lot of changes happened but it's more than we can discuss now You're safe with us. I hope you understand that." I catch Zeke looking over his shoulder at us, and I hear a hiss behind us.

I glance over my shoulder to see Zeke frowning. "We have followers. I didn't think anyone saw us leave."

"Oh God, it's them. They're coming for me," Amber squeals

and begins to shake. I refuse to let her stop, though, and drag her with me as we continue to move forward.

"Come on. We can make it. It's not much farther, and then we have to sprint across a field. But, Amber, if we need to carry you to get you out of here, we can make it happen."

She meets my gaze. "I think I can make it. I don't want to ever go back with them."

Zeke pushes through a door ahead of us, and an eerie red glow greets us. "Give her to me. I can sprint across the field with her while you and Zuko follow."

I push Amber toward him, and he gracefully encourages her to climb on his back to piggyback. We step out of the door into a huge grassy field, and I spy a glowing gate on the other side. It's much further than I expected, and I'm glad Zeke encouraged her to get on his back. There is no way she would have made it that far. I just hope the others didn't struggle too much. It's still a long way to pack land once we get to the other side.

"We need to move now. I can hear them getting closer. I'll try to stall them. Be safe, brother. I'll see you again soon. Ember, take care, and Amber, stay strong." Zuko nods at each of us before stepping back into the door and closing it.

I turn and begin to sprint toward the other side of the field. Zeke follows along beside me, and I glance up to see Amber with her head pressed down into his shoulder with her eyes closed. She appears scared, and I don't blame her. My adrenaline keeps my fear at bay currently, but who knows what will happen when it stops.

"When we get to the gate, we may have to destroy it from the other side. If they get past Zuko, whoever it is could follow us into the earth realm. We don't want the other women to be discovered missing until we have them safely with the pack," Zeke says beside me.

"We'll do what we must," I say as a blast sounds behind me. I pause to look over my shoulder and spy the three brothers glaring at us through a busted door. "Shit, this isn't good."

"Keep moving, Ember. We're almost there," Zeke says, and I turn around to see him a ways in front of me.

I begin to run again but glance over my shoulder. What I see causes my stomach to drop—they're flying toward us faster than we can move.

"Get her through the gate, Zeke. I'm going to hold them off." I stop and spin on my heels to face them.

"Ember, no! You have to come! We'll destroy the gate together!" he shouts, but I refuse to turn to look at him.

"We won't have time. Get her through and get ready to blow it. Only then will I stop to get away. It'll have to be quick. Go, Zeke!" I glare at the three now flying toward me and take a deep breath. The triplets land in front of me, and I let my wings unfurl and be seen.

"Well, aren't you a thieving and deceiving bitch? Is Prospero in on your escape? I doubt that since he's not here. I knew something was up when Persephone showed her pretty little face. So where is my shifter going?" Magi glares at me and reaches for something behind his back.

I frown as he pulls out a sword and his brothers follow his lead, pulling out their own. "She is going home. How dare you take someone from my pack like that!"

"We didn't take her, remember? She was a gift from Greed. How dare you deny him. He will overthrow Lucifer and control this realm. Move aside, so we don't have to kill you. You'll be invaluable to Prospero, it appears, with your breeding," Stole growls out.

"Yes, it's not often Lucifer has offspring. Does he even know you exist? The last child born of his was killed years ago. We made sure of that." Konrad flicks his wrist as if loosening it.

I feel my stomach turn. "You killed his child?"

Konrad smiles viciously. "It was a lot of fun. She was foolish and young. She came with us willingly, and well, I'm sure you can imagine what happened next."

I wanted to hurl, and anger surged through my veins. Taking a deep breath, I let the heat fill me and feel fire encase my wings.

"That's a nice trick. But, of course, we have our own as well." Stole smiles, and I brace myself as his eyes shift and he attacks.

As he moves forward, I release a fire blast that pushes him back into his brothers. It gives me two seconds to whip out the sword I have hidden. I'm thankful now that I have it, even though I wasn't sure about it, to begin with.

Regaining his footing, Stole and his brothers move as one and surround me. I pull up what it was like fighting my mates and release a flurry of counterattacks as they attempt to cut me down. I see surprise in their eyes as they realize I have more skills than they expected.

I maneuver around, continuing to block them and giving Zeke more time to get Amber to the gate. That's all I care about. If I get trapped in here, and they all get free, then so be it. I'll find another way to get home. I just have to keep these assholes from cutting me down.

Each time I try to get them closer together, they throw me off with a different attack. I can't help but wonder if they're communicating as I do with my mates. Then again, they have been fighting for centuries where I've only lived for nineteen years. They have way more experience than I do.

I risk it to glance toward the gate and see Zeke pass through, but it costs me as one of them slices down my shoulder with their blade. I scream in pain and stumble back, barely catching myself. I block the next one, but a shout makes all of us pause.

Ulric and Prospero are running toward us. Ulric is sporting a black eye and looks pissed. I try to take advantage of the three males being distracted and move to sprint toward the gate, but Magi stops me by sinking his sword into my side. I feel it glance off the top of my hip bone, and I fall to the ground as he yanks it out.

"You're not getting away that easy bitch!" Magi yells, and as he goes to swing again, a blast knocks him away, and Ulric stands before me.

"Don't you fucking touch my mate again!" he roars.

Prospero stops beside him, ready to battle but looks at me over his shoulder in confusion. "Mate?" His eyes widen as he takes in my wings and then looks back at Ulric. Stole, Magi, and Konrad stand with their swords raised, watching us.

I look back at Prospero. "Yes, Ulric is my mate."

He looks pained as he looks at Ulric and then back at me. "How long have you known?"

I clutch at my side, willing it to stop bleeding. "Since you came to my pack's land."

He looks surprised, and I'm thankful Ulric continues to watch the three bastards. "You remember?"

I laugh like a lunatic. "Yes. Ulric broke through the memory charm you had put on me the second day I was awake."

He growls, but Zuko bursting through the door and attacking Stole from behind breaks everyone's focus, and chaos ensues. Ulric launches himself at Magi, and Konrad engages Prospero as I lay on the ground, trying to figure out how to get to the damned gate without bleeding out.

Stole goes down, and Zuko lops off his head before sprinting to me. "Fuck, you look bad, Ember. We gotta get you to the gate."

"Like hell, you're not taking her anywhere, vampire!" Prospero knocks Konrad to the ground and turns on us.

Ulric finally takes Magi down, but I can't tell if he's dead or unconscious before Ulric steps between Zuko and his brother. "She is leaving, Prospero. She doesn't belong to you."

"Then I'll make sure she never remembers. I've finally started to feel again, and this is what you do to me? You leave! You're no better than that other bitch. She's here tonight because of you, brother. I understand that now. Well, if I can't have the woman I love, then you can't either!" Prospero roars, and I prepare for him to throw his sword at Zuko and I, but instead, he stabs Ulric in the chest.

"No!" I scream, and a massive blast of power ruptures from me. It sends hellfire directly toward Prospero while somehow managing to encompass Ulric in bright white light. Prospero flies backward and lands on the ground with black flames dancing across his body. They leave welts in places, but he shakes them off and stands, glaring at me.

Zuko moves forward and catches Ulric, and I feel someone pick me up off the ground. I turn my gaze away from Ulric to find Zeke looking down on me. Everything is hazy around us, and my vision swims.

"Get her out of here!" Ulric's words make me focus momentarily, and I find him. He's on the ground behind Zuko as Prospero attempts to get through him to his brother.

"We can't leave him, Zeke. I need him," I whisper, and he shakes his head.

"I have to get you out of here, love. We can't stay."

I move my head and vomit blood before we can move. I begin to cry. I feel like I'm dying, but why? I should be healing, shouldn't I? "Please," I beg, and he frowns.

I gasp as he moves and close my eyes as I begin to feel dizzy. I must be losing a lot of blood.

"Once we're through the gate and it's destroyed, I can give you some of my blood. It'll help you heal. Your healing isn't kicking in because your magic is depleted. It's going to be okay, love," he says against my head, and I cry even harder.

I look up as we approach the gate and notice how pretty it looks. Swirling blues make me think of something from outer space, and I feel like I'm floating as we pass through it. I blink as the sensation falls away and glance up at a dark sky filled with stars. It's warm, and I know we are back on Earth.

The smell of grass and wildflowers fills my nostrils as I glance around. My eyes land on a male with glowing red eyes not far from the gate. He strides toward Zeke and me, and I feel my body grow weak again as my vision gets spotty.

"I'll take her while you get the gate, Prince." His deep voice causes my heart to race.

I look at Zeke, who nods and passes me into the man's arms. I scream as what feels like fire dances down my spine, similar to what I felt when I touched Ulric for the first time but stronger.

The male holds me closer and looks down at me. "Hey, you're going to be okay in just a minute. You're safe. I'm Kai. I'll get Zeke to give you his blood, and we'll get you fixed up. Just hang on."

Tears slip down my cheek as it registers that this is the man Ulric doesn't get along with, and it so happens that he is my third mate. Fuck, is Ulric even going to live? Will I only have two mates? Does Kai feel what I feel?

I mumble as I grip his arm, "Thank you." My vision starts to fade.

A loud boom causes me to jolt, but I know instantly it's not good as more blood rushes from my side. Shit.

"Fuck, Zeke, hurry it up, or we're going to lose her!" Kai sounds urgent, and I faintly hear footsteps drawing closer.

The scent hits me first as Zeke leans in closer to me. He presses his wrist to my mouth. "Drink. It's not too terrible, love, I promise."

I lap at the blood coming from his wrist and fight my darkening vision. I'm going to black out. There's no stopping it.

"You know I have to report this, Zeke. She's his daughter." Kai's words drift to my ears, and I stiffen.

"We'll discuss this later. Let's get her home first. Give her some time." Zeke seems to say it softly, but then again, I can't tell.

The taste of the sweet yet coppery fluid lingers in my mouth, and I feel my magic reaching toward it in my belly. Finally, it seems to know what to do, and I'm glad. I softly smile as my limbs grow heavy, and I stop drinking from the wrist pressed against my lips as I slowly slip into darkness.

CHAPTER TWENTY-FIVE

I feel as if I'm floating in the ocean. The waves push me, and I look up and see Ulric. His wings fan out, holding him above me. I reach for him, but a bright light pulses around him, and he's gone. I cry out his name, but nothing happens. Instead, I feel myself sink beneath the dark waves, descending to the unknown depths below, and then there is nothing.

Sunlight wakes me, and I take in the familiar room around me. It seems like a dream, but at the same time not. I push up from the bed and stretch, letting my wings stretch as well. I look down at my body and realize I'm wearing a male's pair of boxers and a t-shirt. It's then that reality comes crashing back in, and I jolt from the bed sitting in the middle of Adam's room at the pack house.

"Fuck!" I say before bursting into the hall and looking for someone, anyone. *Zeke, where the hell are you?* My emotions are all over the place as everything comes crashing back to reality. I may have lost Ulric, and there is a deep pain resting in my heart. I need to know if he's okay, and I need Zeke. Where is he?

I follow the hall into the family living room and stop as I stare at the group sitting on the couches. They look exhausted but smile when they see me. Adam and Corey are seated on one of the large couches behind a coffee table covered in coffee mugs. My parents sit across from them and immediately stand from the couch and rush toward me.

The windows between the bookshelves let in the bright sunlight from beyond. It distracts me momentarily as I realize how long it's been since I've seen the sun's rays. I forgot how beautiful it is.

"Honey, you're awake! I'm so glad you're okay." My mom wraps me in her arms, and my dad encircles us both.

"We thought we lost you, sweetheart," he chokes out, and I feel fat tears fall from my eyes.

"I didn't know if I would ever get back." I nuzzle into them, breathing in their scents. I pull my wings in closer, and they adjust their hold around me. I missed their hugs.

They step back and look at me, and I meet their gaze as I wipe at my cheeks. "Where is Zeke?"

"He should be back any minute. He went to get some of your clothes. He argued with Adam that you wouldn't be pleased when you woke up in his clothes," my mom says, pushing my hair out of my face.

I chuckle. "I'm not. I hope he gets here soon." I glance down at my body and grimace. At least someone cleaned me up, and my wounds feel healed. It must have been whatever Zeke made me drink. Wait, was that his blood?

My dad grabs my hand and pulls me toward the couch they previously occupied. "Sweetheart, are you hungry?"

I look over at Corey and Adam, who watch on in concern and then down at the table in front of them. "I guess I could eat, yes."

Mom encourages me to sit and places pillows around my wings. "Okay, you stay here with your mate, and we'll go to the kitchen."

A growl escapes me at her words. "My mate is not present.

Please do not refer to anyone else as such."

The room goes silent as they all stare at me. I look them all in the eye, challenging them to state otherwise before my mother nods and pulls my dad from the room.

"You found your mate?" Adam asks hesitantly from across the room, and I meet his gaze. He appears bewildered and sad.

My emotions dance all over my mind as I take them both in. They look weary. I still care for them, but neither one will hold the place of a true mate in my life. It's not the same despite what I had with either of them in the past.

"Yes, I did. I have more than one." I cross my arms across my chest as they both look shocked. I push the painful emotions fighting to rear their head after the battle last night. I still don't know if Ulric is alive, let alone made it. I can't sense him, and I don't know if that's because I'm in a different realm or what. It shouldn't matter, though, should it?

"You have more than one?" Corey asks, bewildered.

"I do. I'm sorry, my brain is a jumble right now. Do you think you can tell me what happened after Zendaya took me?" I drop my arms and lean forward. I wince as my side twinges, and I reach down to feel where I was stabbed. I guess it's still tender.

"When she took you, the entire Turner pack spent days scouring the woods. We couldn't even find a trace. Finally, we gave up after months and returned home. Zeke was furious for the first few weeks before he disappeared. He didn't tell us where he was going, but obviously, he found you." Corey shrugs, and what he said registers in my mind.

"Wait, how long have I been gone?" I look at them as they look away, and then Adam meets my gaze.

"It's been a year, Ember," he says and then stands, moving closer to me. He kneels before me on the ground and looks up into my eyes.

"I thought I lost you. I finally let myself fall for you, and they take you. I have been living in hell since that day. Will you give us another chance, please? I know you found your mates, but maybe you can still care for me as well and help me lead this pack. I want you at my side. No one else." Adam rests his hand on my knee, and I instantly flare my wings out. It startles him, and he pulls it away.

A knock sounds at the door briefly before it opens, and Zeke enters. He tilts his head as he takes in Adam before me and then moves to my side with a pile of clothes in his hands. He seems tense, and I don't blame him.

"I got you something more comfortable to wear, love. Everything okay?" He looks at Adam again, and I let out a sigh.

"Get up, Adam. It can't happen. I'm sorry, but I'm not even the same person that Zendaya took to Hell. Not only have I changed mentally, but physically too. I can't accept my role in this pack as the future Luna. I have other things I'm destined to do. I still care for you, but it's not what you're looking for. You need your mate—the one destined to lead with you. That's not me. What I'll do is help protect this pack in any way I can. Can you tell me where the girls we brought with us are? Zeke, can you sit with me, please?" I rub my head as I try to adjust to where I'm at and how it's possible that so much time passed here when it was only a month or two in Hell.

Zeke sets the pile of clothes down on the coffee table. "Sure."

"Adam, I need to give this back to you." I focus for a moment and pull the ring he gave me off my hand. "Your ring was something that helped me stay safe while in Hell. I had to deceive someone, and it played a key role. The person that is meant for you should be the one to wear it, though."

Adam takes the ring from my hand while he stands and returns to his place on the opposite couch, dejected as Corey clears his throat. "We placed the women in empty rooms on the upper floors. Some of them were confused. The ones from our pack were returned to their families or, in some cases, what's left of their family here."

"So, they're all okay?" I look at him hopefully.

He shrugs. "As far as we can tell, yes. We'll know more soon enough, I guess. Can you tell us what happened to you?"

I sigh and glance at Zeke. *Should I tell them everything?*

He shrugs. *Do you have a reason not to? You've never kept anything from Corey, but I feel that your friendship with them will be crucial despite Adam's broken heart.*

I nod and turn back to them. "Okay, but don't interrupt until I'm finished. It's a lot."

Corey holds up his hand. "Wait, should we let your parents get back first so you can tell us all in one go?"

I nod. "That's not a bad idea. I can change while we wait." I stand, and Zeke grabs my arm.

He stands, holding me still. "They need to leave if you're changing." He turns and growls at them, and both Adam and Corey's eyes flicker with amusement.

"Why just us? None of us are her mates." Adam stands, frowning.

I burst out laughing, and they look at me confused as Zeke continues to glare at them. "Zeke is one of my mates. Just turn your backs. Zeke, knock it off. Set your prince's ass down and chill."

He rolls his eyes but places himself between the males across the room and me. Adam and Corey look curious but turn their backs to us, and I grab my clothes and quickly change.

Once I'm seated, and my wings tucked in close, Zeke slides in beside me and wraps an arm around me before clearing his throat.

Corey glances over his shoulder and sees that it's safe to turn around. He and Adam return to their couch.

Corey looks at me curiously. "Did you say prince in regard to Zeke? I thought he was just a regular vampire."

I tilt my head and look at Zeke. "Yes, he's a vampire prince, and I guess Ulric is technically one as well, right, Zeke?"

He grabs my hand and squeezes it. "Yes, but so are you, love."

My parents choose that moment to reenter, and fuzzy redheads launch themselves at me, and I'm drowning in freckled arms as my sisters sit on top of me.

I wrap them in my arms as the three of us cry. They mutter words that get lost in sobs, and finally, they remove themselves from me as Alpha Gale enters. He looks at everyone in the room before leaning against one of the bookcases closest to Adam and Corey.

"It's good to have you back, Ember." He nods, and I take him in, recalling Zendaya's words.

"Yes, it's good to be home. Do you need something, Alpha Turner?" I ask and stare him dead in the eye.

He tilts his head and looks at me curiously. "I just wanted to see if you were comfortable. I'll leave you to visit with all of your loved ones."

I offer him a smile. "Thank you, I would appreciate that. It seems I have been gone for a long time."

He nods, and I watch him leave before meeting everyone's curious looks.

"I'll explain another time. Right now, let me tell you my story and eat. It's long, so get comfortable."

"Your wings are beautiful, Ember, are you an angel now?" Winnie asks with wide eyes.

"Oh, Uhm, no. I guess I'm part angel?" I glance at my mom, who lets out a heavy sigh.

"I guess I should tell them, now." She sounds resigned.

"You know what, I got it, Mom. I'll start from the beginning and tell you the whole thing. Adam needs to hear it too." I reach for one of the muffins on the coffee table and grab a cup of coffee. I take a big gulp and a large bite, savoring the taste of the cinnamon in the muffin before launching into my story, starting when I found out about Mom's one-night stand.

CHAPTER TWENTY-SIX

W e leave the living area two hours later, and I walk with my hand in Zeke's toward my family's home. Corey and Adam follow quietly behind us. I guess they're afraid to let me out of their sight now. I don't know.

My sisters took the news of my mom's one-night stand better than I expected. Of course, they were shocked that she withheld the information for so long, but then again, none of us ever expected me to be kidnapped to Hell.

I turn and pull Zeke to a stop as my sisters and parents walk on. Corey and Adam stop with us, and I don't mind that they can hear me. "Zeke, did Ulric make it?"

He lets out a sigh and looks pained. "I don't know, Ember. When I was prepping the gate to blow, I saw Zuko dragging him back toward the castle with the help of a few of our guards. Prospero was unconscious on the ground, I think. I can only hope, though. Have you tried to reach out to him?"

"No, I haven't because I can't feel him. Is it because we're not in Hell anymore?"

"Maybe? I'm not sure. I mean, I could feel that you were still

alive, but I wasn't sure where. Is it possible that with everything
that's happened, it's created a block?"

I shrug. "I don't know. I guess we could give it a few days
and try it."

He looks down at his feet as I say that, and I cock my head to
the side. "What? Why did your mood just change?"

He meets my gaze again. "I don't know if you remember Kai
much, but you do know he is one of Lucifer's main men."

Adam and Corey let out a low growl, and I look at them
silently, urging them to shut it. "I knew we were risking it by
asking him for help. So why are you bringing it up? Did he see
something?"

Zeke runs a hand through his hair, and I notice his shoulder
tense. "He did. Ember, he knows who you are, and he's going to
tell Lucifer. He insists that he needs to know that he has an heir
alive."

I feel my stomach drop. "Shit. How long do I have before I
have to go back?"

Zeke grabs my other hand and pulls me toward him gently. I
rest my head on his shoulder, "I begged him for at least a couple
of days to a week. I don't even know if we'll get that much. He
seemed pretty pissed and didn't want to leave you once we got
here."

I step back and look over my shoulder at Corey and Adam
before meeting Zeke's gaze. "There may be a reason for that
other than the fact that I'm Lucifer's daughter."

"Fuck, Ember, are you saying what I think you're saying?"
Zeke looks at me skeptically.

"When you passed me to him, I felt something stronger than
what I felt with you and Ulric when the mate bond started
sliding into place. It burned like hellfire, and there's no way he
didn't feel it too." I rub my thumb across his hand, and Corey
clears his throat behind me.

"So, you now have three mates?" I turn to meet his gaze and then look over at Adam, who looks sad.

"I guess I do, whether he acknowledges it or not. I guess I'll find out sooner rather than later. I'm not looking forward to meeting my father. I saw him briefly at that ball, and I don't want to be put in that group that was with him. They all seemed way too uppity for my tastes. I know I have to go back, though." I turn and look at Zeke.

Adam grunts before he asks, "Why do you need to go back?"

I look back at them, the two guys who have been at my side for years and that I have officially put in the friend zone, but I know I'll be able to trust them with my life. "I have to go back not only to find Ulric, but because from what Zendaya said, it's on me to balance Hell again. The fallen can only be killed by someone in Lucifer's bloodline or by Lucifer himself. I think he's had a hard time having an heir because the fallen commissioned someone to kill his children. If they kill us before we have learned how to fight back, we don't stand a chance. I have to take Greed down before he completely takes over Hell."

Adam nods in understanding. "We'll do anything we can to help you."

"I know you will, Adam, but you have to put this pack first. You need to take your father's place sooner rather than later. I found some things out about him while I was in Hell that aren't good, Adam." I look at the ground, preparing to share with him what I found out about his mother.

"I have my suspicions, Ember. There are things he's done that were supposed to be for the benefit of the pack but don't make sense. Just tell me." Adam squares his shoulders.

Corey places a supportive hand on his shoulders, and I meet Adam's gaze. "Your dad worked with a witch to attain power by sacrificing your mother."

His mouth gapes, and his eyes fill with tears. I drop Zeke's hand and immediately grab Adam and wrap him in a hug.

"Fuck. That's not what I thought you were going to say. He sacrificed her?" he asks, pulling out of my embrace briefly.

I glance over at Corey, who frowns. "Yes, he did. He had help. Unfortunately, I don't know the specifics of which Beta it was, but we'll figure it out."

Adam growls. "Now I understand why James was pushing so hard to work with us and befriend us. They know, don't they?"

I shrug and step back toward Zeke, who wraps me into a hug. "I don't know. It's possible. I don't know who the witch is he worked with to attain the power, but she could be hiding in Alaska for all I know."

"Maybe finding her is part of the balancing you're destined to do? Will you help us, Ember?" Corey asks with a sad frown. He understands that it could have been his father who helped him.

"I will, however, I can. I'll find a way to make sure I can be here to help if I'm retaken to Hell. Maybe I'll be able to come and go rather than be a captive like I was before. I hope so." I look at Zeke, and he shrugs. Neither one of us knows how things are going to work out.

Corey lets out a deep breath, and we all look up at him. "Well, until they show up to take you back, you better enjoy the hell out of being home. Oh, and teach us some of the tricks you learned in Hell. If we're going to face an army of angels and demons sometime in the future, while also weeding out the baddies in this pack, we're going to need to be a hell of a lot stronger."

I laugh and turn to face the direction my family went. "I guess you're right. We'll start tomorrow, though. Today, let me spend time with my family." With that, we begin walking toward my family's home. I plan to spend as much time as I can with them and tomorrow my sisters are going to train with us. There may be a target on their back someday because of me, and I'll be damned if they don't know how to protect themselves. I refuse to let what happened to Amber and those other girls happen to them.

AFTERWORD

Thank you so much for reading my story. If you loved this book as much as I loved writing it, I ask that you please leave me a review. I enjoyed bringing this story to life and letting my imagination run wild. Find me on social media to keep up with upcoming books, giveaways, and sales.

Check out my website here for more info about me and my work: www.thechaptergoddess.com

ACKNOWLEDGMENTS

I would like to thank my family and closest friends for supporting me while creating this novel. It took me much longer than I planned to complete, but here it is. My best support has been my husband for letting me work insane hours on it. He has been there while frustration, writer's block, and pure exhaustion have wreaked havoc on me.

To all my readers, you are the best! You inspire me with your encouragement and I honestly could not pursue my dream in writing if you weren't here.

To my editor Maggie, Beta readers, and ARC readers, where would I be without you? You all gave me excellent feedback and motivation with this story.

Thank you everyone who played a part in the creation of this book. It truly is impossible to name everyone that played a part but you all know who you are!

OTHER BOOKS BY THE AUTHOR

Fae Shifter Series:

1. Releasing Her Power Within
2. Unleashed
3. Revealed
4. The Blood King
5. Coming Soon
6. Coming Soon

Ember Series:

1. Black Flames
2. Coming Soon
3. Coming Soon

Standalones:

Breaking Traditions The Shifter And The Mage

Short Stories

Tragic Magic, featured in "Tales of Kathaldi" edited by Ron L. Lahr

Freedom, published with Red Penguin Publishing, "Once Upon A Time… A Fairy Tale Anthology", edited by J.K. Larkin

Creative Intent

Dog Park Epiphany

New Path

Isla's Wish

ABOUT THE AUTHOR

Madilynn Dale is a reader and author. She lives in the state of Oklahoma and enjoys being outdoors. Her biggest hobby is reading, and she enjoys a variety of books. She is married and has one son and seven fur babies. She currently holds a license as a Physical Therapy Assistant in the state of Oklahoma but is taking time to focus on her son. She holds a Bachelor of Science degree in Kinesiology and an Associates of Science degree in Physical Therapy Assistant sciences.

www.ingramcontent.com/pod-product-compliance
Lightning Source LLC
Chambersburg PA
CBHW070602120726
47909CB00007B/2410